The few portable crew-served guns the amazons had were set for a crossfire. Farther back, down in the warren of the slave-pens, fallback positions were being fortified. The only thing left to do was insure that the Invid victory would be costly.

After a few minutes they heard the sound of heavy footfalls—marching mecha, advancing on their prey without fear or hesitation.

A pair of colossal Odeons rounded a corner, filling the corridor. The amazon gunners waited until the optimal moment, then opened up. The Inorganics seemed to experience paroxysms of pain as fire splashed over them and ripped them apart; then they collapsed in on themselves.

More Odeons appeared, moving with greater caution. The Sentinels and the Praxians held their fire until they couldn't miss, then blasted away. One, its skull aflame, whirled and convulsed, then trying to hold itself erect, went reeling toward a giant column.

A camouflaged panel at the base of the column slid open. Jack Baker was standing there, wide-eyed, as he watched a burning twenty-five-foot-tall mecha stagger directly toward him.

By Jack McKinney
Published by Ballantine Books:

THE ROBOTECH® SERIES

THE SENTINELS® SERIES

THE SENTINELS™ #4

WORLD KILLERS

Jack McKinney

A Del Rey Book

BALLANTINE BOOKS • NEW YORK

FOR WENDE SILVER
PART HAYDONITE, PART SPHERISIAN,
MOSTLY PRAXIAN,
AND ALL *NEW YORKER*—
WITH LOVE

A Del Rey Book
Published by Ballantine Books

Library of Congress Catalog Card Number: 87-91884

ISBN 0-345-35304-8

Manufactured in the United States of America

First Edition: July 1988
Fifth Printing: May 1990

ROBOTECH CHRONOLOGY

1999   Alien spacecraft known as SDF-1 crashlands on Earth through an opening in hyperspace, effectively ending almost a decade of Global Civil War.

        In another part of the Galaxy, Zor is killed during a Flower of Life seeding attempt.

2002   Destruction of Mars Base Sara.

2009   On the SDF-1's launch day, the Zentraedi (after a ten-year search for the fortress) appear and lay waste to Macross Island. The SDF-1 makes an accidental jump to Pluto.

2009–11 The SDF-1 battles its way back to Earth.

2011–12 The SDF-1 spends almost half a year on Earth, is ordered to leave, and defeats Dolza's armada, which has laid waste to much of the planet.

2012–14 A two-year period of reconstruction begins.

2012   The Robotech Masters lose confidence in the ability of their giant warriors to recapture the SDF-1, and begin a mass pilgrimage through interstellar space to Earth.

2013   Dana Sterling is born.

2014   Destruction of the SDFs 1 and 2 and Khyron's battlecruiser.

2014–20 The SDF-3 is built and launched. Rick Hunter turns 29 in 2020; Dana turns 7.

Subsequent events covering the Tiresian campaign are recounted in the Sentinels series. A complete Robochronology will appear in the fifth and final volume.

CHAPTER
ONE

They were the New Paladins, riding forth to answer the trumpet call to a nightmare war.

They were mortals caught up in events that transcended anything they had ever expected.

Many of them were career military people who had learned that wars were often won by those who made the fewest screwups.

But they also knew that everybody screws up sometime.

Le Roy la Paz, *The Sentinels*

"**E**VERYBODY STAY SHARP! LOOKS LIKE WE'RE gonna have to go to guns!"

Jack Baker trimmed the mated Veritechs he was flying —the sleek Alpha fighter was now joined like a vaned nose cone to the bigger, burlier Beta ship. A quick glance over his weapons status displays revealed that the other two Alpha-Betas of his raiding party were still in tight formation behind him.

"Jack, *no!*" yelled Janice Em. She was in the second ship along with Burak, Lron, and Tesla. "You *heard* what Veidt and Sarna said: this world's defenses will respond to *any* hostile action!"

Actually, Veidt had said the legendary protective systems of the planet responded to the mere *intent* of intrusion or provocative act. And that certainly seemed to be the case today, even though the fighters had gone in with weapons and shields down.

"I got a news flash for you: we've *already* got Haydon IV PO'd at us, kiddo," Jack snorted. "Or d'you think this planet's surface *usually* twitches and then starts spitting sparklers at people? Get ready; like it or not, it looks as if we're in for some turns 'n' burns."

One part of him registered the fact that the terrain of Haydon IV wasn't actually twitching; it was *changing shape*, like something from one of those old-time clay-animation flicks. And the things shooting up at the incoming Veritechs were more like swirling vortices or sheets of flame than sparklers.

Whatever they were, they were traveling at such high velocity that Jack saw the VTs had no chance of running for it.

"Activate shields and weapons." Jack tried to sound calm. "And stay close to me." It was too late to go back, so there was nothing to do but *drive on*.

Only he wished there were experienced combat fliers in the other two combined VTs. Janice had been through training, and so had Learna, but neither of them had any dogfighting experience to speak of. He would have preferred to have Max and Miriya Sterling flying at his wingtips.

But Miriya had been stricken, like Rick Hunter and his wife Lisa, by the strange microorganisms of Garuda. And so had another Sentinel, one whose possible death filled Jack with feelings and impulses that bewildered and shocked him . . .

He tried to put that out of his mind; what was happening to the famous Baker cool and concentration? *Damn!*

From the cockpit's rear seat, where she was strapped into the copilot's station, Bela reached forward to clap him on the shoulder. "That's the lad! Kick their flaming arses! I'll loan you the boot!"

The vortices of fire came darting and circling, changing shape and roiling—like silken scarves on the wind. All Jack's sensors were in alarm mode, but none of them could tell him what he was facing.

Fire with fire, he told himself fatalistically, and put a burst of pumped laser into the first one to come into range.

Somehow Tesla got on the tac net. "No, you *fool*! You're signing our death warrants!"

"Don't bother me; I'm workin'," Jack growled.

The cannonfire seemed to have no effect; the vortice changed course a bit and came straight for him. He shot it again. The other VTs chose targets of opportunity and opened up, too.

The vortices flared angrily, and some were jarred, but they kept coming. More came from what seemed to be an opening in the countryside below, like flecks of incandescent paint falling upward.

Jack was still firing when the first vortex hit him. It flared angrily against his shields, sending the indicators toward the danger zones, and it seemed he could feel the infernal heat right through the fuselage. More swarmed after.

The other VTs were struck, too. The vortices spread across them, coating them in a blinding radiance.

"Wake up! Come, come; I have no time for this nonsense! Wake him!"

Rem heard the thick, moist rumbling voice, loud enough to echo and shake the walls. He associated it with the sensation he felt now: bonds still holding his raw, bleeding wrists and ankles, and the cottony blur the Invid psy-scanners had left in his brain.

At the Regent's command, Invid officers applied brief pain to speed up the effects of the reviving injections they had given him. Rem squirmed and moaned, shaking off part of the fog, and opened his eyes.

Rem saw the throne room that the Regent had decreed for himself high in a Haydon IV tower. It was a minor mercy to see the light of Briz'dziki, the local sun, rather than the cold insides of the Invid's nearby hive.

Rem tried to recall what he was doing there, and it came back in a confused, horrifying rush. Capture by the Invid on Garuda; exposure to Garudan atmosphere—why wasn't he dead, or mad?

Or, perhaps he was—perhaps he was both.

No, he wasn't dead; the pain of his shackles was a branding-hot clarity too sharp for that. But mad . . .

As he struggled feebly, he heard a low, mosquitolike humming that quickly built until it shock-waved from one side of his skull to the other. The shackles seemed to grow teeth and gnaw at his wrists, promising to devour their way up his arms and legs, ripping and savaging.

Rem screamed. The Invid stench coagulated with evil glee in his chest—he was sure he would suffocate.

Not mad, then—but even more terribly, a victim of *hin*, the Garudan altered-reality or transcendent state.

Kami and Learna and their people thrived that way—in *hin*—as a matter of symbiotic course, interacting with their environment on a microorganic, even subatomic, scale. Stranded from the synergistic biota of their planet, they would not even be sentient beings.

But to outside life-forms, exposure to the atmosphere of Garuda and to *hin* was a sentence of death by insanity.

Rem fought to hold onto some last shred of reality. The seemingly endless memories of the Optera of long ago, and the paradise it had been—but had he only dreamed them? Images of the Regent's estranged mate, the Regis, and her passion for Zor, whose biogenetic material had been made manifest in Rem's cloning—were they fever-dreams of the *hin*? But they had seemed so real, not hallucinatory; more ordered and in focus than any dream or nightmare.

The Invid officers hoisted Rem to his feet with a clanking of his chains. To Rem's addled and tormented senses, the cold tiles felt like white-green frost that burned the soles of his feet and froze them at the same time.

The Regent loomed before him, twenty feet high, massive and terrible, his mantle spread like a cobra's hood as he gazed down through liquid black eyes as big as manhole covers. Rem felt the *hin* seize him again, making the breath in his lungs congeal and refuse to move.

Rem heard his own whimpering, felt his self-control about to slip from his grasp. He had the abrupt impression that there were things in the shadows waiting to pounce upon him and feast on his marrow, then take his mind and steal his soul. And though a remote part of his intellect could recognize it as the mind-wrenching effect of *hin*, he couldn't find the strength of will to fight it.

"Stand him up straight," the Regent said, when Rem would have pulled himself into a weeping fetal ball. "Hold his head up."

When Rem was standing up and staring, as wild-eyed as an animal with its leg in a trap, the Regent went on. "You're a very difficult fellow, Tiresian. Or should I say, 'Clone'? Or better yet, 'Zor-clone'?"

He held up four-fingered fists on wrists several times thicker than Rem's waist. "Whatever you *really* are, here's something that might interest you. Your Sentinel friends are coming."

Rem couldn't hide a wretched whimper of disbelief and despair mixed with crazed hope. The Regent caught it. "That's right: they are coming directly into my hands. To be imprisoned like you, to be put to the Inquisition like you, and to go through all the pain and mind-probing you've gone through."

Rem was nearly in tears, but the Regent was leaning forward in the colossal throne, drowning him out. "But it needn't happen that way! You can save them, Zor-clone, and save yourself as well! The Haydon IV healers can cure them and cure you, too, this very hour; you can leave with them—if you'll simply say a few paltry words and give me what I want."

Rem *was* broken. Courage and conviction and strength and faith—and even love—are overrated when it comes to defense against torture. Yet the Regent failed to incorporate one thing into his equations—the one factor that no agony could overcome: ignorance.

"Tell me where the last Protoculture matrix is," the Regent hissed. "Tell me where the original Zor sent it—hid it! You have many of his memories—how, I'm not sure. But that one *must* be there, it *must*!"

But it wasn't. If it had been, Rem would have yielded it up in a moment. That escape was closed to him, though.

Rem laid his head to his chest and sobbed. Deep in the *hin*, he felt the sunlight jeering at him, his fear-sweat turning to acid against his skin, panic closing off his windpipe.

He heard the creak as the Regent rose from his chair. "Above all things, I despise stubbornness. That, I punish."

Lynn-Minmei tried to stop the passageway from spinning as she lurched along, her hand held by the mysterious VT pilot; she was barefoot and disheveled, sick with the drinks she had downed but sicker still with her latest and worst glimpse of Human nature.

Not that she'd *meant* to drink a lot; she had nothing but contempt for drunkards. But life as the consort of General T. R. Edwards was a little easier to bear after a round or two. And then there was the drink itself—from Edwards's private bottle—something she had heard the top-echelon officers jokingly call *weed-whacker*.

It was a 150-proof vacuum distillate that had been soaked in fibers from a plant related to the Flower of Life, and strained out again. Brackish; deadly. But oddly smooth and warming.

Best taken by the slow shot glass.

But, she had needed *something* to fortify her as she sat there and listened to Edwards—the man Minmei had thought she loved, the man to whom she had given herself —reveal himself as a devil incarnate.

She was dizzy, and thought she might lose her balance, or her lunch—she had had no dinner. "Wait, wait," she puffed, breathless. Her head spun, and she tasted bile in the back of her throat.

The VT pilot stopped and turned to her, gesturing in a way that made it clear he was concerned about her. Minmei brushed her hair out of her eyes yet again, to study him. "Do I know you? Who *are* you?"

He was tall and lean, and demonstrated a supple strength. Behind the tinted facebowl of his flight helmet, all she could discern was the dark, thick beard. He regarded her for a moment, then answered, "It says right here: REF Service # 666–60–937."

She could *see* that, and his flight officer's insignia and unit flash. But his name tape, stitched over his left breast pocket, was unfamiliar: *Isle, L.* His voice, coming through the helmet's tinny external speaker, was unrecognizable.

Her mystery savior was wearing the unit patch of one of the outfits from Dr. Lang's research facility. Lang had managed to ram through the council an authorization for his *own* security forces, but Edwards had fought the seconding of pilots to the Robotech scientist. So, this was almost certainly one of the fliers who had been selected from the lower ranks and trained on Tirol to fill the cockpits of Lang's personal army.

But what was he doing on SDF-3?

Minmei swayed slowly from side to side, closing one eye in an effort to focus on him. "C'mom, c'mon; I mean, why're y'*doing* this?" She still wasn't sure he wouldn't drag her back to Edwards—maybe to claim some kind of reward or favor.

She was also waiting for the alarms to go off.

Surely, by now, Edwards had realized that she hadn't simply fled his embrace and his bedroom for some fresh air. Even vain, cold Edwards must have admitted to himself by now that Minmei had made a break for freedom.

"You said you want to go to Tiresia, didn't you?" the VT flier was saying. "And perhaps to Garuda, or Haydon IV? I'll see that you get to wherever you want to go, Minmei. But Tiresia's the obligatory first stop."

There was some resonance in his voice, even over the speaker, that she thought she recognized. Minmei sighed and ran her hand through her fine black hair again. Plainly, no VT could make a star-jump; and the few remaining REF vessels that could go superluminal were scarcely the kind of spacecraft you could sign out like a borrowed fanjet.

But there was something in the man's tone, something steely and yet compassionate, that didn't sound like it brooked failure.

She vaguely remembered saying to him, outside Edwards's quarters, that she wanted to go to Tiresia or Garuda, but the beginning of their adventure was an alcoholic mini-blackout. She was not sure what her plan had been, though, except that Jonathan Wolff and Rick Hunter were out there someplace.

She shook her head slowly. "I don't—I don't . . ."

He took her hand again. "Don't worry, Minmei."

Then he led her off again. Minmei lost track of things for a while, but blearily realized at one point that he was shoving oversize deck slippers onto her bare feet. At another point, she felt something sting her arm and saw that he had given her a shot with a medikit ampule.

"Antinausea," REF # 666–60–937 explained. "It makes it tough to see out the cockpit canopy if you heave your cookies."

"Cockpit?" she repeated, trying to figure out what he was getting at. Then she realized that he had her standing near a hatch that led to a hangar deck. There were the distant whines of VTs being readied for flight.

"Wait right here," he said after he led her into the vast, mostly darkened hangar deck. Minmei did not get to ask what he was doing; he was gone.

The antinausea drug settled her queasiness and brought her around a bit, too. She was drawing deep breaths and burping a bit, sitting on the deck, when he caught her hands and pulled Minmei upward.

"All set; just follow me. That's our ship over there."

"Wh—"

And then they were walking among the parked mecha of the hangar deck. Welding sparks leapt and humming maint-crew machinery made noise in the distance, and she could hear men and women yelling or cursing or cajoling or laughing as they sweated to keep the REF's fighting forces operational.

He was leading her toward an armored Alpha, a lusterless gray fighter trimmed in olive drab, bulked by its augmentation pods. It was one of the most formidable ships in the REF inventory, and she didn't think it likely that it had been assigned to one of Lang's "six-month-wonder" pilots.

Minmei saw the boarding ladder before her and it brought back a flood of memories. She was a non-tech person; why did mecha insist on playing such an overwhelming part in her life?

Then somebody yelled from the distance, and more voices took up the cry. She realized woozily that the voices were coming her way. She had both hands on the boarding ladder and one foot on the first rung when she became aware of a ruckus behind her.

By the time she turned around, there were three or four flight-deck personnel laid out flat, unconscious. Minmei blinked at them owlishly. *What—*

Then REF # 666–60–937 was pushing her up the ladder, loading her into the copilot's seat, and then belting her in. Apparently he knew all the right codes; the launch-cat airlock accepted the powerful Alpha fighter and flung it out into space.

Green, looming Fantoma cast its light on them and their ship, and Tirol was a gibbous splotch of orange-brown-gray not far from it. The VT pilot turned his craft toward Tirol.

Suddenly his instruments were squealing and beeping for his attention. "Hot scramble from SDF-3, of course," she heard him mutter. "They want you back. They're coming to get you."

"Then—"

"Sit tight." He hit the auxiliaries for full military power and dove toward Tirol. Eager pursuers formed up for the hunt.

Minmei, pressed back in her seat, looking out at the unknowable stars, felt tears pressed from her eyes by acceleration, to wet the headrest behind her.

"Here they come," said REF # 666–60–937.

In the case of Garudan evolution, there can be no question that a wide spectrum of intracellular organelles developed through the cannibalistic warfare among bacteria that led to an amazing degree of symbiosis. The interactions of the entire Garudan ecosystem, the planet's dominant species included, give weight to those who argue that the evolution of multicellular organisms resulted from the extracellular symbiosis of monocellular organisms.

Like ours, a Garudan's body is composed of about ten quadrillion animal cells and another one hundred quadrillion bacterial cells. But the range of microorganic activity and variety is far greater, and the interaction of the symbionts far more complex.

The upshot is that a Human who is exposed to Garudan atmosphere is like a pocket calculator plugged into a mainframe: it is not designed for it and will quickly burn out.

Perhaps unsurprisingly, in light of recent research, the Garudans have a simple explanation for the extraordinary nature of their planet's ecosystem: "Haydon wished it so."

Cabell, *A Pedagogue Abroad: Notes on the Sentinels Campaign*

VINCE GRANT'S HAND COVERED LISA HUNTER'S forehead and then some. He drew it back, moist with her perspiration. "She's still feverish." He struggled with himself for a moment, not sure if he could or should say what else he was thinking.

Jean, Vince's wife, nodded slightly. The patients were *all* that way: Rick and Lisa, Karen Penn and Miriya Sterling. They were comatose and failing fast, as a result of their exposure to the Garudan atmosphere. They were tied down on gurneys to help control their intermittent seizures.

The shuttlecraft's deckplates vibrated under Vince's

boot soles. "Jean, what if Veidt's wrong, or the Invid double-cross us?"

Somebody had to ask the question. The fate of worlds was riding on what the Sentinels would do. Moralists would say that the lives of four individuals were as important as the life of a planet or the outcome of a war, but Vince didn't have the luxury of dealing with the abstract.

He wiped the perspiration from Lisa's brow with a cloth and pulled the blanket back up under her chin. He looked at the other stricken Sentinels.

Here were four lives that would come to an end unless the virtually miraculous Haydonian healing crafts were brought to bear. But what might the survival of the Hunters and the others cost?

The Invid sounded so accommodating—it could only be some sort of trick. Vince drew a breath and smoothed out his uniform tunic. Given his size, no one—least of all, an XT—was likely to notice the bulge of the Badger assault pistols he was wearing in shoulder rigs under each armpit. If this was a trap, the Regent's hordes would find out how expensive a pricetag such a seemingly simple skirmish could carry.

Vince was not particularly afraid of death. He had long since figured out his attitude about dying, and other people sensed his inner calm. As the shuttle started to cut into Haydon IV's atmosphere, Max Sterling appeared in the hatch, knotting his fingers together, and looked to Vince.

Max had left his place at the controls, permitting Wolff to take over, and come aft to check on his wife yet again. "Veidt's gotten final landing approval," Max told them. He hesitated, then added, "They'll keep their word, don't you think? The Invid, I mean?"

Jean Grant, attending her patients, avoided eye contact with Max; she didn't want to lie, and she didn't want to voice her doubts. Secretly, she thought it was only a fifty-

fifty possibility that Miriya or any of them would be cured
—or that anybody on the shuttle would survive the visit to
Haydon IV.

Vince turned to Max and said, "They'd *better*."

The shuttle came in low over Glike, the principal Haydonite population center. The city looked like something
out of the *Arabian Nights*—so fabulous that they momen-
tarily forgot their fears. Some of the architectural styles
had been borrowed from other worlds—Tiresian columns
and friezes; Spherisian crystal palaces; Praxian statuary and
totems. But most of Glike was uniquely Haydonite: slender
minarets and spires, fantastic white-frost gingerbread mansions, lacy elfin halls that seemed to shine with an inner
light.

Besides flying craft like Veidt's, there were machines
from the various worlds that traded with Haydon IV, and
different forms of Haydonite ship. Jean spotted one, on a
scope, that reminded her of a pilot whale with great, flip-
perlike wings—all curves and a bulging transparent passenger compartment.

There were also flying carpets, or what looked enough
like them to make her think of Scheherazade.

Just then Veidt and Sarna appeared from the flight deck,
where they had been guiding Wolff in his landing approach. They looked as unearthly and remote as ever,
robed and floating a few inches off the deck, their faces as
featureless as those of unfinished mannequins.

"We'll be landing soon," Veidt said in that weird, whis-
pery, processed-sounding voice. "I think you would do
well to prepare yourselves and your patients."

Max returned to the pilot's seat and handled the touchdown with an assist from Colonel Wolff. Cabell and Sarna
looked on. Haydon Control had directed them to a landing
stage in the middle of the city, one of a number of plat-
forms of smoky blue glass sprouting from a central tower.

A reception committee had already appeared to meet

them, standing together on a flying carpet that hovered a few yards above the landing surface. As Vince, Max, and Wolff opened the hatch, the carpet floated toward them and stopped a foot or so off the platform.

As had been agreed, Veidt and Sarna went first to greet the half-dozen Haydonites waiting on the carpet—or, more precisely, floating just off it. Jonathan Wolff took advantage of the moment to look the flying carpet over.

The carpet was thicker than the ones from the tales. It resembled an undulating judo mat, yet it was textured and decorated with exotic, iridescent patterns. It was vaguely rectangular, but he could see that it tended to shift and change conformation. Moreover, the other carpets, sailing around over the city came in many shapes and dimensions, from one-passenger welcome mats to dance-floor-size.

Veidt and Sarna exchanged ritualistic and dignified bows with their people. Since Haydonites lacked arms as well as faces—and legs too, Wolff supposed (although nobody he knew of had ever gotten a look under those hovering robe hems to find out what was underneath them)—the whole ceremony had a reserved, inhuman look to it.

Wolff found that he could tell the males and females apart. The Haydonite men's faces had angular planes, and saucer-size, gemlike things displayed on their robes.

The leader of the welcoming committee was a male, taller and more slender than Veidt. He had a bulging cranium and a deep coppery tone to his skin. A shimmering symbol like a star sapphire's light shone from the center of his forehead. "So, Veidt, you return to bring your disturbances among us yet again?"

But it was Sarna who answered. "You know better than that, Vowad! Our friends are gravely ill, and only Haydonite science can save them! You know the Law; we're obligated to help."

The one called Vowad made an irritated sound. "Yes,

yes—and if it hadn't been this excuse, it would have been some other, eh?"

The others behind Vowad shifted uneasily, and one of them intervened. "Enough! If lives are in jeopardy, it is best the healing begin at once."

Wolff wasn't so sure he liked what he had heard, and he didn't know if he wanted to stake his life on the Haydonites' good graces, but it was too late to back out. He surreptitiously made sure the conventional weapons he had concealed under his clothes were secure, and regretted that it was impossible to carry Protoculture weapons due to these planetary defenses everybody kept talking about.

Sarna turned to the humans waiting by the foot of the shuttle's ramp. "Bring them forth. We go to the Halls of Healing immediately!"

Jean Grant operated a small remote unit. The automated med gurneys on which Rick and the others had been secured rolled forth. Vince was going to ask how the wheeled gurneys were going to get up onto the flying carpet when a part of it extended like an upholstered tongue, at a gentle incline, like a ramp. Max walked at his wife's side.

Once Vince had secured the ship, he joined Wolff, Jean, and the rest on the flying carpet. It didn't give under his considerable weight and felt stable. *More like a flying cloud than a flying carpet*, he thought.

At some invisible command, it rose and wafted away over the city. Though there was no fairing or windshield, the humans felt only a vague stirring of air—despite the fact that the carpet was traveling quite rapidly.

They looked down on a city busy with commerce and trade. As Veidt and Sarna had explained it, Glike was similar to the old-time Hong Kong. It was a place of enforced truce, immune to the military conflicts that had raged around it.

As the others gazed, enraptured, at the soaring beauty

and exquisite elegance of Glike, Sarna went over to Max. "You look tired, Maximilian. You must rest. Won't you be seated?"

He looked around as she gestured with a nod of her head, and saw that the carpet's surface had bunched up to make a kind of lounge chair just his size. He had no idea how she had done that.

Heaven knew he was exhausted, but all he could think of was Miriya; he refused to leave her side. Max gestured toward Veidt and the other Haydonites, now deep in conversation with Cabell, no doubt discussing medical procedures.

"That guy—what's his name, Vowad? Why's he so angry at Veidt?"

Sarna looked at them. "Vowad believes, as many do, that we can coexist with the Invid indefinitely. That any concession we make, any appeasement, is worth it. You already know how my husband and I feel. When Veidt insisted on making his opinions known, the Invid managed to kidnap us both."

Max felt sudden misgiving. "But—the Invid can't attack you here, isn't that what you told us? The planet's defenses would react."

Sarna inclined her head, a strange gesture from one who had no eyes and only contours where a face should be. "Indeed. But there are other ways to bring pressure to bear —the threat of a blockade, or strikes against our trading partners and customers. And, the Invid have attained great influence over some of our folk—with economic leverage and other things."

She moved closer, spoke more quietly. "Vowad is perhaps the single most powerful Haydonite, and I think that it was with his cooperation that Tesla kidnapped Veidt and me. We must be wary of him."

As if he had heard, Vowad turned toward Sarna and called out, "Come, give us your opinion of Cabell's proposed treatment regimen. Surely, my daughter has much to say? You always did when you were younger."

"Yes, Father," Sarna said, and floated back to the group, to leave Max slack-jawed with surprise.

Lieutenant Isle was no Rick Hunter or Max Sterling, but he handled the Alpha with cool deftness, making the most of its brute power and amazing performance, as the hounds gave chase.

Ghost Riders flying patrol between SDF-3 and Tirol, hampered by the fact that Minmei was aboard the quarry, found themselves at a profound disadvantage. Minmei's rescuer fired warning bursts that didn't miss by much, making it plain that he was at no great pains to spare anybody who pressed him too hard.

The sentries yielded, but as the armored Alpha plunged for Tiresia more bogeys appeared on the screens, scrambled from SDF-3. Minmei could hear Isle's breath rasp. "I thought Edwards would be distracted getting the pursuit of the Zentraedi under way," he admitted. "Thought we'd have a little more lead time."

She gave a scornful laugh, shaking her head wearily. "You think T. R. Edwards is going to go after Breetai *personally*? And take a chance that things here will get away from him? You've got a lot to learn, Lieutenant."

The kind of thing I've learned the hard way, she thought. "So, what now?"

He wasn't sure; the decision to help her escape Edwards's sadism had come rather on the spur of the moment. "We'll get you to REF Base Tirol, to Lang's bailiwick, for a start."

"Why? So The Great General has an excuse to kill Lang? Why don't you save everybody the trouble and just drop me off right here?"

He felt at a loss, but brought the fighter onto course for Base Tirol anyway, for want of anything better to do. One plan had been to try to link up with Breetai, but the *Valivarre*, the hijacked Zentraedi mining op ship loaded with the all-important monopole ore, was already beyond the VT's range.

"Stop feeling sorry for yourself," he said in an odd monotone. "It never does anybody any good. Now, tell me what *you* want."

"I—I want Jonathan." She was trying to hold back more tears, because she knew he was right about feeling sorry. "Jonathan Wolff! Just to be with him!"

"So." The word had a hollow, final sound, the way he said it. "Getting to Lang and the council is *still* a first step. Hang on." He increased power again.

"Y-you still haven't told me why you're doing this," she strained to get out, as the mecha thundered under her.

She didn't have a flight helmet, so she could still only hear him over his own helmet's tinny external speaker. "I don't like seeing people pushed around, Minmei."

Just when he should have been enjoying his triumph, Edwards had to suffer the galling news of Minmei's escape.

At first he had thought it was just another of her temper tantrums, set off by news that he had permission to send a contingent after the fleeing Zentraedi and their stolen ore. He realized now, though, that she still thought she loved that idiot Jonathan Wolff.

The half of T. R. Edwards's face that wasn't hidden under his gleaming metal cowl burned red. She was his property, and he had no intention of losing her—not to Wolff and not to anyone else.

Of course, it was out of the question to admit publicly that she had left him. The word was put out, to a limited number of key people, that she had been kidnapped. Minutes later, news reached him of the chase after the armored Alpha.

Apparently the pilot, whoever he was, was neither a Ghost Rider nor some rogue Skull, but rather one of the detached-duty fliers serving the R&D people and council-liaison offices. That hadn't kept him from knocking out several crewmembers and stealing a VT. Edwards looked forward to exacting a fearsome revenge.

But he had no time to waste monitoring the pursuit of the Alpha. There was his flotilla to put into motion, and every second counted, since Breetai was already under way. The ore the Zentraedi had taken with them was the key to a fleet that would let Edwards return to Earth in glory and conquer it.

Once the Zentraedi had been eliminated, it would be time to do away with the bothersome Sentinels. And soon, Minmei would be his wife and rule at his side, an empress over whole planets but his own obedient chattel.

■ ▄ ■ ▄ ■ ▄ ■ ▄ ■ ▄ ■ ▄ ■ ▄ ■ ▄ ■ ▄ ■

CHAPTER
THREE

The place was called Haydon IV, but nobody was able to explain why. It was the third planet out from its primary, so that explanation was null and void. There was no record or myth that gave a clue.

Odd, though; it was the fourth planet the Sentinels were to fight on—Tirol being an REF show.

Oh well. Coincidences were for the scientists; we troopies were just there to shoot 'n' salute.

Susan Graham, from the narration to her documentary film, *Protoculture's Privateers: SDF-3*, Farrago, Ark Angel, *Sentinels, and the REF*

LIKE SCHOOLS OF DEADLY FISH, THE FIERY DEFENSIVE vortices of Haydon IV plastered themselves to the Veritech, glowing brighter and brighter, burning fiercely at the fighter's shields.

"They mean to roast us alive!" Bela said grimly; Jack knew that tone in her voice, the one she took when she had her hand on her sword hilt.

He doubted that the energy defenses would actually do that, though; once the shields went down, the end would be rather swift and spectacular. Even now, the VTs were beginning to lose power; the final fall would be soon.

"Jan, can you spot any large bodies of water downstairs?" Maybe a swan dive into a lake or ocean would short-circuit the vortices, or something.

But she was replying, "Negative. Jack, I'm losing flight control. My instruments say these things are melding with the shields, becoming part of them and making them rigid. Control surfaces are becoming immovable."

It was happening to him, too, and to Learna's ship. The energy was forming a shell, and unless they could break it . . .

Then he yelped as a last, desperate solution occurred to him. "Listen up, everybody! Separate fighters and go to Guardian—correction! Go to Battloid mode, I say again, separate fighters and go to Battloid mode! Maybe we can hatch outta these energy shells!"

The fighters were beginning to tumble and wobble; the mere act of separating them under these conditions bordered on the suicidal. But Kami followed Jack's countdown from her place in the Beta's pilot-seat and at his mark they disengaged. The drubbing they got from the atmosphere almost smashed the two ships into each other, but Jack and Kami fought their controls, imaged through their thinking caps, and managed to get clear.

The fighters fought a terrible battle against the cocooning energy fields—like chicks trying to break through their shells. The ships strained to mechamorphose, to follow that central and perhaps most amazing trait of Robotechnology.

Come on, come on, Jack urged his mecha silently. And at last there was the sliding of components as the Alpha began folding and reconfiguring, its shields following suit.

All at once the blazing inferno burst away from the Alpha in all directions like an outlashing nova. The VT had become a Battloid, Humaniform, like a knight in armor, fists cocked, riding ribbons of thruster fire.

Jack gasped, trying to catch his breath. He checked around and saw Kami's Beta, and Janice's Alpha, with Lron's Beta close-by. All were in Battloid, shimmering with heat waves but still intact and under control.

Jack spotted Learna—a little rocky but apparently getting things under control. But . . .

"Crysta!"

He heard the ursine growling of the female Karbarran, more angry than afraid, as her Beta whirled and tumbled groundward. It was still in fighter mode, its power failing. Jack imaged his systemry and went after her like a high-diver.

Something came into his field of vision and he realized that Janice Em was nearby, her Alpha in Battloid, too, plummeting alongside him for the seemingly doomed effort to save the falling Beta.

"Don't touch it unless your shields are up!" Jack yelled; Crysta's mecha was still aglow with the energy "antibodies." He took a deep breath, and imaged his command to his Battloid. It reached out and seized the Beta.

It was like trying to bulldog a whirlwind. The heavier Beta spun and tumbled, nearly shaking the Alpha loose, the Alpha's amazing Robotech strength notwithstanding.

But Jack clung and, bracing his feet against the fuse-lage, began prying at the wings, straining to help it go into mechamorphosis. At least, to his relief, the Haydon anti-bodies that were infused with the Beta's protective mantle didn't attack him or slide from Crysta's shields over to his own.

Then Janice grabbed the Beta from the other side, and together they fought to save their companions. "Crysta, try for Guardian, do you copy?" Jack had to strain to get out his words as he was thrown around against his harness. *"Guardian!"*

Jack figured that the Beta might be able to achieve the intermediate mode between Fighter and Battloid, and per-haps it would be enough to save those within. Crysta had only recently completed her pilot training, but she kept her cool with bearish Karbarran fatalism, and did her best to obey.

The attempt to mechamorphose didn't appear to be hav-ing any effect, though the Beta's components were straining against one another and seemed ready to fly apart. The efforts of the two Battloids had slowed its fall, though, and Crysta had a bit more control.

Lron, who had been pacing the others in a steep dive, along with Kami and Learna, called out, "Jack, I see water, a large body of it!" There was panic in his voice, but he was calming himself because that was the only possible way to help his mate.

There might be hope yet. "Where?" Jack barked.

"Over in the opening in the terrain, where those energy things came from."

Jack swore: salvation in the lion's den? Not likely. "Crysta, you're gonna have to try to eject. Right now!"

She growled, "I cannot, Jack; ejection mechanism won't respond." There was a kind of abject keening noise in the background of her transmission—the Invid scientist she was carrying, no doubt.

Though the two Battloids had slowed the Beta's fall, they couldn't stop it. "Okay then: we shoot craps. It's *bath time*, Crysta! Brace for a splashdown!"

Lron, Learna, and Kami closed in, too, applying all thrusters to help slow Crysta's fall and shove her ship into position over the large underground lake or sea that Learna had spied. The distant sparkle of the water pinwheeled up and up at them with frightening speed. In the last seconds, they were able to reduce the speed of their fall—then the water smashed into them.

Jack felt as if his neck had been snapped, and he was aware of water bubbling and surging against his canopy. Any conventional aerospace craft would have broken or sprung a thousand leaks, but somehow the Alpha held. Jack broke the surface to see Lron's Beta still fighting desperately to keep Crysta's afloat.

Jack hit his burners and lifted clear of the water on trails of blue flame. Crysta's ship was no longer encased in the energy antibodies, but its fuselage looked broken, and it was no doubt taking on water. Janice Em's Alpha appeared next to it, helping Lron try to keep it from sinking, the water boiling and hissing from the blast of their thrusters, but it was a losing battle.

"Just hold on a second more!" Jack yelled. "Crysta, I'm getting you out of there!"

His Alpha extruded the special manipulator tentacles that were built into all VTs. In another moment, they had stretched forth to open access plates on one of the damaged Beta's nacelles. It only took a moment for them to work the manual controls for the emergency-rescue system.

The entire cockpit module of Crysta's Beta slid free from the rest of the ship; Jack took it up in his Battloid's armored hands even while his manipulators were retracting. "Okay, get clear! I've got her!"

Lron and Janice released their hold on the Beta, and it sank from sight in a fountain of bubbles and froth, steam rising from the water. Jack had risen clear and was sliding the cockpit module into a special fitting on the underside of his Battloid's right forearm.

"Just relax and enjoy the ride." Jack tried to sound lighthearted, but he was scanning his new surroundings and checking out his sensors, expecting another attack. He wasn't so sure the VTs could survive another fight.

"I cannot fathom it," Bela was saying. "Why would this Haydon IV of Veidt's have an underground sea? Is it not, as he and Sarna have told us, a—what was their phrase?— an *artificial world*?"

"That's what they said, all right," Janice Em added. "Only, personally, this wasn't what I pictured."

Nor had Jack. He had imagined a more elaborate kind of O'Neill colony, perhaps, or even a miniature Dyson sphere, but not something truly planet-size.

But it was indisputably an *artifact* of some kind. Beginning at the shores of the lake, fantastic underground mountains reared, looking to Jack like living instrumentality—inorganic versions of living forms and ecosystems.

Veidt and Sarna and the few other Haydonites among the Sentinels had been either unable or unwilling to give exact explanations as to how things worked here, and Jack began to curse them for it now.

Jan was continuing, "If the whole place really *is* an artifact, one of their biggest problems would be managing atmosphere and climate. It makes sense that they'd have huge reservoirs of water and ways of moving it around—under the surface and on it and even over it, as precipitation and clouds—"

"What we should be giving thought to is whether any of those fire-demons still lurk down here," Bela broke in.

"I see none, nor detect any," Lron reported. The others concurred.

"Perhaps the machines cannot see or smell us when we're down here," Gnea, the younger amazon, suggested. "After all, they're used to adversaries coming at them from outer space, not stepping inside their very gates."

Like flies hiding on an upraised flyswatter, Jack realized—which was only a good idea until the swatter's operator discovered the flies' whereabouts.

The opening overhead seemed to be shrinking, and some members of the team cried out, preparing to lift off and escape. Jack yelled for them to stand fast. "You want those air defenses to nail us for good? We're safe for now, and it looks like we discovered a back entrance."

He was less sure than he sounded. The Haydonite defense systems hadn't been challenged in two thousand years (although, granted, they allegedly had cost some local warmonger a few hundred ships that time). Jack had difficulty believing that planetary defenses so outdated could be any match for Robotech mecha. After all, how much trouble would Wolff Pack Hovertanks have with Earth weapons even *twenty* years obsolete?

"Now, we've got a transponder fix on the shuttle, and an inertial track," Jack went on. "It looks to me like there's plenty of room for Battloids to make their way along underground. That's how we're gonna get to Glike."

There was a muted commotion and then Lron's voice came up over the net. "It seems Tesla doesn't agree with your idea, Jack Baker, but a pistol waved at his snout has him quiet once more.

"I for one think this is a good plan you have. We can remain out of sight beneath the city, and if we encounter trouble, we always have the option of blasting our way back to the surface."

Jack bit back his own dark conclusions on what an unfortunate recourse *that* would be. "Jan, you take the point. Lron, drop back and walk drag. I'll be slack man, then Learna, then you, Kami." Jack took up his position at the head of the main body, keeping Janice in sight as she picked out their route.

He had thought about walking point, but he was in command and responsible for looking after his tiny unit from a more appropriate place. Besides, Jan had proven herself to be amazingly capable—adept at military sciences, mecha piloting, small arms, and hand-to-hand. She even excelled at the archaic weapons of the Praxian amazons.

These excellent military abilities, coming from a woman whose former claim to fame was as a female vocalist, didn't make a lot of sense to Jack, but just now he was grateful to have her there. Jack watched as, far overhead, the last of the opening in Haydon IV's surface closed out the last few rays of Briz'dziki.

The VTs waded up from the underground reservoir, shedding waterfalls, as the last of the bubbles rose from Crysta's VT. Jan found a route through a thing that they took for a spillway, some twenty yards in diameter. Though there were some light sources in the labyrinth of living instrumentality, the Veritechs brought up all their wing-lights and spotlights to cut through the gloom.

Jan scouted several conduits and accessways. Twice, the team pulled back to the brink of the sea to start over again because the route had narrowed to a squeeze so tight that the Battloids couldn't get through. The third try was a washout due to extremely high radiation levels; the VTs would protect their occupants for quite a while, but Jack had no idea how long the journey would take, and had no desire to end up as a human night-light.

The fourth try brought them into a sort of pipeline all aglow with the colors of the rainbow. The sensors couldn't determine what the light effects were, but they didn't seem harmful, and time was wasting. "Let's do it," Jack decided.

The team moved along like infantry, or SWAT officers, Lron covering the rear in a kind of crabstep, the enormous rifle/cannon of the Beta held at high port. The pipeline's diameter was about thirty feet, not much higher than the Battloids, and so the mecha moved cautiously.

In some places, the route was lined with pulsing bundles of filament as thick as a mecha's leg—like brilliant gatherings of unshielded optical fibers. In others, intertwinings of mysterious ducting and hoses resembled an incredible Robotech root system. Stupendous struts and support members were the geology of the underground world.

Gradually, though, the "terrain" started changing. The pipeline widened again, and the Battloids had as much room as foot soldiers moving along a highway. A world of dazzling, incomprehensible supertech complexity surrounded them. Light danced and tremendous loads of power surged and hummed.

It was a technological reflection of the nearby *Arabian Nights* cityscape in Glike. But, the manifestations were *above*, as well as around and below. Ziggurat power-management terminals bigger than any Egyptian pyramid; enigmatic things that looked like Van de Graaff generators the size of the Monument City Sportsdome; megastructures of warped, prismatic light that on closer inspection turned out to be mountains of contoured instrumentality.

As their route opened up into a kind of open countryside, they began to lose the oppressive feeling of being underground. That is, until Jan's voice came over the net.

"I'm picking up readings. I think these immunosystems, or whatever they are, are beginning to detect and respond to us again."

"What? Where?" Jack was punching buttons, searching frantically. "I don't see anything." *Don't tell me she's a sensor wizard, too!*

"Trust me, Jack." Her voice was so steady that he believed her. "There's something *big* ahead, something very big. Perhaps the nexus of everything that Haydon *is*, and now that we've stumbled so close to it, whatever it is, it's got a line on us again."

Jack didn't have time to ask her what she was jabbering about, because just then Kami yelled, "Snakes, snakes! *Millions of 'em!*"

Jack whirled even as Kami fired, forgetting the lessons about short, accurate bursts, the Garudan's Battloid hosing its rifle/cannon back and forth like a Robotech fireman.

The others were blazing away, too. Jack could see that whatever Kami spotted wasn't *really* snakes; but the undulating, crackling flows of green and yellow streaming toward the VTs would put that image in the mind of almost anybody—especially a Garudan in the *hin*-altered reality.

Not that Jack had much time to think; Janice Em was right. *Whatever it is we're getting close to, it's got a line on us*.

Like all the other Battloids, he brought his rifle/cannon

up, hoping the stress on Crysta and the captive Invid in the backseat of her cockpit hadn't harmed them.

"Security wheel!" he bellowed over the din of their cannonfire.

The vast space under Haydon IV was lit by stroboscopic bursts brighter than all the pulses of its power routing, as the Battloids formed a security wheel, backing up until their mighty shoulders grazed one another, firing outward to all points of the compass.

A sustained burst usually blew one of the energy snakes to dispersing sparks, and the Battloids soon cleared a ring of death around them. But more serpentines of energy were pouring from every crevice. The things massed, too numerous for even Robotech weapons to deal with, and closed in from every quarter like a worldscape of angry vipers.

CHAPTER

FOUR

*It would be fair to say that I have been less than sensitive to
the plight of the soldier in the past—have held military types in
utmost contempt. I had my reasons, which I have set down elsewhere in these pages.*

*But it's just as fair to point out that since I have become one of
them—shared their privations and sufferings and rare moments of
success, seen their despicable vices and their noble virtues up
close—I am a man chastened.*

From the journals of Flight Officer Isle, L., REF Service #
666-60-937

MINMEI HAD BEEN TO REF BASE TIROL MANY
times, but never via dark alleys and elevated roadway
foundations like some escaped convict.

She would have been curious about this flight officer—
Isle, his nametag said—except that she was feeling sick
again and was exhausted after the harrowing flight from
SDF-3.

They had abandoned the Alpha three miles back under
the shattered remains of a bridge in Old Tiresia. Isle was
successful in dodging his pursuers—they had gone rocket-
ing off in all directions trying to find him.

But why wouldn't he take off that flight helmet? Robotech fighter jocks sometimes felt a superstitious link to
their thinking caps, but really, this was a bit *eerie*.

Lang's R&D research complex was just ahead. Isle
seemed to regard it as safe ground, but Minmei wasn't so

sure. Nor would her savior explain why he couldn't simply land the VT at Lang's bailiwick.

According to the transmissions they had heard during the descent from the superdimensional fortress, Edwards was stripping much of his REF command for forces to pursue Breetai and the *Valivarre*. But Minmei knew that Edwards would never let her go, no matter what the circumstances.

Nevertheless, her small hand was in Isle's gloved one as he led her into an alley across a huge plaza from a rear gate of Lang's domain. But in front of the gate a quarter-mile away, mechanized troops from Edwards's ground forces were confronting Lang's security people. Obviously, Edwards had moved quickly to bottle Lang up and seal him off. Quite probably, Lang hadn't even the vaguest idea why.

Isle was unshaken, reversing field and pressing her back into the darkness. Just then two patrolling infantry went by across the plaza and one almost idly shone his light into it, picking out Isle and Minmei.

Isle turned with iron calm and led her back the way they had come, but by then there was a sound of pursuit: sirens and Hoverbikes and jeeps, tracked vehicles, yelling and crackling static on portable comsets.

A searchlight stabbed down from somewhere high overhead, and then several more lit the area. Isle pressed himself and Minmei up against a wall when one ranged close; then it moved on.

But, with a blaring of engines, a Hovertank pulled to a squealing stop at the far end of a back street, right in their path. Two squads of infantry rushed to block the opposite end, trapping the two between rows of blank buildings.

Isle pushed Minmei against a wall and produced a huge magnum machine pistol, the kind she had heard the soldiers call Badgers; non-Robotech, but murderously effective.

REF troopers were closing in from both sides, men and women alike. Probably, a lot of them were people who had listened to her songs at the service club. Minmei put her hand on the barrel of the Badger and pressed it down toward the ground. It didn't move.

"I can get you away from here." Still that flat, tinny sound from Isle's helmet speaker. "Minmei, I can save you." It sounded like he was offering redemption.

She was shaking her head. "By killing people? If you do, then god damn you! Because if *one more person* dies because of me, I'll kill *myself*!"

She said that last sentence showing her teeth to him, then turned as the spotlights were being lugged into place at the nearer end of the street. Minmei walked toward them as they converged. She had her hands out like a penitent saint.

"Hold your fire! We'll surrender! But I want you to let this man go free, here where I can see it! If you don't release him, you won't have either of us alive!"

She swooned a bit, leaning against a hard evercrete wall, and an indeterminate time passed. There were people around her, flashlight and handspot beams on her, people trying to peel her eyelid back as she screamed and spit and fought and slapped them away, bit at them, and shrieked the most obscene things she could think of.

Then she calmed down. "Let him go," she wept. "Let him go."

Then that most reviled of all voices was near her, Edwards's. "Let *who* go? Who was here, Minmei? Who kidnapped you?"

Edwards was still some distance from her—his weren't the restraining hands gripping her. She gulped air and blinked away her tears and saw that Edwards's troops had secured the area, but Isle wasn't there. He was nowhere to be seen.

She looked to the blank evercrete wall where she had

last seen him. Maybe there were slight punctures in it; the light was too dim to tell, especially with men and women holding her down. But anyway, there was only one person she could think of who could—

Edwards had been about to inflict new fear upon Minmei, some threat to scare her back into line. But Minmei's sudden, maniacal laugh put fear into *him* instead. "You know what you've finally done?" she screamed, frothing. "You've *awakened the dead*! And now your life is *finished*!"

Minmei, gamine though she was, almost pounced on him with fingers extended like claws; it took several groundpounders to hold her back.

"Straitjacket," Edwards said harshly, watching the struggle on the wet pavement.

Rain ran from his alloy cowl and glistening eye-lens, and from the pale fury of his face. "Put her in a straitjacket and get her over to my headquarters."

After the rest had gone, he looked at the wall to which Minmei had looked. In the dim light it was difficult to tell; those punctures were random—products of material defects and pitting and so forth, weren't they?

And yet, *someone* had flown the Alpha that no one seemed to be able to find. *Someone* had been standing next to her in a flight suit.

But Edwards didn't think Minmei would reveal the culprit's identity soon; he could hear her mad laughter and weeping as his security police bore her away.

"Commander! Faster-than-light craft appearing before us, screening our course. Two SDF-escort class, and they're sending challenges."

Breetai looked up from the private calculations he was making. "Patch it through."

He rose from the captain's chair on the bridge of the *Valivarre*. He unhurriedly squared away his Zentraedi longcoat, which was heavy with braid and decorations, all of them paid for in strife and blood. His skullpiece, all crystal and resplendent alloy, reflected the light.

"Attention, *Valivarre*!" came the Human voice. A face appeared on a screen above Breetai, a middle-age Human male's. The man was round-faced and florid, wearing a braided officer's cap.

"This is Commodore Renquist of the REF cruiser *Tokugawa*. On behalf of the Plenipotentiary Council, I order you to heave to and surrender yourself, your ship and crew, and the monopole ore."

The two cruisers were both of the latest type, designed and built by Lang's people. Breetai was a bit surprised; he would have thought Edwards was too unsure of his own position on Tirol to send so many of his faithful off on the mission to bring back the *Valivarre*.

As for Renquist, Breetai recognized the man's name. A lickspittle who had become one of Edwards's servants and been promoted over far more capable officers. Breetai had half expected Adams or Benson or one of the others from Edwards's inner circle to be in charge of any force sent against him, but Edwards must have realized that those traitorous vermin were nothing to send against the *Valivarre* and its hundred-strong Zentraedi warriors.

"You are guilty of piracy and mutiny as well as treason," Renquist was saying, voice shaking a little. "I will remind you of your oath, and give you one and only one chance to surrender."

"My oath and loyalty were given to the duly constituted Earth government, and to Admiral Hunter," Breetai boomed. "Not to your stinking General Edwards, or to you either, coward!"

Renquist's face took on the pallor and distortions of molten candlewax. Sweat started from his brow. *"You misbegotten freak! I'll have you blown to atoms!"*

Too bad the *Valivarre* hadn't gotten more of a head

start, Breetai reflected. His chances of ducking the cruisers would have been good, and he thought it unlikely that Edwards would let half of his main line of defense roam far from Tirol, or be gone for too long.

Of course, Breetai could try to evade them, but the faster SDF escort ships would dog his track easily. Furthermore, fighting a deepspace battle at superluminal speeds was tricky, and the advantage would lie with Renquist and his cruisers and Lang's new generation of weapons. It would be better to settle things here.

Breetai crossed his arms on his enormous chest. "I hardly think that's likely, since you would destroy all the monopole ore left in this region. And none of you will ever get home to Earth, will you? Nevertheless, if battle is what you seek, the Zentraedi will gladly accommodate you. Breetai has never run from a fight. Come, then!"

Renquist's throat worked as he swallowed laboriously; the bluff had failed, and both commanders knew it. In destroying the ore, Renquist would be sealing his own fate. He tried to show determination, but it only came out as a weak bluster. "By god, we beat you devils once, and we'll beat you again! If you don't surrender instantly, I'll give the order to launch!"

Breetai nodded gravely. "Let us not keep our pilots waiting, Commodore."

What Renquist had said was undeniable: the Humans *had* defeated the giant warriors years before. But this time Minmei wasn't there with her songs to turn Zentraedi against Zentraedi, and this time there was no SDF-1 with its final Barrier Shield explosion.

Breetai thought of an expression he had heard Max Sterling use: *We've got 'em over a barrel, and soon we'll have 'em in the barrel!* Only, who would be thus vanquished *this* time?

"He's launching mecha, my lord," a bridge tech said.

But not many of them—certainly not as many as the

cruisers carried. Perhaps it was a probe, or it might be that Edwards hadn't really spared as many of his Ghost Riders as it seemed at first. And maybe there was another element in this situation.

"Order forth our Battlepods," Breetai said in his super-basso voice. "And order the gunners to fire at will at the mecha, but *not* at the cruisers, is that clear?"

Alphas, Betas, and Logans rode trails of blue thruster fire across the eternal night, bearing down on the *Valivarre*. The huge Battlepods of the Zentraedi came out to meet them.

The giants' mecha were like gargantuan headless ostriches—torsos suggesting alloy light bulbs mounted on two long reverse-articulated legs. The chest plastrons were bristled with cannon and missile racks. Officers' pods had, in addition, extra two-barrel gun mounts that they brandished as if they were huge derringers.

The Human fliers were Ghost Riders, loyal only to Edwards, more than willing to slay the giants who had been Humanity's staunch allies not so long ago. They had been briefed on the pods' vulnerable spots and performance profiles; they swept in confidently.

One of the tactics that had given the Humans the upper hand in the Robotech War was developed when Miriya Sterling revealed a weakness in the pods' design. Concentrated fire on a spot just aft the junction of the legs would disable the pods and leave them drifting and helpless.

The first surprise the Ghosts got was in discovering that the pods had been retrofitted to overcome the Achilles' heel, and the second was that the pods' own weapons and accuracy were deadlier than ever. Furthermore, Breetai's pilots had plenty of experience in fighting VTs, while the young Ghost fliers had been trained after the end of the Robotech War. And these Zentraedi were among the very best.

The end result was that the first few moments of combat

saw Ghosts exploding in fireballs and erupting in white-hot wreckage, as the outnumbered Battlepods took an immediate upper hand. Once again, missiles lit the blackness, and beams of raging energy bickered back and forth.

Breetai watched a Logan come apart at the seams like a bursting melon, light and explosive force gushing from it. "We vowed to be your allies," he muttered, "but never your slaves or your victims."

On the bridge of the *Tokugawa*, Renquist watched, mortified, as the Zentraedi drove off his first attack wave with heavy casualties, though the giants had taken a few hits themselves. Operations and intel officers and their computers had a dozen poor excuses and supposed analyses, but he brushed them aside. The Ghosts were simply being outflown.

A face appeared on one of the side screens, a young flying officer. "Commodore, with all due respect, I must protest! We were given definite orders by the council to negotiate with Breetai before any direct action was taken!"

Renquist narrowed his eyes, his jowls quivering. "Negotiate, hell! How dare you? One more word from you and I'll have you executed for mutiny!" At an angry gesture from the commodore, the connection was broken.

But it reminded Renquist of another unfortunate aspect of his mission. As Breetai had guessed, Edwards was too wary to strip REF Base Tirol and SDF-3 of the bulk of his Ghosts and leave himself at risk. Therefore, nearly half the flying group assigned to Renquist was composed of elements drawn from the various other units remaining after the Skulls had been tapped for duty with the Sentinels. And the Jokers, Diamondbacks, and the rest were less eager to follow this departure from council instructions.

But Renquist felt he had now seen the enemy's total strength. After all, there were only slightly more than one hundred Zentraedi altogether! All he had to do was to make sure the Human numerical advantage was absolute.

The Zentraedi had won in a limited matching; but even after the initial defeat, Renquist could double the odds without resorting to any but the Ghost Riders and surely overwhelm the giants.

He turned to a bridge officer. "Launch the rest of the Ghosts immediately and reform the survivors of the first attack wave. This time we're going to crush those alien scum!"

Breetai had expected no less. The Alphas and Betas and Logans thronged at the Battlepods, driving them back or blowing them to smithereens, some of them breaking through and coming for the *Valivarre*.

The ore vessel's gun batteries and missile racks opened up, but she was a mining craft, not a warship; soon, shots threatened to penetrate her shields. Breetai noticed that the Ghosts were being very deliberate, shooting for the engines and control sections, seeking to disable rather than destroy.

The pods could no longer protect the ore ship. Breetai saw a badly damaged officer's mecha, beset by two Logans in Guardian mode, try to ram one of them. But the Logan avoided the kamikaze run and the two Humans got the pod in a crossfire, turning it into a fireball.

Then they turned and, with others, formed up to add their firepower to the final assault on *Valivarre*. Breetai watched them dive in at him, his face like a graven idol's.

CHAPTER
FIVE

She was too brilliant not to see the ramifications of her act. In taking half her race off on the pursuit of the Ultimate Invid Form and the New Optera, she would be forcing her husband to fend for himself in many ways—to confront certain things, to learn certain things. Things that—it isn't inconceivable—could force deevolution to turn end for end.

One possible motive for this is that there was some love for him in her still.

Gitta Hopkins, *Queen Bee: A Biography of the Invid Regis*

A LOW, ANGRY, CHAINSAW GROWL FROM THE HELL-cat made Cabell glance warily toward the thing, but Veidt seemed not to register its presence. The Regent reached down to stroke his pet's head, enjoying Cabell's uneasiness.

Cabell had good reason to be wary of the Invid Inorganic mecha called Hellcats. When the Invid first invaded Tirol, one had tried to tear him limb from limb.

Those sitting on their haunches to either side of the Regent's throne were even larger than the usual, and Hellcats were far bigger than any saber-tooth that ever lived. They were a glassy indigo, their eyes gleaming like ruby lasers. They were armed with razor-sharp claws, sword-edged shoulder horns and tail, and glittering fangs. About their muscular throats were resplendent collars set with gems from many worlds.

Cabell found himself transfixed by the 'Cats' baleful glares, so it was Veidt, looking and sounding serene as he floated there, who spoke. "Mighty Regent! Please accept our gratitude for granting us this moment of your attention. We know what great demands are placed on your time." He bowed solemnly.

"You have no idea," the Regent contradicted in his growling, gurgling voice, "none whatsoever!" His mantle flared and the four-fingered hands balled into fists the size of kegs.

"So do not flatter yourselves. I'm reconsolidating an interstellar empire, and you ask me to turn my thoughts to trifles. Still—*noblesse oblige*, and all that; I want it known that once I hold the universe in my fist, I will not be an unkind overlord." The mantle pulled back a bit.

Veidt bowed his head but looked unperturbed.

The Regent considered the matter with more caution than he would have admitted. The conflict revolving around Veidt, his mate Sarna, and Sarna's "father," Vowad —if such a concept as parentage could fairly be used with regard to Haydonites—concerned the whole planet. And it was one of the things that had worked to the Regent's advantage, he mulled.

Brute force was the standard Invid method of dealing with the enemy, but here on Haydon IV that was impossible. But intrigue, like warfare, was an art the Opterans had acquired after Zor destroyed their idyllic existence. And so, the Regent knew there were certain games that must be played, and played to best effect. Thus, this interview.

"No, you will find me most reasonable and benevolent, as I have been here today," the Regent added, knowing the planet itself was listening. "And how goes the healing?"

Cabell had found his nerve again. He smoothed his flowing, embroidered robes, shrugged to resettle the high, stiff collar that surrounded his head, and stroked the white beard that nearly reached his waist. "Rather well, we think, though it's difficult to tell. The Haydonites are using a sort of therapy employing their arts of nanoengineering. Prognoses are good."

"How fortunate for them." The Regent nodded, but he was silently angry that the effects of exposure to Garuda's biosphere hadn't killed the Hunters and the rest. "And now that you have brought me this report, you may go." The Regent gestured to his bodyguard commander to show the visitors out.

"Just a moment." Cabell stopped him. "There is the question of my apprentice, the young clone Rem. I ask you to release him to us, that he may undergo the treatments, too."

"I am not finished with Rem quite yet," the Regent said balefully, glancing down at them. Even seated, the tyrant overshadowed them like some pharaonic statue. "And as for you, you may go."

Now it was Cabell's turn to bristle; the anger in his voice quite surprised the Regent. "Not until you let me see that boy! Not until we take him for proper care!"

Hearing his tone, both Hellcats came to their feet, spitting and showing their long fangs. But Cabell was undeterred, meeting the Regent's fury with fury of his own.

Veidt spoke before Cabell could, though. "Great Regent! All the galaxy has heard of your vast intellect and spirit. Here now is your chance to prove that you can show mercy. Consider what praise it will win you! Why, word of it would reach even to the Regis herself."

Sly, the Regent mused, studying Veidt. For a race of artificial beings, the Haydonites showed surprising emotion and understanding of motivation.

Veidt had touched a nerve. Very likely, the Regis's spies would inform her of such a matter as the Regent's showing mercy—or if not, his own agents could see to it that she heard. More than almost anything, he wanted to win her back. And while his headlong plunge into deevolution kept him from truly understanding those impulses that guided his onetime mate, the Regent thought that mercy shown to the Zor-clone would certainly please her.

So he said, "Rem has already received the treatments I have permitted your companions to undergo, for I am not through with him as yet. Be that as it may, I will grant you a compromise solution: you may visit him in his confinement, provided that you try to get him to see reason."

The Regent's subject planetary systems, if they were eavesdropping, would no doubt register *that* in the Regent's favor. He was quite proud of himself. He had turned the bothersome visit of Veidt and Cabell around so that he might profit from it in a number of ways.

And, with a little luck, he had bought enough time to come up with a way of slaying the Sentinels once and for all.

Jack Baker shot yet another of the energy serpents, watching it de-rezz into fast-swirling will-o'-the-wisps of light that dissipated and went dark. It occurred to him that those flickering pinpoints of light might be fading only to reconverge and come at him again, but there was no time to wonder about that.

"Jack! Two o'clock!" gritted Learna, who stood to Jack's right, still finishing off a writhing, crackling mass that was headed straight for her from *her* right. Twelve o'clock was the leader's position, of course.

Jack finished blowing away a bunch of the things to his left that were wriggling at him, then traversed his beam and flamed the two-o'clock snakes. He caught sinuous movement to his left again and began hosing down a nearby console with a sustained Protoculture salvo; it was thick with energy serpents, like a medusa.

Bela, in the Battloid's rear—now lower—seat, whistled and made ear-piercing war cries, when she wasn't spotting new targets for him. She seemed to be enjoying herself.

The Battloids' security wheel was surrounded by a sea of undulating glow-shapes; more and more seeped forth by the second, from every crevice and feature of the place. The mecha swept their constant-fire aim around and up and back, but the snakes closed in relentlessly. It was as if the technolandscape had come alive.

The Battloids fought with all the strength, power, and precision that Robotechnology had built into them, but it seemed hopeless. Energy levels were dropping sharply due to the ferocious demands of the weapons systems.

My first real command, Jack thought bitterly, *and my last, too, maybe. Perfect record: no wins.*

Then he thought of the afflicted—Karen and the others —somewhere above, in Glike. And Veidt, Cabell, and the rest of the escorts would be there, too, all of them counting on Jack's team to get through.

But it was Karen's face he saw before him, and it made him fight like a man possessed.

But even the awesome firepower of five titan Battloids wasn't enough to keep back the tide of Haydon defenders; energy serpents struck at the foot of Jan's mecha, sending out bursts of heat and light, and dissolving metal. She lurched, checked herself when her first impulse was to stomp them (which would only have made it that much easier for them to damage her), and zapped them instead, melting decking and sending gobs of incandescence flying.

But while Janice was doing that, another dozen snakes got in close enough to coil and strike at Kami, who was to *her* right. The shields appeared to give no protection whatsoever against the things. In the meantime, several more dropped onto Lron from high overhead and began melting their way through his Battloid.

Jack made himself face the fact that there was no way

out for the Battloids. Snakes were beginning to rain down from the ceiling, and he couldn't see any avenue of retreat for the mecha. It was a command he hated giving as much as a naval officer would hate giving the order to abandon ship, but Jack gritted his teeth and said, "Prepare to eject."

He got no argument; everyone had seen that their current situation was untenable, and knew that getting clear of the Protoculture-powered mecha was their only chance. While listening to the others run through the eject checklist and doing so himself, Jack hit a control stud as he imaged his ship.

His Battloid made a bowling movement. Crysta's cockpit/escape capsule went sliding into the clear along the decking. A rough ride, but better than being consumed by Haydon IV's gruesome defenses. The snakes ignored the module, but kept coming at the VTs.

"You all strapped in tight back there, Bela?"

"Take us for a ride, Jackie boy!" she roared merrily.

Jack hurried his checklist rundown, to catch up with the others. The Veritechs had zero-zero-eject systems, so that occupants could survive a punch-out even at ground level, even at a standstill.

The snakes had gotten through on the decking now, swarming at them, while more rained down from every cranny in the ceiling like some bizarre neon version of an Old Testament plague. "All right, everybody: hit it!" Jack barked. "And once you touch down, keep moving and don't look back!"

Janice had already punched out, pieces of her Battloid blown free by explosive bolts so that her cockpit could be fired clear on blue eruptions of Protoculture power. Kami and Learna went at almost exactly the same moment, lofted through the air along with their passengers.

Jack hesitated until he saw that Lron was away, and then reached for his eject switch. He hit it, then reached up, crossing his arms during the fuse-delay to grab his seat harness, hands to opposite shoulders.

He gripped with everything he had and held his elbows tightly to him so that his arms would not flap around and get broken when the charges went off.

He almost didn't make it; the snakes had gotten through his mecha's shin armor and attacked the systemry there.

A power flux sent the metal goliath reeling, and for a moment Jack thought he and Bela were going to be fired straight into a metal rampart of Haydonite apparatus. But at the last split second, the Battloid responded to his frantic imaging and straightened. The jolt of the ejection felt like it was going to push his head down into his chest cavity.

Bela let out a lusty battle cry, mixed with her deep laughter. Jack was not nearly so boisterous.

Lron and the rest were already scrambling free of their cockpit/escape capsules. Crysta and her Invid passenger came trotting toward the grounded capsules from the spot where her cockpit had stopped after Jack bowled it into the clear.

Even the Invid captives—Tesla and the two scientists—were stepping lively. Jack was fumbling to hit the releases on his safety harness before his capsule smacked the decking, partially crumpling its skin.

He heard Jan's voice over his helmet phones. "Get clear of your capsules! Hurry! The snakes have sensed them somehow!"

Jack blew the canopy and scrambled out to stand on his seat, grasping the windshield frame. Jan was right: most of the snakes were still massing to smother the now-motionless Battloids, but some had turned toward them and were slithering in the direction of the ejection capsules.

"Bela, come on!" He was popping emergency panels, grabbing out gear and weapons from the drop-lockers.

But she was already on her feet, gathering up her Praxian weapons and the REF gear she had brought along. "Right behind you, laddy-buck."

Janice Em had laid down fire with her Wolverine assault rifle, but powerful as it was, it wasn't very effective. The shots seemed to make the snakes take notice of her and move to converge on her. On sudden impulse, she took the weapon and hurled it as far from her as she could. Snakes were on it even as it clattered to the decking, striking at it as if the rifle were a living enemy.

"Get rid of your Protoculture weapons!" she yelled over the net. "That's how they're sensing us!"

Jack had gathered up his own gear, but now he threw aside his Wolverine and his Shiva energy handgun as well. All around him, the others were doing the same. As each discarded weapon landed, snakes piled onto it, striking at it with bites that sent up fireworks and scoria.

The party moved away from the capsules carefully, picking their way among snakes that only seemed interested in getting at the ejection modules. There were detonations from the beseiged Battloids as they toppled or erupted from the effect of the snakebites.

Jack's little command took shelter behind a bank of cognizance relays, ducking away from the final, bright explosions that obliterated the mecha. At Jack's command, those who weren't wearing flight helmets kept their hands over their ears and their mouths wide open, so that they wouldn't be deafened. Wreckage whirled and debris ricocheted off the walls of the machine-cavern.

Jack was already taking stock of his situation, and there was nothing about it that made him want to do victory rolls. True, they still had conventional firearms and the Praxian, Garudan, and Karbarran weapons. And the handheld inertial trackers would give them a direction of sorts. But there were only the limited emergency rations of food and water in the ejection packs, and no viable hope of raising Vince Grant or the others up on the surface with the flight-helmet communicators.

Most of the equipment the team had brought along had been destroyed with the VTs. They were more like a bunch of marooned survivors than a raiding party.

But there was one critical thing in their favor: the snakes were ignoring them. Now that the Battloids were smoking wreckage, the snakes seemed to be dissolving away, perhaps returning to whatever fabrication matrices had given them form. Powerful blasts of fire-fighting gas belched from fixtures all around the remains of the Battloids, extinguishing the fires, and tremendous ventilators created a minor windstorm, drawing away the fumes.

"Walking is good healthy exercise anyway, so my mom used to tell me," Bela said cheerfully, getting to her feet. She was checking over her crossbow and resettling the two-handed shortsword she carried. Clearly, her skintight REF flightsuit was less comfortable to her than the rather daring fighting costume she usually wore.

Gnea, looking like a giant, lissome seventeen-year-old, went to join her friend and mentor. Gnea held one of the *naginata*like Praxian halberds, a polearm with a curved, glittering head and a wicked spike set at the opposite end. Jack had seen the two use their weapons in combat, and had learned the foolishness of underestimating primitive arms.

He checked his inertial locator; there was no use going back, and so Glike was their only hope now. But then he noticed Janice, standing to one side, distracted. She looked as if she were listening to some distant siren song to which the rest of them were deaf.

"It's near," she whispered. "Somewhere close, and it's aware of us." Burak, horned like an auroch, who had ridden with her, looked at her strangely.

"What is?" Crysta asked. She was pumping up the globular reservoir of her long Karbarran pneumatic rifle with its hinged forestock lever. "Janice, what is it you perceive?"

"Haydon IV the artificial world has a mind, an Awareness," Janice said, as if in a dream. "And the seat of that Awareness, its nexus, is not far away."

She knew it was true, but couldn't understand how the knowledge had been given to her. She turned to them. "We must go to it!"

"Huh-uh." Jack was shrugging into his packstraps. "They'll be waiting for us up there in Glike, remember? Admiral Hunter, and Karen and the rest? People we're supposed to rescue? I admit things haven't exactly been beer and skittles so far, but we're not gonna let 'em down. We stick to the plan."

Janice Em found that she couldn't answer. She felt like a double image on a monitor screen, ghostly twins standing side by side. The whirlpool of thoughts and sensory impulses that spun within her had stolen her voice, immobilized her. Vast forces were vying within her.

She had a sudden sense of Lang—not of the Robotech genius's physical presence, but rather of his voice, his intellect. Intentionally submerged memories had surfaced in this moment of crisis. Changes were triggered in the being the REF and the Sentinels—and even Minmei—knew as Janice Em.

As she transformed her companions drew away from her.

CHAPTER
SIX

Anybody who says million-to-one odds are unbeatable never had Breetai standing on their side of the scales at the weigh-in.

Lisa Hayes Hunter, *Recollections*

THERE WAS NO REALITY, NO ORDERLY FLOW OF TIME, no ground underfoot or substantial object that she could touch. She was in a void, without form, as she had been for so long.

Then things began to impinge upon her. It came to her that her name was Karen Penn. Other facts and memories and realizations coalesced.

She was a member of the Sentinels by way of the Robotech Expeditionary Force. Her mother had died in childbirth, and her father held that against Karen to this day. There was another young officer, Jack Baker, whom she—

She blocked that thought out. But there were more—the memory of how she had been poisoned by the atmosphere of Garuda, swept up in the hallucinatory expanded mindstate the Garudans called *hin*, a state for which the human mind had never been intended. Then there were the nightmares, the visions, the visitations of the endless mindstorm of the *hin*. Some had been horrible, some of terrible beauty, but all had strained her grip on her sanity and the very functions of her autonomic nervous system.

The flickering spark of her life had been all but out when without warning something seemed to be fanning it, encouraging it to glow and grow brighter. Then there was an almost physical feeling, as if she were being flushed out with snowmelt water from a mountain river—as if she were wired up with electrodes.

And a chorus of somehow silent voices, singing words she never quite understood, drew her up and up from the verge of death.

Over the preceding weeks, Karen had dreamed or hallucinated many times. Now she had finally awakened. This time, what she saw made her sob a bit, with relief.

Lieutenant Commander Miriya Sterling sat at her bedside, holding Karen's hand. Once the battle queen of the Zentraedi's feared Quadrono Battalion, now wife to Max Sterling, leader of the Skull Squadron, Miriya had fought for the Human race and the Sentinels as hard as she had ever fought for the Robotech Masters—or even harder; love had shown her the way.

Miriya gave Karen a tender smile that seemed out of character with the ferocity of a Quadrono. She smoothed a lock of Karen's hair. "Welcome back."

Karen tried to speak, not even sure what she would say, but Miriya hushed her. "You'll still be weak for a little while; the rest of us were, too. Just rest."

Miriya turned and spoke softly over her shoulder. "Dr. Grant? She's awake."

Another face came into view over Miriya's shoulder, a heart-shaped face with big black eyes and skin the color of dark honey. "Take it slow," Dr. Jean Grant said. "You're gonna be just fine, Karen."

Karen concluded that she wasn't in a Sentinels' sick

bay; that much was apparent from what she could see of her surroundings. The apparatus all around her—what she took to be med equipment—had the look of geometrical sculptures in crystal and precious metals, and abstract shapes of neon and laser light. She recalled seeing the same design technology in the Haydonites' module of the starship *Farrago*. She reached an understandable conclusion.

"Haydon IV?" Jean and Miriya both nodded their heads slowly. "Then, we've done it? We've liberated another planet from the Invid?"

"No, Lieutenant." Lisa Hayes Hunter stepped into Karen's line of sight, Rick following a step behind.

"Garuda was freed," Lisa went on, "but several of us were stricken by the planet's biosphere. Our only chance was Haydonite science, so Vince and Jean and several others brought us here, under a flag of surrender."

"Not surrender," Rick rasped. "*I* never surrendered to the Invid, and neither did you! Besides, they don't rule Haydon IV, at least not officially, so a surrender's null and void."

Karen was startled to see how hateful his expression was, not just in mentioning the Invid but toward everything that had brought him to this moment. She figured the Hunters had already done battle in private.

"I'm *never* surrendering!" he swore.

Lisa looked like she was about to say something but then thought better of it. To cover the awkward silence, Jean got Karen to sit up. There were assorted Haydonites hovering at a polite distance, and through the windows of the Hall of Healing Karen could see the wonderland of Glike, with its flying carpets and fairy-tale architecture.

"Vince, Colonel Wolff, and Max are trying to find Sarna and get an update on what's going on," Miriya said. "And Cabell and Veidt have an audience with the Regent."

Karen Penn tried to phrase her next question carefully.

Everything was a blur concerning the disastrous raid on the Invid base on Garuda, but she felt a sudden fear. "Did we suffer—many casualties? On Garuda?"

That seemed to lessen the tension a little. Jean smiled slightly. "It could've been a lot worse. Jack's just fine, Karen."

Karen blushed and stammered, "I—I didn't mean—that is—" The last thing she wanted was for anybody to think she had a soft spot for that salivating show-off, Jack Baker!

One of the Haydonite healers glided closer. "You will pardon the interruption, one hopes, but time draws near for another treatment for you, Miriya Sterling."

"But—" Karen felt a sudden misgiving. "I thought we were all healed?"

Miriya's expression was mournful. "You are—and so am I, I hope. But there's been a complication in my case."

She rose and patted Karen's shoulder. "You see, I'm pregnant, and we don't know how the Garudan exposure may have affected that." She squared her shoulders and set off in military style, chin high, surrounded by hovering Haydonites.

"That's all the more reason we've got to get out of here," Rick said. "I say we make a break as soon as we can."

"Not until we're sure Miriya's all right," Lisa contradicted firmly.

"What good'll it do to have her healthy in an Invid dungeon?" he snapped. "Everybody knows that what the Invid want around here, they get sooner or later! And I'm not about to let myself be—"

Lisa whirled on him again. "Then go—go on, save yourself! But we're not abandoning Miriya, or Rem!"

They held the tableau for a moment, and Karen was stunned by the realization that they were very close to striking one another.

Just then another Haydonite drifted up to them, cloak

billowing. "We've just received word for you all to hold yourselves in readiness. The Regent has commanded that you appear before him to answer the charges against you."

As Breetai watched the Ghost Riders rush in to finish off his Battlepods and the *Valivarre*, he spoke a single name.

"Kazianna!"

Her face appeared in a small inset on the master screen. "Your orders, great Breetai?"

At another time he would have gazed upon Kazianna Hesh with fondness: the Zentraedi warrior-woman who had somehow come to understand the meaning of Human love and lovemaking, and taught those things to her battle lord. But this was combat, and Breetai was focused completely.

"Strike now, Quadronos!"

Kazianna gave a hungry smile behind her tinted face-bowl. "We strike, my lord!"

From the locks and launch bays of *Valivarre*, new mecha swept forth on brilliant plumes of thruster fire, as a score of Quadronos entered the fray. The Ghost Riders, most of them too young to have served in the Robotech War, were bewildered, not understanding what these high-speed, extremely maneuverable new opponents were.

Kazianna led the way, as swift and agile as a hornet, unleashing the tremendous firepower of her armored suit. On her first attack pass, she flamed a Logan, and moments later a second. Behind her, Robotech harpies poured into the opening she had made in the Ghosts' formation, unleashing missiles and high-energy beams. The giant female warriors of the Quadronos, primed for battle and having the advantage of surprise, began rolling up a fearsome kill score at once.

Aboard his flagship, Commodore Renquist couldn't understand what was going on at first. All he knew for sure was that there were frantic cries over the Ghosts' tactical commo net, and that the computer displays showed the REF fliers taking terrible losses.

After some moments, databanks matched up these new antagonists with file information: Quadrono-powered armor suits containing forty-five and fifty-foot-tall giantesses, clearly veterans of one of the Zentraedi's most feared units.

"Impossible!" Renquist bit out. Those powered armor suits that were left after the war had been adapted for mining, and all intelligence evaluations agreed that the Zentraedi lacked the technical skill to refit them for combat—at least, without Human help.

What Renquist didn't know—what the Zentraedi had chosen to keep to themselves—was that a return to Fantoma and their former way of life had resulted in a resurgence of their memories, the ones the Robotech Masters were supposed to have submerged forever. The grueling mining operations forced a reflowering of the Zentraedi innovative genius.

The Ghost Riders found themselves dogfighting with a swarm of fire-breathing viragoes whose powered armor gave them a distinct edge. The REF mecha were driven back, or simply blown out of existence. The Battlepods, bringing up the rear, mopped up for the Quadronos and flew cover.

Male Zentraedi had a good deal to ponder, Breetai saw with some satisfaction.

He had a commo channel opened to Renquist once again. "Commodore, I'll offer you the chance to withdraw your forces and let us go our way in peace. You can't win, you see."

Renquist was visibly shaken, all color gone from his face. The Ghost Riders had been nearly wiped out, and he wasn't at all sure that the remaining fliers would obey his orders.

But he knew what he could expect from Edwards if he

went home in defeat. "You alien monster! I'll see you in hell first!"

"*Eventually*, perhaps," Breetai conceded, and transmitted a signal to Kazianna.

She darted right through the enemy interceptors and AA fire, as nimble as the legendary Miriya herself, to close in on the cruiser's bridge. Too late, Renquist realized what was happening. Before he could even give the order to clear the bridge, Kazianna let go a tremendous blast at point-blank range, penetrating the shields and bursting the vast curve of viewpane there.

Renquist and his trusted Ghost staff, and Edwards's personal security men, were scorched and blackened, whirled headlong by the outrushing atmosphere, the air flooding from their lungs in a mist despite their every effort to hold it in.

Kazianna had already flung herself away from the cruiser rather than follow up on her advantage. Breetai had no wish to inflict more casualties than he had to. Even as she did so, word came that the few surviving Ghost Riders were breaking contact.

Valivarre and the two cruisers stood motionless, at a face-off, while REF officers struggled with damage control and tried to reestablish a chain of command.

At last Captain da Cruz, of the *Tokugawa*'s sister ship, the *Jutland*, contacted Breetai. He asked her, "Captain, will you accept my offer and part courses under a truce flag?"

"Sir, we will not," da Cruz, a gangly woman with olive skin and iron-gray hair gathered in a tight knot at her neck, responded.

"I understand." Breetai nodded. "My warriors and I await your pleasure."

"Lord Breetai, you misunderstand. It is my opinion, and that of most others in this contingent, that orders were violated when you were attacked. I have had access to certain sealed instructions given Commodore Renquist by General Edwards, and it is my opinion that the Sentinels are now to be found on Haydon IV.

"What I propose is that the *Jutland*—and the *Tokugawa*, as soon as emergency repairs can be made on her—accompany you there on your mission to find Rick and Lisa Hunter and the others. We will render military aid as needed, and escort the admiral and his wife and the rest to REF Base Tirol so that they can make a fair answer to the charges against them."

Da Cruz permitted herself the raising of an eyebrow. "You see, many of us find it difficult to picture the Hunters as traitors, too."

The corners of Breetai's lips turned up. "Perhaps we can help with the repairs to the *Tokugawa*, madam. You might say we've become a bit inventive of late."

CHAPTER
SEVEN

There are more enjoyable things in life than being a hero. Having shingles, for instance.

Jack Baker, *Upwardly Mobile*

THE RAIDING PARTY STARED, AGHAST, AT THE THING that had been Janice Em.

Her skin had become transparent, and the blood vessels and musculature of her face could be seen. Her eyes emitted an eerie light; what there was of her expression seemed flat, unblinking and un-Human.

Jack found that he had instinctively raised his submachine gun. "Wh-what are you, a *zombie*?" He felt stupid even saying it.

Her voice, when it came, had much of Janice's tone and manner. "No; I am an Artificial Person, built in the Tokyo research megaplex. I've acted as Dr. Lang's eyes and ears on the Sentinels mission."

Lron's broad, thickly furred chest rumbled. "I don't like such things—androids running around pretending they are alive!"

The AP was quick to answer, "Oh, but the Janice you know was unaware that she *was* an Artificial Person—an android, if you insist. But I'm still Janice, with all the thoughts and memories of Janice. Only, I'm aware of the other side of my personality at last—that which served Lang. You might say I'm finally whole."

"But why do you reveal this *now*?" Bela asked suspiciously. She had rather liked Jan—admired her for being as quick and strong and skilled in battle as an amazon. But Bela looked upon this being before her—a *Wyrdling*, as Praxians would call it—with wariness.

"Because we mustn't follow the inertial trackers directly to Glike," the AP answered. "The Awareness that oversees Haydon IV is near, and I think it's the key to our dilemma. I saw that there was no other way to get you to detour, though, and if I'd merely slipped away, you'd have come searching for me and put yourselves in greater danger. I understand friendship that well, you see."

She put one hand back to gather up her long lavender hair and hold it out from the nape of her neck. "And there is another reason to reveal myself. To locate the source of this Awareness I must contact it directly, and to do that—I must speak to it."

She reached up with her free hand and pulled a patch of synthetic skin from her neck. She turned to show them the input aperture that had been hidden there. There was a concerted hiss from the two lesser Invid scientists, and Tesla's eyes bulged with fascination. Burak slashed the air angrily with his horns and made a mystical sign of protection.

Jan let her hair fall back into place, and dipped into a pouch on her harness. She came up with connector cord and several different sorts of adaptors. "According to my analysis, one of these will let me link up with this artificial sentience I've detected."

"No! She's not to be trusted," Tesla objected. "An an-

droid? How can we know what her real motive is? Better
that *I* were allowed to converse with this Awareness, my
friends."

Jack looked Tesla over. The Regent's onetime chief scientist no longer resembled a conventional upper-caste
Invid; some time after the awful events on Garuda, he had
undergone some kind of change that he still refused to explain.

He was now almost as tall as the Regent—over seven-
teen feet. His snout was shorter, head more defined, hands
and feet more humanoid than reptilian. His hide was now a
pale green, waxy and smooth.

But most troubling of all, he had grown a fifth digit, and
his hands and his use of them looked quite Human.

Tesla had convinced the Sentinels that he could be of
help on this mission, but Jack wasn't about to trust the
scientist with the secrets of Haydon IV. He moved the
muzzle of his chattergun over to cover Tesla. "Forget it.
You stay away from the machinery down here unless I say
otherwise."

Tesla radiated an unspeakable hatred, but said nothing.
Burak bridled, too, and moved to stand by the Invid. Jack
had long since noticed that there was something between
the two, some secret they shared, but Burak's gesture was
more on the order of a realignment of loyalties.

Burak had been growing a little unstable. He resented it
that his homeworld, Peryton, was far back on the timetable
of Sentinels priorities. Jack made a mental note to keep an
eye on him, as well.

"Okay, uh, Janice." Jack decided that he might as well
go on calling her that. "What d'you need?"

"First, a proper interface." She led them off along the
highway-wide catwalk; they automatically took up tactical
positions and intervals. They passed into a smaller side
passageway, one the VTs would never have managed. The
other raiders were jumpy, expecting Haydon IV to come up

with new horrors, but Jan seemed blithely confident that away from their Protoculture-powered mecha and weapons they would no longer be considered invaders.

Janice's theory might be correct, but Jack still thought longingly of all the firepower they had been forced to abandon.

Janice appeared to be finding her way like an Indian in deep forest, listening and kind of sniffing the air currents as well as searching the future-tech terrain with her gaze.

As they trailed along, they grew hotter. Lron and Crysta shed their outsize flight suits completely, abandoning them except for helmets—and the commo equipment in them— and the harnesses that held their gear and weapons.

Jack, Kami, and Learna removed their helmets as well, attaching them to their web gear, and the two Garudans put on their special breather masks.

At last Janice stopped in another vast open place big enough to hold a cruiser. Before them was a surprisingly delicate-looking affair that reminded Jack of a filament-bright cat's cradle the size of the REF headquarters building back on Tirol.

There were tiers of instrumentation all around; Jan selected one right away. It only took her a moment or two to figure out which adaptors to use, in which configuration, and then she was ready.

Jack volunteered to make the connection. As he stood by with the plug in his hand, Jan seemed to revert to her Human side again. "If you see me go into overload, get the plug out at once. I mean, right away, okay Jack?"

"Sure; right." It hadn't occurred to him that she was risking her life—if that was the correct term. He nervously worked his fingers in his flight glove, hoping it would insulate him from any power surges.

With Jan holding her hair aside again, he took a deep breath and plugged the adaptor into the outlet in her neck. Banks of peripheral instrumentation came alive in light of various colors and a deep humming filled the chamber; the humming rose in pitch until it sounded like a synthesized choir.

A glow sprang out from Janice Em, and Jack nearly pulled the plug, but she managed in a breathless voice, "Don't . . . don't."

Jack stepped back to watch as she was bathed in radiance. He thought he could sense conversations being held all around him, and the flow of rivers of information. He spun to see how the other raiders were weathering.

Bela and Gnea were unafraid, but had closed ranks. Lron and Crysta had their weapons in their hands, but didn't look like they were going to blow holes in anything; their service in the Sentinels had taught them a certain self-control.

Kami and Learna were looking about them in rapture, and Jack wondered what they were seeing and hearing. They were inhaling through their breather masks, drawing the atmosphere of Garuda, with its myriad microscopic symbiotes, into their lungs. He knew they were in the expanded mindstate of *hin*, and wished he could know how the systemry of Haydon IV was manifesting itself to them.

The two lesser Invid POWs, Garak and Pye, were cringing in a corner, but Tesla had drawn himself up to his full height, hands reaching into the air imploringly. He lurched toward a stack of control panels and indicators like a long-lost lover.

Jack squeezed off a short burst into the decking in the scientist's path, tracers drawing bright warning lines, ricochets glancing away into the distance. Tesla stopped as if someone had slapped him out of a trance, gazing down at the dully gleaming bullet-smears of lead at his feet.

Jack had the submachine gun up to his shoulder, Tesla bracketed in the sight blades. Tesla moved back a step, and then another, until he was back where he had been standing. Jack stole a quick glance aside at Burak, who was fingering his Garudan small arm, a thing that looked like a grappling hook.

Burak looked indecisive, but it was plain that he was furious with Jack's intervention. Then a hand fell on Burak's shoulder: Bela had shouldered her crossbow and held her shortsword in her other hand. Gnea held her halberd ready. There was no struggle, only an understanding that Burak was to lower his weapon and stand his ground, or else see his head fly from his shoulders. He chose the former option.

Wise decision, Jack thought. *Otherwise those ladies would probably have your horns on their living-room wall, kid.*

"Look!" Jack pivoted, seeing what Crysta was bellowing about. His jaw dropped.

Janice Em was still wrapped in a strobing aurora, but she was *changing appearance*. One moment, she was the Janice who had sung with Minmei and later joined the Sentinels. The next, she was the Artificial Person she had revealed herself to be. Then she was something even more disturbing—a transparent Human being or a Spherisian. And after that she flickered, seeming to be a Haydonite, with their smooth lack of features, an ectoplasmic robe flowing around her as she hovered above the decking.

The brilliance grew more intense, so that they could barely endure it. Jack thought about spraying a burst into the machinery or turning a random control, but decided that might get them into even worse trouble.

A wind swept through the mammoth chamber, and somewhere in the center of the light Janice was shifting through various forms—some Human, some not. Kami was baying in hysteria, and Tesla was screaming, while Lron had both hands clapped to his ears. Gnea and Bela, arms outspread, swords lifted, were war goddesses howling a banshee challenge to the elements.

Just when it seemed they couldn't bear it anymore, the

light faded and the sound died away. The air lost every breath of movement. In the stillness that followed, the raiders collected themselves and blinked away the dazzling lights circling before their eyes.

Janice Em stood once more in her Human form, the disconnected interface jack in her hand. "Are you all right?" Bela ventured.

"Yes, quite, thank you." She sounded distant, but then she beamed at them in a very *Homo sapiens* smile.

"I'm fine, and I found out what we need to know."

"But . . ." Jack realized his submachine gun's muzzle was pointed her way and quickly lowered it. "What was all that shape-changing about?"

Janice looked up at the web of light. "You might say that Haydon IV has been teaching me a few things about my own capabilities and potential. The Tokyo project teams and even Dr. Lang, I'm afraid, didn't quite realize them all."

She collected herself, turning her attention to matters at hand. "But that's beside the point now. We must be on our way."

She had bent to pick up her own weapons and equipment. "And we must hurry. The others are in danger, up above in Glike, and we have to get to them at once."

"Huh? Hey!" Jack trotted after to catch up, as Jan started for a nearby column of instrumentality. The others fell in behind, Gnea and Bela in particular making sure the Invid kept up and got into no mischief.

The column was the circumference of a spaceport control tower, stretching from the floor to the ceiling. As Jan approached it, a section of flickering indicators slid aside, revealing a small compartment.

Jan turned on her companions, silencing their objections, demands, and threats. "Listen: I'll answer any question you want, explain everything I can, on the journey.

Only, we *must start now*, and this is the first step on the road to Glike."

Jack blew his breath out, cheeks bulging like a bugler's. "If I survive, I'm never volunteering for anything again. Okay; let's march."

The place wasn't too cramped; they had about as much room as in a half-filled elevator. None of them was particularly surprised when the compartment closed up again and there was a feeling of movement, straight up.

"First question," Jack said tiredly. "D'they have rest rooms on this flight?"

"You should've thought of that before we left." Janice Em grinned back at him.

The medics had injected her with something calculated to speed along her sobering—making her neurotransmitters block the acute depressant effects and raising her P3 waves. But Minmei was still writhing between a pair of Ghost Rider security people as she was dragged before Edwards in his office on the top floor of Base Tirol HQ on Fantoma.

She had tried to bite, scratch, and kick, but the REF people were used to hand-to-hand combat, and even though they were under orders not to retaliate, they had kept her from inflicting any significant damage. Exhausted, she was pushed forcefully into a chair and kept seated.

Her face was smudged with dirt and tears. Through a sort of blur, she saw a figure move and heard Edwards's voice. "Wait outside," he told his troops.

She heard the brittle fury in his voice and became truly afraid for the first time. She had seen his moods before, knew he was capable of anything when he was like this— even of murdering her on the spot.

She wiped her eyes and tried to stop crying. Edwards

was standing behind his desk, hands clasped at the small of
his back.

"Who was the pilot who helped you escape?"

"Go to hell," she choked.

He walked unhurriedly from behind the desk. "Where
did you think you were going?"

"God damn you!"

He moved with stunning speed, grabbing a fistful of her
hair and winding it painfully, making her cry out, holding
her in her seat with his other hand.

"Do you really think you can ever be free of *me*, Minmei? I *never* yield anything that's mine; you should know
that by now." His voice was very soft, as if it calmed him
to be hurting her.

Minmei resisted ineffectually for a moment, then gave
up. "Go ahead! Do what you want! You think being cruel
makes you strong? I've known *real* men, and compared to
them you're a pitiful excuse for a Human being and a miserable failure as a lover—"

Her own scream cut her off, as he gave her more pain.
He had her wrist in a hold that felt like he was about to
break it, and he shook her head back and forth slowly to
emphasize each word. "Your Jonathan Wolff's dead by
now, like Hunter and the rest. Were you going to join the
Zentraedi? They got in my way, too; they're finished."

He knelt, pulling her face around to his. "I told you
there are things I know, things I've learned since we got to
Tirol, that will give me unlimited power. Unlimited *control*. You may not love me willingly, but *you will love me*."

Nothing Minmei had ever heard had terrified her like
those words. She could feel his hot breath on her; it sick-
ened her.

"Now, you're going to tell me everything I want to
know, and all the rest of it. And in the meantime we'll just
keep you nice and calm."

The general reached out with his free hand and buzzed

for the guards. All her blathering about awakening the dead—it had to be mad raving, of course, he told himself, but it still bothered him. And yet a search of the area had turned up no sign whatsoever of the pilot who had spirited her off SDF-3, nor could Edwards's agents produce any clues.

The dead might mean a number of things, but Edwards suspected he knew whom she meant. Preposterous . . .

He flung her at the guards. "Lock her up, dry her out. I want no one to get word of this. Complete cover-up. Tell the interrogators to keep me updated."

After the guards had dragged her out, Edwards gazed out the window.

He could hardly know that, far across a distant landing-site hardtop, a man in a pilot's suit was staring back through a telebinoc at the silhouette so far away that was a mortal enemy.

Lieutenant Isle lowered the telebinoc. All the elaborate security systems and complex equipment and weaponry between him and Edwards were just an abstract problem in mission planning now; just a layered project requiring the proper application and strength of will.

But the battle itself was joined.

■ □ ■ □ ■ □ ■ □ ■ □ ■ □ ■ □ ■ □ ■ □ ■ □ ■ □ ■ □ ■

CHAPTER
EIGHT

If Sartre's right and the history of every person is the story of failure, then something's outta whack here.

Commander Vincent Grant, quoted in *The Sentinels*, by
Le Roy la Paz

I F GLIKE WAS ENCHANTING FROM THE LANDING STAGES
and spires of the city, it was overwhelming from the van-
tage point of a Haydonite cone-flier.

Vince, mesmerized by the fantasyland view, blinked in
surprise to realize that the cone was hovering, with its
disk-rim up against a landing stage, over the summit of a
skyscraper that suggested an inverted icicle. The transparent dome under which he, Jonathan Wolff, and Max had
been standing now parted, providing a debarkation gate.

But the landing stage was empty. Max turned to their
Haydonite pilot suspiciously. "You said you were taking us
to Sarna."

The Haydonite was smaller and more slender than either
Veidt or Sarna and had an emerald cast to her skin. In the
center of her forehead was a star-sapphire pattern of light
that came from no apparent source. Her features were no

more pronounced than those of any other Haydonite the visitors had seen, and yet there were contours that somehow gave her face an individuality. The offworlders had learned that the Haydonites were far from anonymous.

She bowed serenely. "She will be with you presently. You will, after all, wish some privacy for your consultations. There are dangers in this city, as well you know. And now, if you will pardon me, I have other pressing matters to which I must see."

Vince led the way out of the cone-flier, and in another few seconds it was lifting away into the sky of Glike, among the flying carpets and lolling skybarges.

It was windy and chilly up there, but the view made it worthwhile. Jonathan Wolff unlimbered a telebinocular and looked around. Max glared out angrily at the Oz-like urbanscape; he was worried about Miriya and the rest, wishing some direct action were possible.

Vince said, "What I don't get is this business with Vowad, Sarna's father. I mean, *jealousy*, from a *Haydonite*?"

The emotions of the synthetically spawned Haydonites were usually too subtle for the other Sentinels to detect, or were deeply suppressed. And certainly their family ties were tenuous by outsiders' standards. But the situation between Sarna, Vowad, and Veidt was apparently the exception.

Haydonites didn't so much reproduce as literally *create* their offspring, as a sort of art form. The young incorporated characteristics of the elders and selected innovations, as esthetic essays, as well.

Wolff lowered the telebinocular. "From what I've been able to pick up since we've been here, Vowad is the ultimate expression of Haydonite development, their Number One," he said. "And Sarna was, sort of, his crowning achievement. Except, she didn't behave quite the way she was supposed to. Got all enthused over Veidt and some

radical ideas he had, like resisting the Invid encroach-
ment."

"Where've we heard *that* before?" Max murmured.

"Thing is," Wolff went on, "I get the impression that if
anybody could keep the Invid from having their way on
Haydon IV, it's Vowad. Only, he doesn't seem inclined to
do it."

"The whole thing's a little slippery by Haydonite standards, I suppose," Vince said. "The Invid ease their way in
with trade arrangements and diplomatic missions, cultural
exchanges and all that, and the next thing you know,
they're entrenched. Bribed the officials; intimidated or
blackmailed the bureaucrats—they've got all the leverage
they need around here, more or less."

And if the planet's vaunted defense system ever really
existed, the three had come to realize, it found the Invid
infiltration/subversion operation too nebulous to deal with.
So long as the Invid made no overt moves, they were safe
from retribution. And violent transactions *between* offworlders were, so it seemed, exempt from interference by
planetary defenses.

Wolff raised the telebinocular again, scanning. "Heads
up," he said softly.

A flying carpet was approaching, a hooked-rug size. In
another few seconds, Sarna alighted next to them.

After receiving news that Rick, Lisa, and the others had
recovered, she said, "We haven't much time. Matters here
are much worse than Veidt and I ever thought when we
proposed this plan. We have to get you all off Haydon IV
as soon as we can."

Before they could press her for details, she hastened,
"You brought your seeing devices? Good; look over there,
at the juncture of the Sky Road and Silver Way."

Eventually they focused on the point she was indicating.
Vince watched for a moment, then breathed an uncharac-
teristic, deliberate string of obscenities.

"Yeah; this changes things," Wolff added sardonically.

Far away and below, a slave coffle was being moved along by Inorganic guards toward a rearing, adamantine Invid stronghold that looked brutally out of place in exquisite Glike.

The prisoners, headbanded with metallic straps that glowed with instrumentation, were dirty and disheveled. It was easy to see that they were big, rugged women wearing the remains of their fighting costumes, walking with heads held high, herded by their captors.

"Praxians," Max said softly. "The missing Praxians. They're *here!*"

Sarna was nodding measuredly. "They were not, as we thought, exterminated; the Invid have many more than that here in the city and elsewhere on Haydon IV. Many, many thousands."

In contrast to the usual lack of extreme emotion in Haydonites, there was loathing in her voice now. "And my father, Vowad, permits it. Permits anything, to preserve his oh-so-important serenity, and this little . . . Shangri-la, as you Humans might say."

They lowered their binoculars as she went on. "The Regent has brought the proper pressure to bear; he'll have you all in captivity soon, if we don't move quickly. I've arranged for—"

But she got no further, as the sun was blotted out overhead by flying carpets over half an acre in area. On them stood Inorganics: Scrim and Crann and Odeon, weapons ready, along with the Haydonites who were doing the actual flying.

The three REF fighters pulled their Badger assault pistols, ready to fight for their lives, but Sarna said, "No! If you fire first, you'll have done what they want. And Miriya and the others will suffer the more for it. Stay where you are and let me speak for you."

The flying carpets landed so as to ring them in with the

sheer drop of the brink at their backs. Vince, Max, and Wolff formed their own security wheel, but kept their machine pistol muzzles pointed at the landing stage surface. They had a few other surprises on their persons beside the Badgers, but going up against Inorganics without mecha of their own would amount to a suicide mission.

They recognized Vowad right away by the bulging cranium and deep red flesh tone, and the enormous lavender star sapphire set in his forehead. He was standing beside the Invid Regent, the Regent's two Hellcats flanking them. The other Haydonites there bore what Vince had learned to recognize as emblems marking them as Respected Elders —the "Old Guard" of the planet, who had made their peace with Invid subversion.

The Inorganics lumbered off the carpets, deploying to encircle the Sentinels. Among the mecha were Armored Officers, somewhat evolved Invid in powered armor, standing some eight feet tall or so, brandishing weapons. Vince couldn't figure out why the defenses of the planet didn't respond to such a show of force—unless either the defenses were a myth or the Haydonites had decreed that those defenses not interfere with the Regent's troops.

The Regent and Vowad alighted, the Hellcats stalking along a pace behind. "You Humans are born troublemakers," the Regent observed. "Always scheming, never still."

"It keeps us amused, kicking you off planet after planet," Jonathan Wolff conceded mildly.

The Regent growled, and his Hellcats showed their fangs in furious screams. Vowad, seeing his daughter among the Sentinels, intervened before the 'Cats could pounce.

"You will accompany us to where your other companions are being held! There you will be examined for positive identification, and officially remanded to the custody of the Regent, for trial on charges of war crimes."

"Like hell," Max Sterling said, thumbing off his pistols' safeties. "Might as well die right here."

But Sarna leaned to whisper in his ear, "Please! Trust me; there's a way out of this yet, but you *must* play along for a while. For Miriya's sake, and your unborn's!"

Slowly, unwillingly, Max returned the Badgers to their underarm rigs. Vince and Wolff hesitated, then did the same.

"Veidt or I will send word to you as soon as we can," Sarna whispered as the Invid closed in.

The Regent loomed before them. "How splendid it feels to have your . . . *company* . . . at last!"

Covered by Inorganic guns, the three men were disarmed and ushered aboard the largest flying carpet. Vowad stayed behind, drawing Sarna aside, as the Regent and his troops and prisoners lifted away. The two hovered there, the wind rustling their long robes.

"I detest these uncontrolled emotions you've acquired through your contact with the Sentinels. I command you to stop this foolish sedition," Vowad hissed at her. "I forbid you to bring down the wrath of the Invid upon us."

"Command? Forbid? Those are words only the Invid may use on Haydon IV now; you've seen to that."

"Stop speaking like a madwoman, Sarna! These attitudes of yours are insanity! You never talked like this until you met that accursed Veidt!"

"But, Father, *you* have the power to unleash our defenses against them—to fight the Invid!"

"And perhaps destroy our whole world in the process?" A gesture of his head indicated the departing Invid and their prisoners.

"What is your Invid war to me? What are the Sentinels? Just a tick of the eternal clock of Haydon IV; a single moment in our lifetime. When they have all passed away, we will be as we have always been and will always be. I will not risk this perfect place for the petty squabbles of the lower orders."

"It seems your decision to withhold information from the council was well conceived," Exedore said.

"Regrettably, yes," Lang answered, showing no regret at all.

Anything said before the council went straight to Edwards's ear, and both scientists had thought it unwise to let Edwards know that there was any monopole ore left here on Tirol.

"In my opinion, the battle lines are drawn, and we're only awaiting the opening shot," Lang added. Exedore, who had seen centuries of war, nodded.

They felt safe speaking their mind there in the center of Lang's research facility, satisfied that it was debugged and that the people he had gathered around him were loyal. Besides, his latest project was complete: one of the SDF Escort-class cruisers had been adapted with a spacefold drive.

It had taken every gram of ore recoverable from the analysis labs and every speck from the secret cache Lang and Exedore had amassed with Breetai's help. At last there was a way to contact Earth, to pass along a warning of the Robotech Masters' intention to seek out the world to which Zor had sent the SDF-1 and the mysterious Protoculture matrix—provided the rest of the Plenipotentiary Council could be swayed.

Exedore and Lang sat together, waiting, before the lab's main screen. The heated debate of the last five hours had them all exhausted, and the one-hour interlude before the vote, during which each member was to weigh the pros and cons, had come as a welcome chance to catch their breath.

A tone sounded and the screen lit up again, split so that the other ten council members' faces appeared there.

Former judge Justine Huxley said, "The moment for the vote has come. If there are no further objections, council members will be so good as to enter their ballots."

Exedore and Lang complied, not hiding their vote from each other as they keyed in their codes. The tabulating computer came up with the result instantly.

"By a two-vote majority, Dr. Lang's proposal to send the refitted SDF-7 class ship back to Earth, with warning of the peril constituted by the Robotech Masters, is carried."

"I would reiterate my point that the voyage be undertaken as soon as possible," Lang was quick to put in, "and my recommendation that Major Carpenter be put in overall charge of the mission."

Suddenly, Edwards's face replaced all others on the screen, flushed with fury. "You're all making a mistake you'll regret! That's the only spacefold ship we've got, maybe the only one we'll have for months or years to come!

"Who knows what Carpenter and the others will run into back there? I'll say it again: the only sane course of action is to wait until we've got an armada and return to Earth in overwhelming strength!"

"Are you saying that the majority of the council has lost possession of its mental faculties?" Exedore asked innocently. Edwards made a wordless sound of rage and broke the connection, so that the council's faces returned to the screen. After a few quick directives to the effect that Lang and Exedore should begin organizing the voyage, the meeting was adjourned.

"Edwards never seems to learn his lesson," Exedore remarked. "Even though the bulk of his Ghost Riders failed to return from their mission to apprehend Breetai, he speaks as though he has the military might to enforce his will."

"So I noticed—and it makes me wonder." Lang had had his own people circulating among REF personnel, and the overwhelming majority were on the side of the council, but still Edwards carried on as though he had a hole card.

Then there was this strange business about the pilot who had tried to save Minmei. Lang could discover nothing about the man—sometimes he doubted if witnesses were right, and wondered if the pilot existed at all. Edwards, for his part, insisted that Minmei had escaped confinement and was probably being harbored by friends somewhere in Tiresia.

But that didn't jell with the Edwards that Lang knew: what he had, he rarely let slip away from him.

Edwards glared disgustedly at the blank screen.

Idiots! The council was asserting itself more and more, now that the general's power base of Ghost Riders had been cut so drastically. It was a pity he couldn't give them a *real* taste of the power he wielded, but that would have been showing his hand too soon.

All his efforts to infiltrate people into Lang's organization had failed, too, so there was little chance of getting his own agents onto Carpenter's roster. Devil take the luck! He wanted every spacefold ship for his own master plan, and the idea of an unwarned Earth, softened up by the Robotech Masters, was quite appealing.

But he still had his options. Perhaps it was time now that he allowed himself a diversion. He opened a commo channel.

"Medical? Give me an update on the patient."

"No appreciable change, sir," a clinician's voice answered.

Incompetents! Not fit to be called therapists. All they had managed to do was drive Minmei into near catatonia.

He felt a sudden hunger for her, a need to reassure himself that she was still in his power.

"Perhaps a little personal contact is what's needed," he said. "Remain where you are; I'll be right down."

CHAPTER
NINE

To paraphrase the Human aphorism, "I think, therefore I scram."

Cabell, *A Pedagogue Abroad: Notes on the Sentinels Campaign*

THE INVID ENFORCERS OF THE REGENT'S HORDES were nothing like that class of mecha the Regis was developing. Hers were bigger than Battloids, mounting enormous cannons, her most powerful fighting machines, while his were scarcely bigger than the Armored Officers.

Three Enforcers entered the Hall of Healing now, driving Cabell and Veidt before them, as the others looked up. Vince, Max, and Wolff were waiting there, as well as Rick, Lisa, and the rest. Vince's arm was around Jean's shoulder, while Max held both Miriya's hands. There was still some distance between Rick and Lisa.

Veidt turned to the lead Enforcer. "I wish to speak to these prisoners alone."

The mecha's voice sounded like a warped audio disk. "Those are not the Regent's orders! Count yourself lucky that you are not confined as well!" The Enforcers stayed where they were, weapons ready.

Veidt made a helpless shrug as he turned to his friends. "Those of us who believe in freedom are doing our best to obtain your release," he said.

"Not likely to help much, is it?" Max asked bitterly. "We've already been measured for slave headbands and restraining devices and cages. And you're telling me the people who sold us out—*your* people—are gonna find the backbone to help us now? Dream on."

Miriya shushed him. "If it hadn't been for the Haydonites, we four would be dead right now."

Max lowered his head, speaking so they could barely hear him. "Maybe that'd be preferable. Maybe we'd *all* be better off that way."

His face went deathly pale as he said it; everyone there was aware that Miriya was pregnant.

Veidt regarded Max for a moment. "I trust you'll change your mind in time." He came about, the hem of his robes swirling, and wafted out the door. One Enforcer left, and the other two remained on guard by the door.

"Did you get to see Rem?" Jean asked Cabell.

"No. A great joke of the Regent's, promising to allow us to. What he really meant is that we're all to be imprisoned along with him."

"What a sense of humor." Rick grunted. "I wonder if he does weddings and funerals."

He was looking around at the alien lab equipment, speculating on what among it would make the best improvised weapon—because he had no intention of ending up in a cage. And surely the Invid jailers would be there to fit the Sentinels with slave headbands any minute now; there wasn't much time to act.

All of a sudden Cabell started using common Terran English of a sort. "We must ayk-may an eak-bray. Eidt-Vay

will be aiting-way." Cabell said it as though he were leading them in prayer, or giving them a quiet pep talk.

One of the Enforcers shifted, bringing its heavy rifle to
bear. "Stop! No communication in offworld tongues, or
we'll bind and gag you all. Healer, make the final checks
that the Regent has ordered, then all of you stand ready to
be transferred to the laboratories of the omnipotent Regent!"

The Humans, meanwhile, had been absorbing what Cabell told them. Lisa found a moment in which to chuckle at
the irony. Apparently Cabell had learned more than just
science in his dealings with Lang, Dr. Penn and the rest,
and with the Human Sentinels.

*We've got fifty-skillion bucks worth of taxpayers' money
in Robotech paraphernalia*, it occurred to Rick, *and now
the whole shebang's riding on one old alien coot talking in
pig latin!* Somehow, it seemed appropriate.

It was like sending vital battle signals with a child's
decoder ring from a cereal box, but it seemed to have
worked. And the remark about the Regent's laboratories
had everyone there determined to escape or die trying;
there *were* fates worse than death.

Even as the Enforcer guard was delivering his warning,
Jean Grant surreptitiously adjusted a control on the lifesigns monitoring equipment. Oscillators oscillated and
alarms buzzed; lights flashed and electronic tones made
urgent warbles.

The Enforcer swung its barrel around. "What's this?"

Jean pretended to be studying the healing devices. "I
think their thalmic excrescences have formed a medullary
fistula!" To her former patients she snapped, "Quick, all of
you! Lie back down! Your refraction's stuck in the optical
reciprocator!"

The Enforcers were teetering a little, overwhelmed.
"Wh-what are you saying, female? Explain yourself!"

Jean demonstrated her impatience. "They're having a

relapse, you big worm-in-a-can! Quick, you and your partner go get help! Get the healers! Get the Regent! Can't you see they're dying?"

Karen was the first to pick up her cue and fall back on the floor moaning. Lisa gaped at her for an instant, then went into her *own* pretended fit, staggering around and twitching exaggeratedly, making some very strange faces. Rick caught on and flopped to the floor in a 'gatoring paroxysm; Miriya swooned onto a treatment couch and began uttering piercing sounds of pain.

The two Enforcers were so nonplussed that for a moment they nearly *did* turn to go get help. But they caught themselves and covered the prisoners again. "Stand fast, you! None of your tricks now!"

"Trick? Does *this* look like a trick?" Jean said, pointing to the incomprehensible sound and light show of the Haydonite medical apparatus.

And I hope you don't say yes!

The Enforcer stumped over to the machine to have a look for itself, motioning Jean aside with the gun barrel. She only moved a step or two away, but that didn't bother the Invid; she was nothing but an unarmed female Human. The second Enforcer moved up nearby, covering the oddly contorting afflicted ones just in case they were planning something. Unnoticed, Vince Grant slipped from sight between two stacks of equipment.

The first Enforcer gazed at the baffling displays of the instruments while the supposedly relapsed patients drooled, howled like dogs, and went into vigorous spasms. Jean watched from a step away, her hands behind her back.

"What does all this mean? Explain!" the Invid demanded.

Jean produced one hand so that she could point. "It's all right there on the middle scanner! See?"

As the thing leaned in for a closer look, she whipped around the power-delivery cable she had yanked loose and

thrust it against the armored [...]
pure energy swathed the thing, [...]
Jean made a silent prayer of than[...]
insulation kept her from being fried a[...]
the field generated by the furious curre[...]
hair stand on end.

The radiant wrath of it drove her back aft[...]
ond or two, though, forcing her to drop the [...]
Enforcer was still shuddering and lurching; Jean [...]
she might have succeeded in mortally wounding the[...]
bryolike Invid inside, or the systemry of its mecha.

The second Enforcer was angling for a shot at her, careful to keep the afflicted Sentinels and Max and Wolff in its
field of fire. But as it raised its massive rifle, a hand pulled
the pistol from its belt. Vince Grant took a quick step back
and shot the thing straight in the back of the helmet.

Smoke and steam and green goop burst from the gap in
the Invid armor, along with the smell of incinerated tissue
and forge-spatterings of molten alloy. Vince had to dodge
quickly as the second guard collapsed backward, nearly
pinning him.

The other captives were all on their feet now, closing in
on the fallen Enforcers. "D'you think they got off an
alert?" Max wondered.

"Probably not, but that doesn't mean we're in the
clear," Wolff surmised. He gingerly touched the fallen rifle
of the one Jean had zapped; it was warm, but intact and
apparently still functional. He hoisted the rifle onto his
shoulder.

Vince passed his pistol to Rick and took up the other
rifle. Lisa took the zapped guard's handgun before Max
could grab it. It was shaped something like a giant Protoculture staple gun. "Rank Hath Its Privilege, and all that."
She smiled.

Max gave her a lopsided smirk. "Use it in good health,
Lisa. Only, let's get goin'!"

...hat. Rick weighed
...ay, grateful that the
... fire with enemy
...He paused in the
...behind him, ready

...At the first corner,
...most shot him.

...d sailed away at
...l after him. They
...up to the roof of

torso. Crackling wreaths of
...ending it into convulsions.
...s that the cable's thick
...s well. Nevertheless,
...nt made her short
...r only a sec-
...able. The
...thought
...em-

...Max demanded as
...held drifted him out onto the sunlit roof landing stage.

"We can keep surveillance on anything that transpires in the Halls of Healing," Veidt replied. "After all, one is well advised to keep a close watch on patients. Quickly now: put those on."

He pointed toward a pile of sleeveless Haydonite robes lying on a medium-smallish flying carpet. They dove at the disguises, tumbling onto the carpet. It took some reshuffling for Vince to wind up with the longest garment, and even then his legs were exposed from midshin down. He settled for kneeling, the bulky Invid rifle held between his knees.

The others were more easily concealed, and in another moment Veidt had the carpet aloft. Lisa realized that there was no way to confine her hair, or for the others to keep theirs from flying, un-Haydonitelike, in the wind, but there was no help for that now. At least the high collars helped camouflage them somewhat.

Of them all, only Miriya hadn't recovered completely. Max kept one arm around her as she hung onto him woozily.

They passed through complex traffic patterns of carpets, cone-fliers, offworld aircraft, and Invid vehicles, but Veidt negotiated it with no apparent effort, and nobody appeared to notice them.

"Veidt, I don't know what your plan is," Rick called out, "but we've got pressing matters of our own. One of them is that the Praxians are—"

"Are being held as slaves by the Invid," Veidt anticipated. "I am well aware of it. And we're on our way now to do something about that. It's the most likely starting place for our effort to dislodge the Regent from my world."

Rick wished once again that it was possible to call the Sentinels' cruiser—the *Ark Angel*, as they had dubbed her —for a pickup, but knew now that that would only result in an uneven battle the Sentinels' flagship couldn't hope to win. Besides, there was every possibility the cruiser would be attacked by Haydon IV's "antibodies."

Wolff saw that the flying carpet was on a course toward the Invid stronghold at the juncture of Sky Road and Silver Way, where he had seen the amazon POWs earlier. He braced himself, wishing he had had time to pick up a gun.

But under Veidt's guidance, the carpet began descending just before reaching the stronghold, to settle onto a landing hardtop on the roof of the building next door, overlooking the broad boulevard. "The next slave work party should come along just beneath us," he said.

"What, you expect the few of us, with four small arms, to eliminate Inorganics?" Wolff scoffed. "If it's so easy, why didn't you do it before?"

"As you know, direct physical violence is not the Haydonite *forte*," Veidt pointed out. "But since there is no longer any route of escape from the planet, aiding and abetting it is our only recourse.

"And besides, the women will be guarded by Enforcers and Armored Officers, not Inorganics. More to the point, the successes of the Sentinels have given other Haydonites the encouragement they needed to lend us aid."

"It's just as well things worked out this way," Lisa said,

checking her pistol. "We couldn't leave the Praxians here, enslaved."

Again, that keenness in Lisa to fight took Rick somewhat by surprise. *Looks like something I'm gonna have to get used to.*

"Other things will be working in your favor as well," Veidt continued, "and I haven't long to explain them."

The line of Praxians moved tiredly, after a grueling day of work in the Invid warehouses and shipyards. The Central Slavepen loomed before them.

Of course, the Invid didn't need the labor of the tens of thousands of women they had captured in their conquest of Praxis; there were drones and automata enough to perform the work. But it made sense to keep them busy and exhausted, and to utilize them. Besides, the practice pointed out to the Praxians—and the Haydonites and various offworld races represented in Glike—exactly what happened to those who defied the Regent.

The Enforcers on the ground and their Armored Officer who skimmed overhead in his open, single-occupant skirmish ship kept careful watch on their captives. Sometimes, after an eighteen- or twenty-hour work shift, the females became rebellious, unwilling to reenter their cells. That was when it took a good jolt from the slave headbands or a nerve lash to keep them moving.

Sure enough, one of the habitual troublemakers broke from the line just as she was about to pass through the portals to the slave kennels. She was shorter than most of them, and solid, round-faced and olive-skinned. Heedless of the rebukes of the headband and the nerve whip, she was still defiant.

"I'm not going back into any cage!"

"You have been warned," the nearest Enforcer said, activating the POW/slave's headband. Writhing in pain, she would be flung into her cage despite what she had said, and so would anyone who stood with her. It was tedious work for the Enforcers, but they had nothing better to do anyway. They *lived*, literally, to serve their Regent.

But on this bright turquoise Haydon afternoon, the timetable was suddenly thrown out. The headband didn't respond, and the defiant one stood there, showing her white teeth in a fighting sneer, hands up in combat posture, feet positioned and ready.

The Enforcer tried again, but there was still no response. Another amazon, with a long flame-red braid, stepped from the ranks, and two more came behind her. The Enforcers registered the fact that there was some sort of malfunction and prepared to reestablish order in a more direct way, with sonic lashes and warning shots—or with armored blows and Protoculture blasts, if it came to that.

But as the first Enforcer raised its weapon, an Invid rifle beam hit its helmet squarely and blew it apart. Another rifle bolt hit the next nearest Enforcer, drilling through it in a split second. Pistol blasts peppered the skirmish ship and the Armored Officer in it, who, taken by surprise while flying low and slow, emitted smoke and flame. The skirmish ship went off kilter and slewed toward the road surface.

The warrior women of Praxis quickly realized that an ambush had been mounted, and that the despised headbands could no longer deal out punishment. There were people on the upper landing stage—Tiresoids, though they were wearing Haydonite robes for some reason—urging them on.

The warrior women didn't need much urging. With a chorus of cries like angry Hellcats, they sprang at their enemies.

CHAPTER
TEN

The DNA sings its four notes
Cytosine, adenine, guanine, thymine,
In infinite configurations
As though Bach were God,
Or vice-versa

Mingtao, *Protoculture: Journey Beyond Mecha.*

OW DO WE KNOW THIS ISN'T THE DEMENTED malfunction of a berserk android?" Tesla bawled, plastered up against the rear wall of the travel capsule. Garak and Pye were hunkered down near him.

Jack was checking the action of his submachine gun nervously, making sure for the tenth time that the magazine was loaded with exploding armor-piercers. "*You* don't get a vote, so it doesn't matter what you think. And the rest of us believe Jan."

He tried the magazine release again, to make sure he could eject an old and insert a new one smoothly. He was about to say something else when Bela broke in.

The big amazon turned on Tesla, holding her sword. More than twice her height, the Invid sucked his gut in, afraid she was about to split it open.

"Yes. I believe my people are being held prisoner here.

Yes, I believe that Veidt and some of the others are in a conspiracy to throw your species out, and yes, I think the Regent's reign on Haydon IV will end today."

But she turned to Jan anxiously, in spite of that. "Can't this thing move any faster?"

"We'll be there soon," Janice Em tried to reassure her. "But I must tell you that the battle's already being joined."

It was unnecessary to ask where that information had come from. Jan's inexplicable link with the Awareness that resided in Haydon IV had already proved itself beyond doubt. Elevators, funiculae, bucket transporters—they had all come at Jan's beck and call, speeding the raiders on their way.

And the Awareness had told her things, things the others couldn't hear. She knew of Veidt's saboteurs' remote-canceling of the power system that energized the slave headbands; of the escape of Rick and the others; of the risky battle plan they were following. She knew that Veidt himself was ignorant of the fact that she had tapped into the Awareness.

She had also been shown the origins of the hatred between Vowad and Veidt, and the reason Vowad was the linchpin of the entire battle.

Jan also knew things the Awareness had chosen to tell her alone, at least for now—things about its defensive systems. Better than anyone on the planet, she knew how time was pressing on the Awareness, the rebels, her own raiding party—the entire focal point of events.

One thing she didn't quite understand was why the Awareness of the planet had accepted her. It was barely translatable into Human terms, but in some ways the Awareness had seemed to *recognize* her, as if some message had been built into it to awaken at the instant when the synthetic mind of Janice Em made contact with it. That troubled her greatly, but there was simply no time to address it right now.

The travel capsule began to slow. "Game time," Jan said.

"Are you sure you've got the terminus pinpointed?" Jack asked, taking up a firing position just before the doors, the submachine gun raised. The others were kneeling or standing behind him, readying Karbarran pneumatic rifles and Garudan clawguns and dart-throwers, and grenades and all the rest, in a hedgehog of conventional firepower.

"Just as I said," Jan went on, reading signs none of the others could even perceive. "The Central Slavepen command post."

To the astonishment of Enforcers and Armored Officers who hadn't even been aware it was movable, the central pylon in the middle of their command post swung open. They were preoccupied with the first reports of a slave uprising and mystified by the fact that they couldn't get any response from the slave headbands.

But every Invid there heard it when the first Armored Officer to spot the raiders squealed an almost ultrasonic peal of alarm.

Kneeling and standing in two ranks, Jack and his party began hosing fire all around the command center.

Although the weapons of the fallen Enforcers were outsize by normal Human standards, they were not too unwieldy for the robust amazons. The guns were appropriated at once. With piercing yells, many of the women took great pleasure in ripping off the inert headbands and hurling them to the ground and stomping them flat, or twisting them into junk, or, among the brawnier, simply snapping them in two.

By that time, a flying carpet was settling nearby, carrying the Tiresoids who were robed as locals, but flown by a real Haydonite.

Rick had intended to make a quick announcement to get

things on track, but Lisa beat him to it. She flung off her robe and leapt to the shining pavement while the carpet was still a yard above the road, holding her pistol high and firing it twice to get their attention.

"Warriors of Praxis! We are Sentinels, allies of your great fighter Bela! We've broken free of the Regent and we mean to raise rebellion! Are you with us?"

Some of the liberated slaves fired into the air too, to signal their intent, while the rest cheered Lisa and those whom the amazons naturally assumed to be Lisa's followers. The rest of the Sentinels were also shedding their disguises, and though several of them had the obvious drawback of being male, the Praxians hailed them. At least the big dark-skinned fellow with the rifle was amazon size —and more—and looked encouragingly tough.

"The power to the slavebands is out, but we're not sure how long that will last," Lisa went on. "We have to strike at once! Your queen and your sisters are right there in the Central Slavepen. Here's how we're going to get them out."

It was basically the plan the Sentinels had thrown together while waiting for the slaves to pass by, but she had inserted a few refinements of her own. Rick had to admit he was impressed. The amazons, all drilled in the disciplines of warfare, split up into squads and moved out with little confusion or delay.

Inside the slavepen command post, things had begun going disturbingly wrong.

A short time before, the power-relay system that energized and controlled the slave headbands had simply gone dead. Almost immediately, reports had begun coming in from the working parties at various Invid installations and en route that the Praxians were in revolt. The cages where the captives were quartered had become a bedlam, too, and the amazons were apparently trying to bend the bars apart with their bare hands.

Word had been sent to the Regent, and troops were already being deployed to trouble spots from elsewhere in the city and the countryside.

"At least one bunch is still under control," an Armored Officer observed in his single-sideband voice. A remote screen showed a column of returning prisoners shuffling through the main entrance of the complex, heads bent in dejection and exhaustion.

"Perhaps the malfunction isn't systemwide," another suggested, then the two turned their attention to deploying reinforcements. But no one in the command center had noticed that the instrumentation on the slaves' headbands was dark. And they had turned away before realizing there were no Enforcers or Officers driving them along.

Nor were any Invid looking at the screen as the women turned not toward the cargo elevators that would take them down to their cages, but rather toward the building's arsenal.

Invid dashing around to respond to the emergency took no notice either, and the slaves' dejected heads helped with the deception. That is, until the Praxians reached the door of the arsenal itself.

An Armored Officer barred their way. "Stop! Where are your overseers?"

Zibyl, the round-faced, olive-skinned one who had shown defiance outside the complex, led the line. Now she looked around in feigned surprise, saying, "Why, I don't know, Great Master; they were there not a moment ago. Perhaps they stopped to speak to another Master. Shall I go look for them?"

She took a step back the way she had come. "Stand where you are," the Officer shouted. It automatically took a few steps in that direction, too. "Slaves aren't supposed to be in this area unaccompanied!"

As it did so, several of the women slipped past, behind its back, silently entering the arsenal.

"I see no overseers," the Officer was saying. "And I see no function lights on your headbands. In fact, some of those women back there have no headbands at all! All of you, line up with your hands against that wall while I contact—"

The Invid got no farther. From the tattered remnants of her fighting costume Zibyl pulled the pistol Lisa had given her. The Officer was just facing back toward her when she squeezed the trigger. The beam was set at minimum dispersal, a star-hot line no wider than a pencil's lead.

Zibyl was wearing a fey smile.

The Officer went windmilling back as green goo and little meteor sparks spurted from the rupture in its helmet. Zibyl shot it again, dead center in the chest, and twice more; the Invid flopped to the floor with a deafening clang of heavy metal.

Just then there was a yell from the rear of the column, "Enemy fire-team coming!"

"Stand clear!" yelled Zibyl, planting her bare feet more firmly and raising the heavy Invid pistol with both hands. She stood her ground, her jaw set, as her sisters dove or dropped or sprinted out of her line of fire.

Four Enforcers lumbered around the corner like walking tanks, their steps resounding up and down the corridor like locomotives being hit with battering rams. They were unlimbering their rifles.

Zibyl took careful aim at the leader, determined to buy time and ferally willing to die just so long as she could take some of the more hated slavemasters with her. She thought she might get one or, with extraordinary luck, two, before they cremated her on the spot.

Zibyl got off the first shot but missed with the unfamiliar handgun. The Enforcers were bringing their heavy weapons to bear, muzzles the circumference of stovepipes zeroing in on her, when Zibyl heard a rich contralto behind her bark, "Sister! *Hit the deck!*"

Zibyl did. The three Praxians who had womanhandled the Enforcer assault weapon out of the arsenal and into the corridor had set it up on its tripod. The gunner had to sit on another woman's shoulders to aim, and she fired.

The shot got the lead Invid where the creature's naval would have been if it had had one, and burned it in half. The Praxians traversed the beam and cut the next Enforcer in two.

More amazons poured into the corridor from the armory, blazing away with pistols and rifles. Zibyl spun around on her stomach and fired, too. In moments, the Enforcers were smoking debris in a spreading pool of green slime.

Zibyl rose to her feet, coughing at the smell of it, and hollered to her Sisters, "What are you waiting for? They know we're here now! Get weapons, quickly; we haven't much time!"

"They've been discovered," Veidt said, as he seemingly stared off into space. "The alarms are going off now."

Vince took a deep breath. "Okay; everybody keep low."

He pushed off from the wall with his shoulders and stepped from concealment behind the flying buttress of the Central Slavepen. The coast was clear. Vince loped toward the entrance, Wolff right behind with the other Invid rifle. Lisa, Rick, and Jean were next, along with the still-unsteady Miriya Sterling, who was being helped along by Max. Cabell came just behind, looking dignified even in this frantic endeavor, and with him floated Veidt. Karen Penn brought up the rear, covering with Rick's pistol.

Rick had dithered a little before making the decision to give Karen his pistol, but it came down to a matter of practical necessity. Karen had the skill and training for the job he had assigned her, and it was only sensible that she be armed. Max wouldn't leave Miriya, and Rick himself wanted to be up toward the front, where he could see what was going on and help make decisions, even if this *had* turned into Lisa's show. To his relief, Lisa had made no objection.

The automated weapons installations guarding the main entrance were silent, just as Veidt had promised. The fugitives made it through the door and onto the big rotunda beyond. They kept to the shadows along the walls, working their way in the opposite direction from that taken by Zibyl and the others. They were headed for the slave cages.

Enforcers and Armored Officers, along with a scattering of scientists and other Evolveds, were running back and forth, taking no notice of the interlopers at first. Vince, leading the way, was thankful that the Invid had decided to make their Glike slave operation an Enforcer- and Officer-run facility; if there had been Inorganic bipeds, the Sentinels and the Praxians would have had little hope of coping with them.

The checkpoint to the slave cages was a guard station one quarter of the way around the gleaming green circle of the rotunda. They were nearly there when a passing Officer noticed them and skidded to a halt, heels striking sparks from the superhard substance of the floor.

"Halt! Identify yours—" was all he got out before Vince waxed him with a sustained burst from the rifle. Guards were just becoming aware of the danger when Vince and Wolff went charging at them assault-style, firing on every other footfall as they fast-walked. Rick dashed for the fallen officer, to relieve it of its sidearm.

Karen rushed forward to help Vince and Wolff, laying down rounds with the pistol. The guard station had been stripped of all but three soldiers in the emergency, and they only lasted a few quickened heartbeats once the shooting started.

But at least they left behind more weapons. Everyone was armed now except for Veidt, and Cabell, whom Rem had once warned, *Stay away from guns or you'll end up burning your foot off!* Even Miriya was in the fight, insisting on having a pistol. After studying the Haydonite-installed equipment for a few moments, Veidt judged that escape from the slavepens could be cut off by Invid in the command center, or even there at the guard station if the stations were retaken intact.

Wolff solved that with his usual panache. Cycling the heavy security lock doors to open all through the slavepen maze with the station's controls, he then brought up the rifle's mouth and blew the controls to wreckage.

"One problem down, but they'll be sending reinforcements here any time now," Lisa said.

Wolff ran a fingertip over his superbly groomed mustache. "Then, dearest Captain, may I suggest that we not *be* here at that time?" He turned and set his rifle across a control console, checking fields of fire, preparing to hold the position while the others effected rescue. At Lisa's command, Karen stayed with him, handing her pistol to Jean and taking another rifle in its place.

Rick had readjusted his own Invid rifle's sling so that he could lug it, leveled in firing position, at waist height with the sling over his left shoulder, right hand on the grip and trigger. It was unbelievably heavy, the sling pressing deep into his flesh. He said, "Everybody ready? No objections?"

No objections. The Sentinels descended into the slavepens of Haydon IV.

CHAPTER
ELEVEN

Awright, so the mecha are in dinged-up shape and the weapons barrels are shot out and the replacement parts stocks are all gone. Boys and girls, we're all functioning beyond manufacturer's specifications.

Rick Hunter, quoted in Mizner's *Rakes and Rogues: The True Story of the SDF-3 Expeditionary Mission*

"*I* FORBID IT!"

Vowad hovered before Sarna as she sought to take control of the giant flying carpet. Some two acres in area, it would hold all the Sentinels and all the freed slaves, too—provided that any of them survived the uprising.

And it wasn't every Haydonite who could command and control such a carpet alone. But she was the daughter of the greatest intellect of her species.

Nevertheless, Vowad blocked her way as she tried to take control of the carpet there on the immense landing surface at the summit of the city's tallest tower—the roof of her home.

"I forbid you to become involved in this *bestial* business!" Vowad ranted. "Let the lower orders settle their own vendettas! Let them kill and kill one another if that's what they want so badly! You have a far higher destiny!"

"Why do you always talk like a god to me," Sarna asked him, "but bow your head like a slave to the Invid?"

Hearing that he went rigid, the only movement being his robe's hem wafting in the breeze. She went around him, took control of the vast carpet, and bade it rise into the air.

Moments later, she was streaking for the Central Slave-pen.

Bela stabbed her shortsword tip in the elevator floor to jam the doors open.

The Invid in the command center were preoccupied with reports of a firefight at the arsenal, and the sudden silence from the guard station by the slavepen entrance, when Jack and his raiders opened up.

The two ranks put out the heaviest volume of fire they could, aware that the Invid would respond very quickly, and that the pneumatic reservoirs of the Karbarran long-guns would empty rapidly. Even the submachine-gun magazines would last only three or four seconds at full auto. The Sentinels were all, including Burak, on the firing line; Gnea and Bela had abandoned their traditional weapons in favor of automatic weapons.

Tesla, Garak, and Pye cringed in the furthest corner of the elevator, making no move to either interfere with or break past their captors.

In that first onslaught the team threw the command center into complete chaos and irreparably cut the Invid chain of command. Explosive armor-piercing bullets could penetrate vulnerable spots even in Enforcer alloy at such short range; the unarmored Invid were targets assigned to Burak, the ursinoid Karbarrans, and the foxlike Garudans.

And the vital equipment that made the Invid nerve center function was everybody's bull's-eye.

Components exploded and clear-polymer indicator faces blew apart; power connectors shorted and splintered hous-ing became deadly shrapnel. Invid who had been calling for mass execution of hostage-slaves only a moment before died, clutching terrible wounds.

"Fire in the hole!" the amazons yelled, as per REF training. With their teeth they had yanked out the pins of the stick grenades they held in each hand. Now they lofted them off in assorted directions as the rest of the raiders hugged the floor.

The Praxians had been careful to angle the throws so that the pylon/elevator would shield the party from the blast and shrapnel. The Sentinels clapped their hands to their ears and opened their mouths to reduce the effects of the explosions.

The world seemed to jump, and there was a whirlwind of shredded tissue and equipment outside the elevator doorway. When Jack looked up, he saw the dead and dying and heard the moans of the injured—but that was mere background. Tottering toward the elevator was an Enforcer, its armor pitted and lead-smeared by impacts. It was lurching, and Jack could see green Invid soupy stuff leaking from its right knee joint.

"LAW!" he yelled, even while he was emptying his chattergun magazine at the thing, lead-smearing it some more. But the Enforcer was bringing its rifle sights into alignment with the elevator car.

Janice Em shouldered Jack aside, out of the doorway. She peered through the sights of the light antitank weapon, fixed the Enforcer in the reticle, and pulled the thumb-trigger. The Enforcer took the shaped charge in the middle of its abdomen and swelled, its armor cracking open like a hard-boiled egg with an expanding yoke. By then Jan was on the floor with her head covered. The blast went toward the ceiling, but left all of them partly deaf.

Jack shook his head in an effort to stop the ringing. "Everybody on your feet!" Bela was shouting. "Move it!"

The raiders rushed out into the command center to find that secondary blowups from the systemry had done even more damage than the bullets and the grenades had. There was smoke everywhere, and the stench of the cracked-open armor; a few small fires still burned.

"If you see any Protoculture weapons, grab 'em!" Jack called out.

Gnea looked around at the devastation. "This equipment is useless! Janice Em, you said you would be able to find out where Arla-Non and our other sisters are being held!"

"And I shall." Jan didn't seem to need direct physical connection to Haydon's Awareness now that she had interfaced with it once; instead, she went straight to a small terminal and punched up a schematic.

She studied the glowing displays for a moment then switched off the terminal. "There: that's our route."

She pointed toward a column on the far side of the command center, an even bigger one than they had arrived in.

The raiders hurried over toward the column. Lron and Crysta had Invid rifles now, and Kami and Learna pistols. The Garudans were still keeping a wary eye on Tesla, Garak, and Pye. Jack himself never let Burak stray from his sight.

Some unseen manipulation of Jan's caused the second column to open and reveal another elevator whose existence the Invid had never suspected.

"Other Sentinels are already in the complex, and battle's begun," she said. "But the Invid are rushing reinforcments here."

"Everybody in," Jack said, standing by the doors of the second elevator. When the three Invid captives hesitated, Gnea and Bela prodded them with still-hot rifle muzzles.

"Why can't you just release us?" Pye wailed.

"We might still have use for you, worm," Bela said, ominously guttural. Her whole world had died; she had no forbearance with the Invid anymore and would just as soon kill them.

"The suffering you've endured is nothing compared to the suffering you've inflicted, so do not try my patience!"

Jack got them all boarded, even Burak, who seemed to be in another of his strange, incommunicative moods. The elevator dropped toward the subsurface levels.

Rick led his group at a fast walk, stopping himself whenever he found that he had broken into a trot. Stumbling into an ambush wouldn't help anything right now, even though he felt each ticking second as a possible loss of Praxian lives.

Just before they had started down, they had heard the distant firefight, realizing that Zibyl's bunch had armed themselves and were keeping the Invid busy. But it would still only be a matter of time before the Regent arrived with fresh troops and mecha, enough to crush any resistance the escaped slaves could put up.

Lisa had yielded the point position to her husband, but continued to conduct herself as overall commander of the contingent. Rick, Max, Vince, and Jean accepted that, as they accepted the fact that Veidt and Cabell were determined to come the whole distance despite the fact that the Haydonite couldn't—and the old sage wouldn't—use a weapon.

Their path led down through a complex refurbished in Invid style, feeling more like a walk through a living organism than a raid on a prison facility. But on the third level below the surface, they encountered the first of the cages.

The Praxian slaves were being kept in big ironwork affairs suspended from the ceilings, more like captured birds or sideshow exhibits than prisoners of war. When Rick spotted the first cage, the women crowded into it looked at him listlessly for a second or two, then suddenly realized what they were seeing.

One dragged herself halfway to her feet, fists clasped on the bars. "Sisters! Look here!"

It was easy to see that the women knew *something* was up; the cold evercrete floor below their pens was littered with twisted and broken slave headbands. Evidently the Praxians had lost no time getting rid of them once the bands were deactivated.

In another moment the prisoners were murmuring and exclaiming to one another, but there were no shouted greetings or hails. The Sentinels were unknown to the Praxians, and this just might be some new Invid ploy. Still, the amazons jostled to see what was going on, making their cages swing and turn.

Someone made her way through the press of captives to the bars of the first cage. She was one of the tallest there, powerfully built, with a long leonine mane of sun-bleached hair. The colorful rags of her fighting costume were faded and threadbare, and her high, soft hide boots were worn through, yet she had a regal manner, her head erect.

"Who are you, and why have you come?" she demanded. "Are you allies of the Invid?"

Lisa recognized the woman from pictures she had seen on Praxis. "We're allies of your daughter Bela, Your Majesty, and of others who fight the Invid!"

Queen Arla-Non tossed back her mane proudly. "Then, you're our allies, too."

Rick had gone to study the mechanisms that suspended the cage, while Vince, Max, and Jean fanned out as security. Even Miriya was on alert, holding her pistol ready.

Veidt was standing near a systems juncture, in some kind of trance. Cabell went to look over Rick's shoulder, offering his input. It was some kind of complicated drum-and-gear affair, needlessly primitive.

"Don't touch anything till we can—" Rick was saying.

"Perhaps this tiny lever," Cabell ventured, flicking it.

Arla-Non and her sisters shouted angrily as the cage

dropped. Rick let out a squawk and rammed in the manual brake, which luckily held, and the prisoners were jounced every which way among the bars.

"Hmm, interesting," Cabell allowed.

The cages were lowered without further mishap, and Sisters of Praxis crowded one another, stepping free. Arla-Non clapped Lisa and Jean on the shoulders. "Thanks to you, Sisters! And to your male subordinates as well!" She clasped forearms with Miriya.

Rick looked a little startled, but Vince gave a casual chuckle and Max muttered, "Oh, we were just along for company."

Those who had been freed were only a small fraction of the amazons being held in the center, and that in turn was only a part of the total number of Praxian slaves on Haydon IV. Arla-Non dispatched her warriors to the other cellblocks, to continue the liberation. Miriya and Lisa handed over their pistols, so the rescuers wouldn't have to go unarmed.

Just then Veidt came floating back. "Sarna will be here soon, but I fear the other news isn't good. The Regent is mustering his troops for an attack on the Central Slavepen. And . . . there is some other intellect in contact with the Awareness of Haydon IV. I cannot discern it well; a synthetic mentality, I believe."

"No time for that now," Rick said. "We've got to make sure Wolff and Karen don't get overrun up above, and we gotta get the Praxians armed. This thing's just *begun*."

Lisa conceded the sense of that. Once Arla-Non understood the situation she organized her women immediately, as capable as any field commander the REF fighters had ever seen. She gave orders by squads and platoons, and her warriors jumped to obey, some racing off to help in freeing the rest of the Praxians, the rest forming up to carry the battle back aboveground.

"What about patrols down here?" Lisa asked.

"We know the schedules of the regular patrols, believe me," Arla-Non said, "and we should be able to deal with them, at least for now."

The group set out, and Arla-Non was as good as her word. They ambushed the one skeleton crew of Enforcers that came their way, a pair walking guard. The newly acquired weapons were quickly distributed.

But as they were heading toward the surface, Karen Penn came loping tiredly from that direction. She had obviously been through some heavy fighting. At her back came a squad of the women from Zibyl's group, somewhat the worse for combat.

"That bunch from the armory got to us," she explained breathlessly to Rick. "We have most of the ground level secured. But a mob of Enforcers and Officers showed up and set up a crossfire at the entrance. Nobody can get in or out, and we think they're bringing up Inorganics."

"Other escape routes?" Rick asked.

Karen shook her head. "All covered, and the crossfire's murder."

More and more Praxians were showing up now, liberated from other cellblocks. Although there were thousands in the place, Rick knew that didn't mean much unless they were armed. "All right, let's get upstairs and see what we can—"

The entire complex trembled and shook as distant impact made the building rumble.

"Something heavy," Max remarked.

There were more voices, and streams of Praxians began coming from the direction of the surface. Many were wounded, some looking like they wouldn't make it. From among them came Wolff, supporting—practically carrying—Zibyl, whose head lolled.

"Inorganics got some licks in," Wolff explained. "Scrim and Odeons, mostly. We blew the slavepen entranceway and brought the roof down on 'em as they charged; no other option. But that won't stop those demons for long."

So much for improvised rescue plans, Rick thought.

"A good try anyway," Arla-Non judged grimly. "We prefer dying free to living in cages, and at least we can do that."

She was right. Zibyl's troops were weighted down with armaments, some carrying two of the heavy Invid rifles, or enormous makeshift packs loaded with ammunition and explosives. The other amazons surrounded them, grabbing weapons, preparing to make the Invid pay.

As the Praxians rushed to set up fields of fire and pre-pare ambushes, Lisa got Veidt's attention. "What about Sarna?"

He shook his head slowly. "The streets are filled with Inorganics, and there's no way she can land there."

Lisa was curious about Veidt's expanding powers now that he was back on Haydon IV, but she had no time to ponder it.

Moments later there was a tremendous explosion from the distance, and Wolff said aloud to himself, "The Inor-ganics."

The few portable crew-served guns the Praxians had were set for a crossfire. Further back, down in the warren of the slavepens, fallback positions were being set up. The only thing left to do was insure that the Invid victory was costly.

After a few minutes, they heard the sound of heavy footfalls—marching mecha, advancing on their prey with-out fear or hesitation.

A pair of colossal Odeons rounded a corner, filling the corridor. The amazon gunners waited until the optimal mo-ment, then opened fire. The Odeons seemed to experience a rictus of agony as fire splashed over them and ripped them apart; then they collapsed in on themselves.

More Odeons appeared, moving more cautiously. The

Sentinels and the Praxians held their fire until the right moment, then blasted away. One, its skull turret aflame, whirled and convulsed, then, trying to hold itself erect, went reeling toward a giant column.

A camouflaged panel at the base of the column slid open and Jack Baker was standing there, wide-eyed, as he watched a burning twenty-five-foot-tall mecha stagger directly toward him.

CHAPTER
TWELVE

*Well, naturally I wanted a war! But I didn't want a war I might
lose!*

> The Regent, quoted by Lemuel Thicka in *Temple of
> Flames: A History of the Invid Regent.*

SARNA CIRCLED THE CENTRAL SLAVEPEN WITH HER
enormous flying carpet, peering down at the turmoil below.
The streets were crowded with Scrim and Crann and
Odeon, and even a few Hellcats, but no more fire seemed
to be coming from within.

Still, she could not set down in the nearby plaza, as she
had planned. The Invid had not yet started firing at Haydonites, but they would attack her if she dropped down
among them. And, more to the point, the slaves wouldn't
be coming out that way now.

The city was in turmoil, with Praxian slaves abandoning
their work assignments, tearing off the inert headbands,
and either fleeing their overseers or attacking them head-on
with whatever weapons came to hand. The amazons fought
with unflinching courage and great skill, but the Invid garrison was large and troops were being rushed in from all

over the planet. It could only be a matter of time before the uprising was crushed.

The defenses of Haydon IV itself were staying out of the battle, and Sarna knew why. It would be easy enough for the vast intellect of Vowad to persuade the planet's systemry that this was a limited conflict in which the Invid were in the right, technically, but needed no help in reestablishing order. Thus, the glory of Haydonite civilization was safe from all-out warfare.

Sarna herself had attempted to get a message through to the Sentinels' cruiser—still orbiting far beyond Haydon's defensive limits—to let them know what was happening. But her father had interfered with the transmission somehow, and there had been no response.

Veidt was deep within the complex somewhere, along with the other Sentinels, and Sarna wasn't about to abandon them. She gathered her resolve and sent the immense carpet sailing down toward the roof of the Central Slavepen.

"No!" She heard the cry even as the carpet came to rest, as gently as a feather. It was Vowad, on a circular mat. He brought it in on her own carpet, confronting her.

"This is madness! Come away with me at once!"

She shook her head. "My friends are inside here."

Vowad was vibrating with anger. "They're doomed! And you are, too, unless you come away with me this instant!"

"You could prevent that, Father. Call down the wrath of Haydon IV upon the Invid!"

"Sarna, it is my duty to *preserve* our world, not see it destroyed!"

"Then go," she said, "and leave me here. For I swore a different vow."

Jack Baker threw his hand up and skipped back as the burning Odeon bounced off the column and crashed onto its back.

Bela and Gnea were already crowding to get past him, to Arla-Non, and it was a bit like being caught in the middle of a buffalo stampede.

"Mother!"

"Your Majesty!"

There was no use in trying to restrain them. They had been frustrated enough by the sudden stopping of the elevator. The complex's power supply was disrupted from the attack on the command center, and from the sapper charges set off by Wolff. The ensuing counterattack by the Invid hadn't helped either. By the time the elevator was moving again, Janice Em was the only calm one aboard.

Now Arla-Non waved from the shelter of an Invid design feature not far away, a thing that looked like a dendrite. Lisa and Rick and some of the others were there, rather dumbfounded.

"Look out!" Jan burst past Jack to sweep the air with fire from her Enforcer rifle. Everyone else saw what she meant, and also fired at the skirmisher ship and its Armored Officer that had come barreling round the corner for a low-level recon. Flier and Invid flew apart like a clay pigeon.

There was a lot of confusion then, particularly regarding the odd-looking being who only halfway resembled Janice Em at this point. Finally, Jack got them to understand that there was a bolthole: the elevator could take them clear to the roof.

"That will do," Veidt told them all. "Sarna is there, with the carpet."

Lisa had done some quick mental addition. "But we can only ferry up twenty or thirty at a time. We've got to hold on down here in the meantime! It might be hours!"

"Good; that will give us a while longer yet to kill Invid," Arla-Non said blithely.

Wounded were being taken aboard for the first trip, but there were also plenty of functionals to protect them once they got up above. Rick took Max's arm. "Get Miriya up there, too. Now! Don't argue with me, *dammit*."

Max was indecisive for a second, then gripped Rick's arm and turned to get his wife and unborn child to safety. Rick discovered that Lisa was staring at him strangely.

She gave him an arch look. "You're not going to insist *I* be evacuated with the injured and helpless?"

Rick sighed, and his face colored some. "Not you, Tiger." Her answering smile warmed him.

Veidt was staring into the elevator. "So, the Awareness has seen fit to aid us. And you are not what you seemed, Janice Em. Still, you must be eloquent! We have a great deal to discuss."

"But not until later," Jan said. "I want you to take the elevator to the roof; it will respond to you now. I can do more good down here." She hefted the Enforcer rifle she held.

Veidt inclined his head slowly. "And, more to the point, Sarna is up there now, eh? And, unless I miss my guess, Vowad?"

Jan had learned how to read much of the hidden information of Haydon IV. She knew how matters stood among the three. She nodded. "There may still be time to convince him, but I'm not the one to do it."

Without another word, Veidt entered the elevator among the wounded and the vengeful. Jan turned to Rick and Lisa. "I guess I don't look much like my PR photos, hmm?"

There was a yell from the battle line as another Inorganic attack began. Rick watched the elevator doors close as it began its ascent. The Sentinels' misson had been rife with mind-boggling shocks and surprises; that Janice was an android seemed to fit in with the unbelievable scheme of things.

"You look pretty damn good to *us*, Jan."

Sarna and Vowad were locked in a battle of wills, the huge carpet vibrating under them. If he couldn't *persuade* his daughter to come with him, he resolved, he would *force* her to come, by taking the carpet under his command.

But she was fighting him with more mental force than he would have believed she could marshal. Though she was of his stock, she lacked his ages of training and experience—and yet something within her was making her very nearly her father's equal in willpower.

But the battle became moot as a structure on the roof swung open and the elevator appeared with its cargo. Wounded amazons were assisted onto the carpet, and ablebodied ones ran to set up firing positions. Max led Miriya to the carpet and eased her down.

They ignored Vowad, who was screaming, "Go back, go back! This war must not spill over into the city at large!"

But it was too late. Before much more could be said, an ogrelike Crann clambored into view, its sensors having detected activity on the rooftop.

The Praxians and Max opened fire right away, but Crann were perhaps the most powerful of the biped Inorganics, and the thing just kept coming, firing back. A hole was burned through the carpet, and several of the wounded were killed instantly as the Crann advanced.

People were diving for cover that wasn't there; Max left Miriya's side and went straight for it, dodging and laying down rounds with an Enforcer rifle.

The Crann ignored him, swinging its weapon muzzle back and forth, immolating everything it saw. Then the beam swung toward the three Haydonites.

Veidt tried to ram Sarna to safety, but she saw that her father was paralyzed with shock or fright.

"No!" she cried, and eluded her mate to drive straight at Vowad, her robe fluttering over the rooftop. She struck her father with her head and upper torso, knocking him out of the line of fire, but the Crann's beam struck Sarna dead center, and she went flying to the roof's surface, her robes burning.

Veidt was there at once, smothering the flames with his own body, feeling more helpless than he had ever felt. But Max got to them in another second, using his jacket, and even Miriya had staggered over to help.

Meanwhile, the amazons had zeroed in on the Crann. Their massed small-arms fire found some vulnerable point in its reverse-articulated knee, and as it lost balance it also lost footing there at the edge of the roof. The Crann plunged from sight, but they heard the impact as it struck the street far below.

Max didn't know much about Haydonite physiology, and what he saw of Sarna's wound reinforced that; the weird textures and shapes, the unfamiliar fluids and systems, looked part organic, part synthetic. But he thought that the damage was too terrible for her to survive. She confirmed that when she spoke, her voice a faint bubbling.

"Father, you see? What is Haydon IV under the Invid but a beautifully appointed slavepen? War might destroy us, but it can never defile us the way enslavement has."

She had no expression that a Human could read, but the note in her voice wrenched at Max's heart. Vowad raised his face to regard the wounded and dying among the Praxians, the determined-looking women who showed their suffering in every line of their faces.

Then Sarna spasmed. From deep within his faceless depths, Veidt let out a wail that was terrible to hear. With no arms for a last embrace, he dropped until he lay draped across the corpse of his mate, and the sound of something he had learned among the Sentinels came from him, a sound no Haydonite had ever made before. Veidt wept like a lost soul.

Max's mouth fell open. From the eyeless visage of Veidt, tears were seeping.

"Ah, Veidt: you are my love," Sarna managed, though the voice sounded far away, as if it were coming now from outside her body. "And all of time and space will not keep us apart." Then she shuddered again, and was still.

It took the others a moment to realize that a new sound was rising to drown out Veidt's sorrow. Vowad floated there, head thrown back, blank face raised to the sky. Max somehow knew that if the Haydonite had arms, those arms would have been thrown wide, hands clenched to fists.

The sound that issued forth from somewhere within Vowad was animal pain, and animal anger.

"More Inorganics!" yelled a woman who had leaped to the roof's edge. The alarm was repeated by others all along that part of the building.

Max rose tiredly, ignoring the pain of his burned hands, to take up his gun. The amazons were right; at least there was time to kill some more Invid before the final defeat was nailed down. Too bad the Sentinels had to end this way. . .

But just then, with Vowad's shriek echoing off the buildings of Glike, the world began to shake.

It wasn't like an earthquake; it was more like the whole artificial planet Haydon IV resonating like a tuning fork to Vowad's pain. The sky seemed to shimmer like a pan of water being struck and struck again on its rim. A deep sympathetic vibration was felt by everyone there on the roof. Even more amazing, the Invid teeming in the street below stopped what they were doing and stood stock still.

Then there was a sound to be heard all through Glike, like wind-whipped flames—like the surging of a funeral pyre's inferno.

Those on the roof abruptly saw movement all through

the city. From hidden crannies and the very seams of the Oz urbanscape, incandescent colors emerged in shapes that seemed alive. And all at once the Invid in the street below were attacked by a moving ant-army of shapes.

Max yelped and leapt back as one scampered past him, brushing his ankle. It didn't hurt, but the contact made his skin tingle and feel a bit numb. It was obvious, though, that the thing wasn't after Max; hundreds, thousands of others like it were emerging from every crevice and homing in on the nearest Invid.

And then he realized what the thing was: a miniature humanoid figure, whose likeness Max had seen often enough to recognize it: *Zor!* The humunculi-Zors were the size of a kid's toy model, made of kaleidoscopic colors, bounding through the air or running at unbelievable speed to take on the Inorganics.

The myriad Zors were seeping from the fabric of the city to attack the Regent's troops. Apparently, the *ghost in the machine* that was Haydon IV's Awareness knew the Invid mind well—and had chosen to form its antibodies in the image of the Regent's most hated foe.

In seconds, the Invid mecha were battling enemies that knew no surrender or retreat. Blasts from Protoculture weapons disintegrated Haydon IV's antibodies, but in the time it took to shoot one, a dozen more tiny Zor simulacra rose up to attack. As the antibodies fastened themselves to the Inorganics, coating them, the war machines began to glow.

Unlike the contest in which Jack's raiders had fought beneath the planet, the antibodies weren't in unending supply now. There were limits even to Haydon IV's power. As Inorganics everywhere blazed away at the tiny demons fashioned in Zor's image, fewer and fewer appeared to take their places.

But the city was still blanketed with antibodies eager to hurl themselves onto the mecha. As Max watched, a Hell-

cat, coated with the shifting, coruscating colors of the antibodies that had plastered themselves to it, rolled and spat
and flopped, clawing at itself uselessly. Its destructive aura
grew brighter, and a moment later it was ruptured by a
dazzling explosion, vanishing from sight.

Elsewhere, an Odeon staggered drunkenly, firing into
the air, as antibodies engulfed it. It tried to decontaminate
its arm with blasts from its hand weapon, but only succeeded in blowing the arm off. A moment later it, too,
blew apart.

Max spun on Veidt. "Hurry! Get that elevator back
down for the others! Quick, before this whole complex
goes!"

Veidt was still stretched out across Sarna, oblivious to
everything around him. At length, Vowad regained some
part of his composure.

"I will go," he said. In a moment, he had started the
elevator back down in a race to save as many others as he
could.

CHAPTER
THIRTEEN

YOUR TAX DOLLARS AT WORK

Graffito found on Sentinels
barricade in the Central Slavepen,
thought to be attributable to
Bela

WHEN THE REGENT HEARD OF THE REVOLT AMONG
the Praxian slaves, he took command of the situation himself. He left his hive just outside the city and called for his
Land Cruiser—the grotesque mobile ground fortress that
was the centerpiece of large-scale Invid surface action.

When he was told that the Sentinels were in some way
responsible for the slave uprising, he sent word to his tor-
turers to prepare for a much more demanding schedule. But
once he was informed that the antibodies of Haydon IV had
turned against him, he instructed his personal flagship to
stand ready against immediate departure.

Not that he counted the battle lost yet; the Haydonite
defenses had been designed to eliminate most of an invading force before that force got to the planet's surface, and
the Invid were already at close range. The Regent had an
advantage no invader had ever achieved before.

"Destroy all power sources!" he ordered. "Obliterate the planet's energy production centers! The Regent was certain that without power, the antibodies would quickly de-rezz into nothingness.

Those Invid not engulfed in Zor antibodies immediately began destroying all power sources they could detect, which meant razing things at random. The biped Inorganics, in particular, destroyed ages of craftsmanship and art in minutes, turning their aim haphazardly from one target to the next. Minarets toppled, domes shattered, and delicate mansions collapsed like fragile pastry crust. Fires flared up, and smoke began to block out Briz'dziki, Haydon's sun.

Then commo relays showed the Regent the nature of the antibodies. Zor, *again!* The Regent's entourage ducked and ran from his berserk blows; he lashed out at the consoles and instrument panels around him. He wrenched the command chair from the deck, flinging it against a bulkhead so hard that the chair dented the plates.

Zor! The perversity of the Haydon IV machinery! The towering affrontery of it! "I will have this planet or I will destroy it!" the Regent roared.

Though he was in a part of the city that had been spared the appearance of the antibodies, the Regent thought better of his plan to travel on the ground. He called for a Terror Weapon troop dropship; but of the three on Haydon IV at the moment, two were elsewhere on the planet picking up reinforcements and the third had been destroyed while hovering near its landing pad not far from the Central Slavepen.

The Regent changed his instructions, and the Land Cruiser swung toward the starport. Time to make a break for his flagship, while he still had other cards to play. A screen relayed the scene from the Land Cruiser's brig, showing him that Rem was still firmly chained there. The Regent stroked his mammoth Hellcats and contemplated the horrors he would inflict on the clone when all this was over.

Even Jack and his team, who had seen the Haydon antibodies in action in other forms, had difficulty believing what they were witnessing. From the very walls of the dungeons came doll-size Zors in every color, setting upon the Inorganics, bringing them down and blowing them apart.

They were a reminder, too, of Rem, who was still held captive by the Regent.

In the slavepens, the counterattack on the Praxians and the Sentinels stopped cold. The main danger to the defenders now was the deafening sound of the Inorganic volleys and the reports of the mecha being blown apart.

Nevertheless, the Inorganics had taken a considerable toll on the antibodies. When the simulacra-Zors flickered away to carry the battle outside, like torch flames on the wind, there were far fewer than there had been at the start. The Invid destruction of Haydon's power-delivery systems was beginning to tell.

Vowad reappeared with the elevator for the next load of evacuees, but now there was no rush. Arla-Non had her other injured ready, but many of the others wanted to be part of the campaign there underground, sweeping the Invid from the complex and searching for any other enslaved Praxians.

"What would be most useful," Lisa told Vowad, "would be smaller flying carpets, to support the Praxians elsewhere in the city and on the planet."

Vowad spoke in a monotone, still numb with the enormity of Sarna's death and his own act of vengeance. "I will see what can be done," he said, "but most Haydonites are busy rescuing themselves and their dependents. The city is dying."

Still, Arla-Non sent a platoon of her amazons up with

Vowad, to help secure the roof and stand ready in case the opportunity arose to rescue other Praxians.

When the elevator left, the Sentinels and the released slaves began a careful advance over the ground the Invid had held only minutes before. There was nothing but debris, smoke, and puddles of metal.

The Praxians returned to the armory and continued their plundering. Outside the Central Slavepen, Rick and the rest found the immediate area quiet, though the sounds of battle came from close-by.

Vowad appeared, this time on a much smaller carpet. "I have summoned others," he said, "and they will take you and yours anywhere you wish."

High above, Rick could see, some carpets of varying sizes were lifting off, some to take the wounded to the Halls of Healing, others to descend to the street and await passengers, all commanded by Haydonites unfamiliar to him. He realized that the Haydonites had somehow subdivided the huge carpet Sarna had brought.

Maybe there's only one real carpet, it occurred to him, *and all the little ones are just temporarily detached pieces*?

Arla-Non's troops boarded the carpets by assigned units, to be borne off to rescue more of their Sisters. Bela had assumed the status of her mother's second-in-command, and Gnea was a kind of aide-de-camp. It was odd to see the hard-driving Bela deferring to someone so readily, but Arla-Non wore an invisible cloak of authority and majesty; Jack didn't blame Bela one bit.

Vowad was still next to Rick and Lisa. "We have attempted to contact your *Ark Angel*, but the Invid still interfere with our transmissions; things beyond the Haydonite atmosphere are not always within our control."

"That's all right," Lisa said gently. "There are more immediate things to think about." The raiders had heard the news of Sarna's death and Vowad's sudden conversion.

Lisa had suffered her own losses in war and knew how deeply it hurt.

"Yes." Vowad nodded. "Power levels are dropping, due to the Invid destruction. Inorganic reinforcements are being airlifted into Glike, and the outcome hangs in the balance. But that is not what concerns me most. The Regent is reported to be on his way to the starport, his ship standing ready. Your friend Rem, the Zor-clone, is still his prisoner.

"I fear the worst."

Jack Baker did not have enough time to say hello to Karen Penn when he saw her. "So, they finally kicked you outta sick bay, huh?" Then it was back to fighting for their lives as the Inorganics pressed the battle, down in the slave warrens.

Now, up on the open street, he sought her out in the chaos of battle. Sliding around a flying squad of big, gladsome amazons off to collect some more Inorganic scalps, he skirted the smoking remains of a skirmish ship, and finally spotted her. She was listening to the sounds of conflict, but she was staring off toward the cloud-high towers of Glike.

"Um," he began, and found himself at a loss. "You sure you're okay? No aftereffects?"

She flashed him a smile. "Yes. Thanks, Jack."

She looked back to the skyline. "Well, what's wrong then?" he persisted.

"Nothing's wrong, Jack. It' just that...all this... maybe it's just as well that Glike be leveled, to start from scratch."

"Huh? Look, these're our *allies* now, y'know!"

She turned a hateful expression on him. "Allies, hell! They're not the first beautiful culture to put up with rot and evil in its midst, just so people could have their aesthetics and their comfort and their personal peace."

Jack felt the color rising in his face. *She's giving me speeches now?*

She looked to the city again. "The glory of Greece was built on slavery, did you know that? I don't care what kind of crap they tell us about it; if I'd been there I'd have bombed the Parthenon, smashed everything slavery bought them—"

Jack felt heat flushing his face. "Penn, don't you start preaching history to *me*! I was just saying—"

"Whatever comes out of the ashes of Glike will be better than what went before, even if it's Stone Age, because Haydon'll be a free planet—"

Jack shook a fist at her. "Will you shut up and listen? I'm saying I agree with—"

"Who're you telling to shut up?"

"Penn! Baker! *Front 'n' center!*"

They were both breathing hard, about to mix it up again, when Rick Hunter's sharp summons cut through the gathering slugfest. Their training kicked in, and they double-timed over to Rick, rifles at sling arms.

Veidt was standing near the Hunters, and so was Janice Em. The Artificial Person had resumed the aspect of a Human female. Rick quickly explained the tactical situation, and Rem's dilemma.

"There's no time to muster a full-scale strike at the Land Cruiser," Rick finished. "But Veidt's ready to try to get a commando team in by carpet. Colonel Wolff, the Garudans, and the Karbarrans will be diverting the Regent's attention and providing fire support. Well?"

"Count us in, S—" Karen had begun answering for them both, by habit, but she stopped, looking aside at the young man who was part friend, part title-fight opponent.

Jack gave a slightly insubordinate smile and touched fingertips to his forehead—more of a wave than a salute. "Like she says, count us in, Admiral."

Jack, Karen, and Veidt boarded Veidt's poker table–size

carpet and lifted away. Rick didn't even have time to turn around; Vince Grant was standing there. "Bad news, Rick: Tesla and Burak are gone."

"What d'ya mean *gone*? Gone where?"

Vince was shaking his head. "Slipped off while we were getting ourselves organized. Somebody said there's a skirmisher ship missing."

Vince indicated Garak and Pye with a nod of his head. "Those two claim they don't know. I think they're lying; something's got them frightened, even more frightened than the Haydon defenses. Where would Tesla and Burak go?"

Rick blew his breath out. "I don't know, and we can't worry about it right now. Just put out an all-points to pick them up. And don't go after them yourself! I need you right here."

Vince showed disappointment. "Aye, sir."

Rick returned to his wife to find her dealing with another problem. "New deepspace blips on the detectors," a Haydonite was saying. "We think they're Invid."

The skirmisher ship flew low over the contested city, streaking toward the cluster of glowing, shadow-dappled domes that was the Invid hive on the horizon.

Burak held his breath, expecting the antibodies of Haydon IV to hurl themselves into the air at him at any second. But the words of Veidt came back to him, that *intent* had everything to do with the responses of the defense system. And, certainly, Tesla's intent had nothing to do with invasion and conquest—at least not today.

Burak was perched on the scientist's shoulders, gripping his robe and harness for dear life, as Tesla piloted the flier along at breakneck speed, using suicidal maneuvers to avoid the mecha and miniature Zor fire-demons that fought through the air.

Burak had unconditionally accepted that his planet's fate

and his own Higher Destiny, his Messiah-hood, were tied to Tesla's own.

No interceptors or withering fire rose to incinerate them as they sped toward the hive; Burak felt sure that Tesla's growing powers had taken care of that problem. Tesla brought the flier in for a landing at the mouth of an opening that led into the central dome.

Burak was beyond any thought of resistance by then. Tesla led him in through a virtually abandoned hive. What Invid there were were disoriented and of no consequence; they stepped aside, kowtowing, at Tesla's imperious orders.

Then the two arrived in the most holy place in any hive, the chamber set aside for those Flowers of Life that had blossomed, or held promise of blossoming. Here, to Tesla's wild exultation, they found plants that had actually borne Fruit.

Burak had begun to recognize a pattern, that the Fruit of each world was different from that borne on any other. And the Fruit brought forth by the worlds once touched by Haydon himself—worlds the Sentinels were trying to free— were the most pronouncedly varied of all.

In this case, the Fruit were eggplant-purple cylinders, round-bottomed and quiveringly gelid. Tesla cupped his hands around one gently.

"See-eee?" The word was more a whispered breath than a spoken sound. "See how the light shines through them? These are new, just grown! They've become ripe in the last few minutes—no more than an hour! Not even the Regent has tasted such Fruit as these!"

Tesla suddenly turned on Burak, who was standing close, watching curiously. The master scientist struck out at the Perytonian jealously, a blow that would have killed if Burak hadn't ducked. "Back! You shall have none!"

Burak backstepped warily. "I want none. I only want you to keep your bargain."

Tesla had seated himself cross-legged on the soft sward of the arborium, a little pile of the Fruits in his lap. "Good."

Burak squatted on his haunches, to watch Tesla sink his long snout into the Fruit, slurping and slobbering at it, runnels of purple juice flowing down his chin, neck, and chest. Soon, something pulsed within the Invid. In moments, a light shone from him that threw Burak's shadow on the dome walls.

Burak hunkered down, shielding his eyes a bit, to witness the next step in Tesla's Flower-induced metamorphosis.

CHAPTER
FOURTEEN

> *Lang was first among the Humans to notice it, the "dovetailing," as he called it, of the worlds specially touched by Haydon and those that held such interest in more recent times for Zor.*
>
> *He pressed me for details and I had to point out that the Zentraedi are the last ones to query in matters of history. But nonetheless I expressed my vast yearning to know the truth of it all, and hoped Emil would come to feel the same way.*
>
> Exedore, *SDF-3 and Me*

THE LAND CRUISER ROCKED FROM THE FORCE OF A tremendous explosion. Knocked from his feet, the Regent rose again in an even more furious temper.

"What was that?" Surely the Zor antibodies were not blowing themselves up?

A scientist bowed. "It appears that some of the outworlders have joined in the battle, Divine One. That was apparently a Karbarran shuttlecraft loaded with conventional explosives and sent at us by remote control. Fortunately, it was of insufficient power to penetrate even our outermost hull."

"Naturally," the Regent snapped. The cruiser, bigger than an aircraft carrier, was a moving mountain of weapons and armor on treads as wide as a Glike boulevard. He thought again about ordering his gunners to open fire and raze the city around him as he withdrew, but that would run the risk of attracting the antibodies. His own life was all-important to the Invid cause, far too vital to risk for mere retribution.

It was too bad this entire part of Glike seemed to have been evacuated; he would have taken consolation in grinding the miserable synthetics under his mobile fortress's treads. It might, in part, make up for his having had to abandon his Flower of Life orchards just as they were about to bear Fruit.

Perhaps he would still be able to retake his Haydon hive. With this thought, he ordered his techs to relay the view from the automatic monitoring equipment inside the orchard. But where he had expected a view of luxuriant Fruit of the Flower, he found himself gazing at an outlandish yet somehow familiar-looking monstrosity that sat gorging itself. Off to one side hunkered a young Perytonian.

"By the Protoculture!" the Regent howled. The two-way channel being open, the thing squatting in the hive orchard looked up at the communications pickup.

"Ah, the Divine, the All-Knowing, the Omnipotent Regent," the thing purred. "Thank you for your hospitality. How delicious, this Fruit of yours!"

"T-Tesla?" the Regent whispered.

"Yes, Tesla! And soon, you'll know what the godlike powers of the Flower *really* are, for Tesla will demonstrate them to you!"

The Regent's anger was so great that he was tempted to turn the Land Cruiser around and go back to obliterate the hive and Tesla. But there was no time; tactical displays showed enemy forces overwhelming the city garrison with the help of the accursed Haydonite antibodies. The Regent cut the communications link with a smashing blow of his fist.

"Increase speed!" he howled.

The scientist cowered. "We are at maximum speed now,

All-Powerful One. Crushing our way through the city makes the going somewhat difficult."

Another scientist added, "We have detected vessels emerging from superluminal drive in deepspace, but have as yet been unable to make contact."

"Well, make sure my flagship is ready to lift off the moment I arrive," the Regent roared. If those *were* Invid ships, he would fry Haydon IV from a safe distance; if not, he would be ready for a strategic withdrawal in the fastest vessel in the Invid fleet.

"And where are our reinforcements?" he added.

"They are being delivered now to the eastern and northern sectors of the city, Mighty One, for diversionary counterattacks to facilitate our withdrawal. We are also monitoring a droppage in city power resources, and a corresponding decrease in antibody activity."

Perhaps it would be possible to win after all. How the Sentinels and the Haydonites and the Praxians would pay! He began planning an elaborate, days-long festival of torture and executions, but the daydream was smashed to pieces moments later.

"Signal from the approaching starships, Omnipotent Lord," a technician said. With that, the face of Breetai appeared on the screen.

The giant felt an unsmiling satisfaction. He had somehow known all along, in his bones, that the Regent was not dead. There was no way the creature could have been tricked or yielded up his life so easily.

For a few seconds, the Regent found that he couldn't catch his breath. Breetai, the Zentraedi's most brilliant commander, and, after the late Dolza, their most powerful warrior!

Breetai glared at the Regent. "We're coming for you," he said, and nothing more. The screen went blank.

The Regent sent his staff scurrying with angry blows

and kicks. "More speed! I'll kill the first one to offer me excuses!"

His ace in the hole might be of crucial importance after all. The Regent faced his brace of pet Hellcats. "Go, and fetch the Zor-clone to me!"

They sprang away, and the Regent summoned a lackey. Quietly, so that the others present couldn't hear, he directed, "Have my personal battle armor prepared."

The carpet was barely big enough for two heavily armed Humans and Veidt, and jostling was a hazardous business indeed. But somehow Jack and Karen managed to keep their footing as the thing whooshed through the sky. How Veidt maintained his place, levitating *above* the carpet as he did, was something the Humans couldn't understand.

They came up on the Land Cruiser from behind, as it ground Glike under it, making its ponderous way toward the starport. Figuring speed and distance, Karen calculated that they only had a few minutes to find and save Rem.

"How're we gonna find him, in a crate that size?" Jack said over the sound of the air rushing by them.

"I can sense his whereabouts," Veidt responded simply. With the trauma of Sarna's death, Veidt seemed changed —more intense, more capable, but cold and remote. A terrible price to pay for increased powers, Karen reflected sadly.

She brought her mind back to matters at hand. "I'm more worried about how we're gonna get *into* that tin can."

"Vowad has arranged for...a diversion," Veidt said. Even as he said it, kaleidoscopic flames licked up from the rubble around the Land Cruiser's treads and the buildings about to be crushed under them. The flames circled and formed a swirling whirlpool, a scintillating funnel of Haydonite antibody power. Up and up it rose, until it stood two hundred feet high. Then it shifted, flashing, and took form.

"Oh my *god*!" Karen breathed.

It was a fiery image of Zor, straddled-legged, blocking the Land Cruiser's path of retreat.

"Kill him! *Kill him!*" the Regent yammered, laying about him on the Land Cruiser's bridge. "I, your god, command you to kill Zor for once and for all!"

When the Land Cruiser loosed its awesome barrage at the unmoving figure, Veidt was ready.

He wove the carpet in among the volleying supercannon and lesser gun batteries. The salvos were disintegrating the cityscape before them, but had no apparent effect on the colossal Zor.

High on the aft part of the cruiser's hull, a rack of missiles was rising into place from its shielded pod. As the pod doors opened to allow it to rise, Veidt swooped through, into the space between the hulls. Karen and Jack found themselves clinging to one another, trying to keep their footing, praying the Haydonite knew what he was doing.

Jack was so scared that he couldn't even enjoy the embrace.

Veidt seemed to know the entire layout of the cruiser, every nut and bolt. An ammo elevator to the launcher's magazine gave them, in turn, access to a utility core. In seconds, they were racing down a passageway scaled to mecha size, high over the heads of the preoccupied Invid.

Veidt flew them to a remote part of the cruiser's belly. They stopped before a compartment with a giant hatch. "Rem's cell," Veidt explained.

But the hatch was open. Karen and Jack piled off, rifles

ready, to peer inside. The Regent's two Hellcats, having cornered Rem, spun on the intruders.

The 'Cats pounced at the Humans even as Jack and Karen brought their muzzles up blazing.

Clad in his heavy, powered battle armor, the Regent railed and raved as his cruiser's most powerful cannonades failed to have any effect on the enormous figure of Zor that stood blocking his way.

"Have my flagship lift off and open fire!" he shrieked.

As the order was relayed, a tech said, "All-Powerful One, there is an unidentified flying object approaching!"

The Regent looked at the monitor to which the tech was pointing. Sure enough, something was racing forward right along the upper hull, weaving in between gun and missile batteries, too close to the cruiser to be fired upon.

"I—I—" The Regent felt his head spin. He saw a Haydonite flying carpet with several figures riding it. As it zipped past the bridge, two resplendent objects were tossed and bounced off the forward hull just in front of the viewport.

The Regent shoved aside the crew members who were trying to see what had been dropped, and had a look for himself. There on the deck lay the two mighty collars, mounted with gems from all the Invid-dominated worlds, that his pet Hellcats had worn. The Regent let out a piercing screech, and was about to direct all fire at the fleeing carpet, when yells of horror burst from his crew.

The giant Zor was moving.

The fiery image strode forward, straight for the Land Cruiser, even as the flagship rose from the nearby starport and began firing at it with all guns. The Regent bleated in pure dread and hurled techs out of his way, charging for the bridge's hatch.

The towering, demonic Zor dove at the cruiser in apparent slow motion, arms spread and fingers curled, as if to enfold it. The collision sent waves of light racing outward like waves in a pond when a rock is thrown in. Multicolored flames flared up along the cruiser's bow as the figure began to merge with it.

High on the hull, an emergency ejection port opened and a metallic shape shot straight up like a sub-launched missile. Riding the propulsive power of his augmentation modules, the Regent arrowed away toward his flagship.

Below him, the cruiser was already half engulfed in the destructive force of Haydon IV's defensive system. A series of explosions ripped the war machine apart like an overtaxed boiler and leveled that part of the city.

In that moment, gazing down as he ascended on his suit jets and reflecting upon the sum total of defeats and reversals, the Regent retreated into uttermost devolved depths. While his powered armor's automatics made the linkup with the flagship and guided him into its airlock, and the vessel itself lifted away from Haydon IV at maximum boost, the Regent abandoned temper tantrums and frustrated rantings for the impersonal malevolence of a serpent.

The Regis would never understand his choice of deevolution, but then she had never sampled it. She had never known how, in its purest form, the devolved state took away the pain of introspection, of reflection, of shame and regret and misgiving.

She would never know the mindless hatred and untainted hostility and the personal peace that state could bring. But for her mate, it was a chosen way of life.

His defeats were forgotten now that he had submerged his higher self; he luxuriated in a rancor so all-embracing that it satisfied him like a drug. But in that trance, contrary to the accustomed blankness, a Vision appeared. It defined itself, coming into mental focus, thrown up before the Regent's eyes by the depths of his loathing and his thirst for revenge. It was an answer to his dilemma.

It was the face of General T.R. Edwards.

Like other worlds the Sentinels had visited, Haydon IV had its shrine to the godlike being after whom it had been named.

This one did not occupy a mountaintop or city plaza or polar ice cap. Rather, it stood at the center of a burnished alloy plain three hundred miles in diameter, the only feature of a landscape that was otherwise as smooth as a looking glass.

Unlike other worlds', Haydon's icon wasn't carved from ice or hewn from the living rock of a peak. Instead, a projected, ghostly image of the legendary figure stood nearly a mile high. It bore a resemblance to a Haydonite in that the features were smooth, anonymous; the arms were within the high-collared cape, so that Haydon looked very much like the inhabitants of that world. Only the hint of flowing hair contradicted it.

The Terrans had been surprised to realize that, by Haydon's own decree, no precise image of him had ever been made. And so he remained shrouded in mystery just as the projection stood wrapped in its long cape.

The Sentinels and the freed Praxians had offered to provide an honor guard for Sarna's funeral, but Vowad and Veidt declined. Together, they boarded a small carpet and undertook the journey with the body of the beloved mate and daughter.

Soon the leveled city was left behind and the idyllic countryside of Haydon IV rolled by beneath. But the two kept their gazes straight ahead. During that long flight not a word was exchanged between the two, each being lost in his contemplation.

When at last they hovered before the projected figure, there was no need to say anything aloud. They had already communed their sorrow to the very planet, and to one another.

Nevertheless, Veidt, having picked up new customs in his travels and travails, bade the figure of Haydon, "Take her into your keeping, she who was everything in this life to me. Grant that her words were true, and that we will be together again!"

He wasn't praying to Haydon, but rather addressing a higher power that even the Haydonites only dimly understood and could not fathom by any application of mere logic.

Still, the image of Haydon moved, as the living Awareness of the planet willed it. Arms appeared from beneath the cape, and eyes, like Human eyes, or Tiresian, came into shadowy resolution. The open palms beckoned.

Sarna's body rose from the carpet, poised and erect as though she lived once more. As the father and the husband watched, she was drawn into the valley of Haydon's cupped palms.

Vowad struggled within himself, moved by the words Veidt had spoken and by the wretched grief of the moment. Sarna was gone, her essence having passed to some other plane of existence, therefore it was illogical to base decisions on what would please her. And yet . . .

Sarna's body had vanished into the cupped hands of Haydon. A glow rose from between them, lighting Haydon's smooth face and the sky above. The two mourners heard many voices raised in wordless music as the light intensified. Then all at once it was unbearable, and they had to look away.

When they turned back, Haydon was lowering vast, empty hands. In moments, the projection stood as it had when they appeared. They stood looking at it for long minutes.

"Veidt, I—I would like to be friends with you from now on, if you will it."

"Thank you, Vowad. It will give her great joy."

CHAPTER
FIFTEEN

So it's eloquence or violence,
'Cause no one believes in coincidence!

The Robotones, "Protoculture Junction"

THE CALL FROM HIS SECRET FACILITY UNDER THE
Royal Hall didn't awaken Edwards; he slept less and less
nowadays, animated by his relentless hunger to wrest control of the REF, and by his frustration that Minmei, still in
solitary confinement, was steadfast in her refusal to so
much as speak to him.

His first impulse was to call his security convoy over to
the Royal Hall with lights flashing and sirens wailing. But
in the cautious head-on power games he was playing with
Lang and the rest of the Plenepotentiary Council, he
couldn't afford to attract attention to the secret advantage
he held. So the trip was low-profile.

With Ghost Rider guards flanking, Edwards picked his
way through the catacombs under the gargantuan Royal
Hall, coming at last to the carefully guarded installations
that was under his personal control.

"We have a contact signal, sir," the officer on duty explained, "but no response to our acknowledgment. We just get the same word in code."

The officer turned up the volume and the speakers murmured Edwards's name over and over.

Edwards issued terse commands. The room was cleared, leaving him alone with the apparatus. It took a bit of remembering, but he had been careful to learn how to operate the devices himself.

"Edwards here."

There was a moment's silence, then he found himself looking into the face of the Invid Regent.

I knew it! Edwards exulted. Perhaps it was in some measure a function of the strange insights he had gotten when he had taken that brain-boost from the captured Invid equipment, but perhaps it was just as much a matter of his innate suspicion. In any case, he had never believed that the creature strangled on Tirol by Tesla was the *real* Regent.

"You took your time answering, Human," the Regent said.

"I'm here now. What do you want?"

Each was inspecting the other with the same thought: this fool could be the answer to my problem!

"There have been . . . unfortunate mishaps," the Regent said. "Your enemies and mine now hold Haydon IV."

Edwards bit back an insult; he had to appear absolutely calm. The failure of his Ghost Riders to return from the pursuit of Breetai had been clear enough proof that the Zentraedi had probably linked up with the damned Sentinels. But to hear that they had triumphed again was almost enough to make him doubt his own high destiny to rule all Creation.

But no; here was the Regent, a sign that Edwards was, indeed, the Chosen of the Gods.

Edwards resisted the impulse to taunt the Regent; he

would need the creature's goodwill for a while longer yet.
"That's too bad. What are we going to do about it?"

The Regent hid his satisfaction at hearing that Edwards
would willingly be a part of the Regent's web of machina-
tions. "I am on my way to the Home Hive on Optera now.
Once there, I will contact you with details of our combined
effort. The Protoculture willing, we shall wipe the Sentinels out of existence."

"I look forward to that day, my good friend," Edwards
said in a butter-wouldn't-melt voice.

The two broke contact with an identical silent thought:
*Just wait until I no longer need you, you gullible simple-
ton!*

On Haydon IV, the sorrow over Sarna's death and the
deaths of thousands of others, and the destruction of Glike,
was lessened somewhat by the somber satisfaction of having evicted the Invid.

Once the Regent departed in his flagship, the Invid simply lost their will to fight. The mopping-up hadn't taken
long. By the time Breetai's *Valivarre* and the two REF
cruisers were making planetfall, most of the fighting was
finished

They found a city where triumphant amazons were cele-
brating their liberation, patrolling the city with weapons in
their hands and heads held high. The Haydonites, too, had
undergone a change: gone were the days when they could
stomach Invid tyranny over themselves or others. The ruins
of Glike had the air of a monument to the trans-species
hunger for freedom.

In the wake of the struggle, the other Sentinels were left
in various moods and states. Vince Grant and his wife
hugged, rejoicing in the victory, but were melancholy in
the knowledge that there was so much more yet to do.

Jack Baker and Karen Penn, watching over Rem in a

Hall of Healing, found that they didn't despise one another quite so much. "Glad you made it, Penn," Jack blurted.

"Thanks for . . . for riding to the rescue, Lancelot," she tried to joke, but she couldn't bring herself to say it lightly as their eyes met.

Across from them, Janice Em was gazing down on Rem, too. She saw images of Rem and Zor and—something else; impulses fought in her for dominance. Although it was contrary to her programming, an undeniable tide of emotion welled up in her every time she looked at the clone. She longed for a chance to ask Lang what it all meant, but despaired of ever having the chance; the war seemed to have taken on a life of its own.

For Breetai there were cheers and accolades, and kisses, too, though his sixty-foot height made those a little impractical.

Lisa didn't care; she insisted that the Zentraedi lift her high so that she could plant a wet one on his cheek. She had the interesting experience of seeing one of the universe's biggest blushes up close. There was a tallish female Zentraedi close-by, someone Lisa had heard called Kazianna, who frowned a bit at Lisa's display of affection.

Lisa understood the possessive look she was seeing on Kazianna's face, and lingered a moment, literally grabbing Breetai's ear. "Well! Congratulations!" she said slyly. The ear grew red and warm in her grasp, but Breetai was grinning like a schoolboy.

As for Lisa and Rick, there was something between them that hadn't been there before the Haydon campaign. It was the unweighted love that had come into being when it was proven in battle that there was no inequality of courage—or concern—between them. Each was an accomplished fighter now, and it was understood that each would have dangers to face. And so each felt equal love for the other, and apprehensions, and pride. And each felt the immeasurable value of every moment they shared.

The Karbarrans and Garudans managed to contact the members of their respective races who were on Haydon IV, and enjoyed the particular pleasures of hometown manners. It pleased the other Sentinels to know that word of the exploits of Lron, Crysta, Kami, Learna, and the rest would be carried back to their homes.

Max Sterling took no part in the impromptu celebrations because he spent every waking moment by Miriya's bedside and often slept there as well. She had lost consciousness shortly after the Regent's flagship lifted off, and had sunk into a deep coma less than an hour later. Even the Haydonite healers were mystified by her condition, which was caused by some interaction of her impossible pregnancy, exposure to the Garudan atmosphere, and the exertions of the battle in Glike.

Tesla and Burak had reappeared. Tesla was now taller, more Humaniform. Most notably, he had a mouth, and spoke with it. Things were so disorganized in Glike that there wasn't much time for comment. But everyone who saw him groaned, either out loud or mentally. *Jeez, he was bad enough as it was! But now that he's got a mouth to shoot off ...*

Breetai's news that Tesla had strangled the simulagent had everyone looking at the scientist with renewed suspicion, of course, and there was vague talk of bringing some kind of war-crimes charge against him. But Tesla managed to deflect it, for the moment anyway, by pointing out that his victim was an Invid espionage agent and that, in any case, Tesla himself was technically a POW. The waters thus muddied, he remained at liberty and at least nominally a Sentinels collaborator.

Tesla had considered parting ways with the Sentinels, but faced the conclusion that his key to Ultimate Transformation lay in visiting the other worlds that had felt Haydon's personal touch—Spheris and Peryton. And the only reasonably safe way to do that lay in the company of the

Sentinels. Besides, trying an escape would risk the wrath of the Karbarrans, the Praxians, the Humans, and the rest, and even with his enhanced powers, Tesla secretly trembled to think of what that meant.

And so when he was finally brought before the leadership, Bela pinking him in the side with a shortsword, Tesla deflected their accusations and inquiries about the changes the Flower's Fruit had wrought in him.

Instead, he said in his blandest voice, "We have a common cause; you must put aside your hatred and mistrust, and work with me in friendship."

The core group of the Sentinels were in favor of roasting him alive, or at least putting a leash and exploding collar back on him, but the very bylaws of the Sentinels and of Haydon militated against that. And so, when the Sentinels came together to deliberate on their next move, Tesla had his say.

"My people are a peaceful race; who can deny this? Did we not live in tranquility for a million eons, until outsiders taught us crime and sin and hate? As the Regent and Regis were deranged by this experience, so have our rulers warped the Invid.

"Have I myself not committed murder most foul for your cause? I, who never raised a hand in violence to any living thing before in my life? But as you are willing to wage war for peace, so I have done in my own way."

There were angry faces all around the new conference hall that had been raised by Robotech mecha and Haydonite science there in the ruins of Glike. Many glowered and murmured, but there was no arguing the facts. Janice Em, wearing the aspect of her android self as she sometimes did these days, looked over at Rem to see his reaction, wondering what the opinion of the genetic heir of Zor would be. Rem's face was resolutely unrevealing.

As for Breetai, he was studying Janice Em and wondering about Lang's motives in creating her. Fortunately for the android and her creator, the Sentinels seemed to regard her as their ally and comrade in arms, rather than as some REF version of the simulagent.

Tesla's strange new mouth, almost doll-like, formed his words with an uncanny grace and lilt.

"But my people deserve a chance to redeem themselves and make restitution!" Tesla pressed on. "I have had a chance to learn peace and restraint and *love* in my time among the Sentinels, and—"

Here his voice broke in calculated fashion and he made a show of holding back tears. "Destroy the Regent and the Regis, yes! But *return to us the Flower of Life*, or give us whatever world upon which the Flower choses to prosper. And then we will be the harmless, inward-turning, compassionate Invid of old. A thousand generations of genetic heritage call out to us to *be* so! And if Fate grants it, I would take humble pleasure in making my small contribution to the Destiny of my species.

"We were given life, as you were! Let us live!"

That subject was tabled for the time being, but the Sentinels leadership exchanged troubled looks. Tesla might be a complete moron militarily, but he was a consummate politician.

Maybe the two go hand in hand, Rick thought, reflecting back to Senator Russo and his ilk on Earth.

Other matters came to the fore and were more quickly and decisively dealt with.

Breetai argued strongly that *all* the Sentinels, liberated Praxians included, should return to Tirol to fight Edwards's scurrilous charges. It looked like he would carry the question, not through guile or politicking, but simply through the force of his conviction.

Rick looked around, wondering who was going to muster the counterargument. But he remembered that Baldan of Spheris was dead, and Teal, the other leading Spherisian, was still closeted and caring for Baldan's death-growth.

The only notable Perytonian, Burak, had been silent and impossible to talk to ever since the Garudan campaign, somehow under Tesla's spell.

And Spheris and Peryton were the last two worlds on the Sentinels' tactical charts, the last two from which the Invid must be uprooted. Rick scanned the room and realized that there were few Spherisians—and none who would speak—and no Perytonians at all, aside from silent Burak.

Rick was as surprised as anyone when he heard himself address the assembly.

"I've fought against Great Breetai and alongside him, and in all this time, to my recollection, I've never actually found the nerve to *contradict* him."

At that comment, there were rumblings of laughter from the Zentraedi, seated like Norse gods in immense chairs around the walls of the room. Kazianna put her hand on Breetai's shoulder, and Breetai placed his hand on hers but kept his attention on Rick Hunter. Size meant nothing in the arena of debate, and Breetai, as canny as any Borgia or Caesar, knew that.

"We congratulate ourselves for the work we've done, as we should," Rick went on. "But what about Spheris? And Peryton? Things there are as bad as they were here on Haydon IV, don't you think? Or maybe worse?

"So the choice is between going on to end the misery the Invid are inflicting on those planets, or going back to clear our names. Well, here's my vote: I have to live with the memories of what I *do*, or *don't do*, not what people say about me. I say we go on, and Edwards be damned."

He resumed his seat amid an almost equal mix of cheers and objections. But Lisa was looking at him with a peculiar cant to her chin.

No more barnstorming, live-for-today, seat-of-the-pants daredevil, she thought. *He's someone else now, like we all are*. Older but wiser. And yet he was arguing the cause he had argued *against* before, when Burak wanted to turn the timetable upside down. A sense of fairness, maybe.

Lisa reached over beneath the table and gave her husband's hand a squeeze. Rick looked a little startled, then gave her a squeeze back.

After the lesser questions were resolved, the session settled into a collision between the two factions. Breetai's point was a valid one, even a frightening one: if Edwards got control of the council and undermined Lang's authority, the general might wrest control of the new fleet of space-fold ships. That in turn could make him unstoppable.

But there were many who felt as Rick did, having fought the Invid oppression on several worlds now. Among the most determined of these were the freed Praxian slaves.

The dispute cut across lines of species, gender, and even family, however. The goliath voices of the Zentraedi and the roars of the Karbarrans and the objections of the Humans and the other races' outcries threatened to turn the debate to a riot.

Rick had barely spoken since his first statement. But when it seemed the Sentinels were about to lose their sense of purpose and revert to sheer quarreling, he rose again.

"Um, I don't see where there's anything we can do but compromise. Someone has to answer Edwards's charges, and someone has to fight for Spheris and Peryton, *now*!"

He dipped into his pocket and pulled out a good-luck piece, a Kennedy half-dollar his father had given him. "What d'you say, Breetai? I'd trust you with either mission. Heads, you go to Spheris and I face Edwards?"

He showed both sides of the coin, to prove there was no fix.

Breetai had eased off his chair to kneel by the table. His face cracked wide in the first true smile he had allowed himself in some time. Breetai held out his palm, as big as a desktop. "Flip it here, Rick Hunter."

Rick did. Breetai caught it, clapping his palms together, and opened his hands again to show them all. It was tails.

There would be plenty to do tomorrow, but for the time being, everyone needed an adjournment.

When all the others were dispersed and they were strolling under strange constellations, Kazianna Hesh took Breetai's hand. "It's not the outcome you looked for, I know, my love, but still I think it's not an unfair one."

"Perhaps. But I tell you this: Edwards will be stopped, even if I have to do it alone."

She kissed his cheek. "Breetai, you will never face any danger alone again—not while I draw breath."

■ ■ ■ ■ ■ ■ ■ ■ ■ ■ ■ ■ ■ ■ ■ ■ ■

CHAPTER
SIXTEEN

The military scholars missed the point entirely. Max and Mir-
iya, indisputably the greatest Robotech warriors of all, were serv-
ing the source of their prowess by laying down their arms for a
time. Life made them do it—the life growing within the onetime
Quadrono commander, fathered by her erstwhile enemy.
Life, triumphing over death.

    Theresa Duvall, *Wingmates: the Story of Max and Miriya*
    Sterling

T HE WORK TO REBUILD GLIKE AND REPAIR DAMAGE
done to other parts of the planet during the terrible clash
between Inorganics and antibodies had begun literally
while the dust was still settling.

If Haydon IV's world-size instrumentality had been intact, it could have accomplished the rebuilding at a miraculous rate. But much of that instrumentality was either
disabled or obliterated or completely exhausted. The Haydonites threw themselves into the job with a religious fer-
vor, though, and they had help.

The tens of thousands of freed Praxians were among the
most willing to help. The warrior women were a homeless
race now that their own planet had been destroyed in the
upheavals following the Invid conquest and Genesis Pit ex-
periments. Many thought sparsely populated Haydon IV
might offer them a fresh start.

It was plain that Arla-Non longed to lead her amazons on a holy war against the Invid, but since only a few could go along on *Ark Angel*, it was the queen's duty to stay with the majority of her subjects, to guide and govern them. Arla-Non expressed every faith in Bela, though, and confirmed that in rituals that the Praxians barred all outsiders from attending.

The contingent that would return to face Edwards's charges before the council was led by Breetai, along with Vince Grant and Jonathan Wolff. While many of the Diamondback and Joker REF fighters wanted to volunteer for service to fill the depleted ranks of the Sentinels fliers, that was voted down. If Edwards made his power play, it might require every loyal pilot in the REF to put down a coup.

Jean Grant, like Max Sterling, refused to leave the planet as long as Miriya was still in a coma and unable to be moved. Miriya had stabilized, but the outlook was still bleak. Nevertheless, Jean had immersed herself in learning the healing arts of the Haydonites, blending them with her own in the hope of curing Miriya.

Cabell had wavered, thinking that he could be of some help if he stayed, but the others said his insights to the functioning of Protoculture and Robotechnology might be more important than ever in the battles ahead. He spent a night closeted alone with his thoughts, and announced in the morning that he would be remaining behind. Rick thought that the old sage had sensed something important about Miriya's situation, but Cabell refused to talk about his motives.

As for Max, he decided that rather than simply sitting and waiting, he would devote himself to the effort to rebuild the planet.

"I'm sure Jean and Cabell and the Haydonites can make her well again," Max told Rick as the Sentinels prepared to depart for Spheris. "You'll see. By the time we're set for the final assault on Optera, I'll be back in a VT and so will Miriya."

"I know you will," Rick said with conviction he didn't really feel. "We can't have you guys missing out on the grand finale."

The two shook hands and Lisa kissed Max's cheek. Soon, the SDF-7 class cruiser was lifting off. Gaps in the rank and file of their fighters had been filled by several hundred amazon volunteers, but in Rick's opinion the force was still woefully inadequate in terms of mecha.

Originally, production facilities on Karbarra and—it had been hoped—Haydon IV were to have kept the Sentinels' complement of war machines at full strength. But production problems had arisen on Karbarra: a fundamental inability of the Invid-designed manufacturing equipment to turn out satisfactory Earth-style mecha, no matter what adjustments the Karbarrans tried. As for Haydon IV, it simply wouldn't have mecha-production capability soon enough to be of any use.

But Sentinels' mecha had played very little part in freeing Haydon IV and, from all reports, would be even less useful on Spheris. Time would tell: Rick and Lisa were anxious to survey the situation on Spheris, at the very least, as soon as possible. Like many of their companions, they now grew frustrated and ill at ease in between blows against the Invid empire.

T.R. Edwards knew a particular triumph as the special council meeting convened. There was only one item on the agenda: Edwards's renewed request for martial law and what amounted to emergency dictatorial powers. To the general's vast satisfaction, Lang and the other opposition had been either unable or unwilling to block the meeting.

At Edwards's urging, the entire session was being transmitted over the Base Tirol public-information channel. He was gambling that, in addition to winning over the council, he could get the subordinate officers and noncoms and enlisted ratings of the REF to hail him as well, paving the way for his eventual takeover.

Now Edwards made his case again, complete with charts and display-screen aids. The excuse this time was that Edwards promised he could squeeze more monopole ore from Fantoma if the military was given complete run of the operation, up to and including drafting Tiresian laborers. Lang and Dr. Penn didn't even seem to be inclined to dispute the facts and figures Edwards's people trumped up, and Exedore had not even deigned to attend.

All was going well when the wrist communicator on Lang's forearm toned. He sent an acknowledging signal through it and waited politely for Edwards to finish.

But before the vote could be called, Lang got the floor. "My colleague, Lord Exedore, informs me that my communications center has received a signal that is of central importance in this issue."

With that, Exedore's face appeared in the central screen, a billboard-size panel that dominated one end of the council chambers. "Here is the transmission received just a short time ago."

Before Edwards could object, a familiar and, to Edwards, despised face—as handsome as a media star's—appeared. "This is Colonel Jonathan Wolff, transmitting from the bridge of the REF vessel *Valivarre*. With me are Commander Vince Grant and Lord Breetai. We have with us all the monopole ore that was mined on Fantoma.

"Escorting us are the SDF cruisers *Tokugawa* and *Jutland*, which accompanied us on operations involved in the liberation of the planet Haydon IV from Invid domination. It is our intention to turn over the monopole ore to Dr. Lang's production facility and to answer the charges being made against us and other Sentinels.

"All we ask is that the council now, by public vote, insure us the fair hearing to which we are entitled by the

REF Code of Military Justice and by United Earth Government law. Members of the council, we await your word."

Wolff's expression softened a bit. "You're our friends, our comrades in arms—some of you are our loved ones. We haven't played you false." He showed just a touch of that debonair smile of his.

Lang was back on his feet as the message ended. "They won't have to wait long for *my* decision! I say yes, let these people have their fair and public hearing!"

When the question was called, Justine Huxley, Obstat, Rheinehardt, and others opposed to Edwards were quick and loud in their vote of support. Edwards's faction on the council did some grumbling, but most either abstained or went with the momentum of the opposition. Few were inclined to deny the Sentinels due process in a role-call vote. Also, they all knew how critical the monopole ore was.

Edwards had gone white with anger. *That blithering idiot, the Regent! Why hadn't he warned me that this might happen?*

For that matter, why hadn't Edwards's *own* communications-intercept people discovered this plot? It pointed to the possibility that Lang was aware of the technical eavesdropping Edwards's organization was doing, and had exploited it to his, Lang's, advantage, lulling Edwards and then using some unknown "back channel" of contact with Breetai.

This was a major setback, and one piped through the orbiting SDF-3 as well as all of the REF installations on Tirol—

Edwards was rocked physically by a sudden realization. Wolff's face and voice had gone out over the PI channel!

Minmei's jailers had turned some switch that activated the telescreen built into the wall of her cell just as T.R. Edwards made his triumphant entry to the council chambers. The screen, installed in the cells for interrogation, agitprop, and "motivational" purposes, had always been dark before.

Minmei watched Edwards's performance with a trapped animal's dumb despair. The appearance of Jonathan Wolff convinced her that she had at last lost every shred of sanity.

But it was too real, too vivid, to be a dream or hallucination. She slowly rose from her narrow bunk, crossing the little cell, and touched her fingertips to the screen. Tears washed her cheeks.

She heard his words, "You're . . . our loved ones. We haven't played you false." Minmei closed her eyes and pressed her lips to Wolff's lips on the screen, sobbing.

She had been shut away in her quarters on the *Ark Angel* all through the Haydon IV campaign, unable to break away from her own private struggle.

At her request, the ship's techs and artisans had made the compartment as much an imitation of her crystal world as they could with mirrors, prisms, and fanciful formations that suggested underground strata. There, Teal of Spheris labored over the brilliant, multifaceted form that was all that remained of her fellow Spherisian, Baldan.

Teal had refused to touch or even look at it at first, after Baldan was trapped in his merging with the geological substance of Praxis. Baldan had been a fellow prisoner of hers, in the clutches of the Invid, nothing more! To touch the thing that had looked like a football-size crystal meant taking on responsibility for it, and meant entering a rapport with Baldan's essence that would make them mates.

It wasn't fair! Teal had no desire to be responsible for a child or be in rapport with Baldan. She had never asked to be involved in this mad Sentinels crusade! Teal had her own plans, her own life to live.

And yet, when she had stood looking down at it, Teal had known that if she failed to carry out the rite of Shaping, Baldan would pass away forever and the egg would lose the forces of life it carried. With strange tears in her transparent eyes, she took up her ceremonial blade and began Shaping.

And she stayed at it all through the voyage, and the battle on Haydon IV, when the SDF-7 flagship could do little but hold its station. Teal laboriously calculated each cut and guided the newly-carved Spherisian in its growth. It was a trial as taxing as any gestation period or rite of passage. But at last, near the end of her strength, Teal looked upon a healthy adolescent male who was the image of Baldan and still growing quickly.

She wasn't surprised when Bela, returning from Praxis, requested entry to her compartment. It was Bela, along with Miriya Sterling, who had returned to the Praxian caverns to retrieve the egg when Teal refused to. Bela who, absurdly, had threatened to raise the child herself, when the amazon hadn't the first idea about *Humanoid* children, much less creatures of living mineral.

Teal granted permission to enter. Bela, usually rowdy and often gruff, was subdued and tentative. But when she looked down on the child, she was aglow. "But—why are his eyes closed? Why does he not move?"

"He has been regaining the knowledge that Baldan left behind in him," Teal explained. "And preparing himself for true birth. I waited, hoping you and Miriya could both be here."

Teal explained what must be done. Each took one of the statuelike figure's cold hands, kneeling by him. Where a Spherisian parent would ordinarily have done so alone, Teal had the Praxian lean close, their heads together, so that they could both breathe upon the child's mouth together.

One, twice—and on the third, a strange aura of blue radiance leapt from Teal's mouth to the infant's. Bela felt the odd sensation of Spherisian life-force stirring about and through her.

The cold hands tingled now, not with heat so much as

with animating force. Some eldritch piezoelectric effect, Bela wondered? The fingers were no longer stiff, but supple in the manner of living crystal. Bela's Praxian eyes, like those of a bird of prey, grew wide, watching the boy's eyes flutter open.

"Wh—what have you called him?"

Teal held her son's hand in her own. "I call him Baldan. Baldan II. I couldn't bear to name him anything else."

She sighed. "Love is so inconvenient."

Veidt had also insisted on coming along on the continuation of the mission, saying that Haydon IV held too many sad memories. No one had any objections, but every other Haydonite had elected to stay behind and rebuild the planet. Rick suspected Veidt preferred it that way.

Getting the new Praxian recruits squared away was something the Hunters felt safe in delegating to Gnea, Bela, and the other amazon veterans, plus ship's officers. The couple managed to get free of other official responsibilities after the initial confusion and returned at long last to the quarters they shared.

Rick leaned his head back against the hatch once it closed. "A lo-oong day at the beach, babe." Lisa chortled tiredly and nodded.

They hadn't been there since the start of the Garudan mission; it was odd to be back in the quiet, by the bed they had shared too long a time ago.

A change was apparent in Lisa. Though she still wore the body-suit uniform of the REF, her damaged government-issue boots had been replaced with a pair of Praxian footgear, like over-the-knee moccasin wrappings, of soft hide resembling chamois. Her long hair was held back with a knotted band of crimson, satiny fabric Bela had given her.

She also wore a weapons belt around her hips, with a pistol tied down to one thigh and a long Praxian fighting knife to the other. Many Sentinels wore sidearms as a matter of course, but this was something new in Lisa.

In fact, Rick was packing, too. "We're a little over-dressed, aren't we?" he asked, unbuckling his gunbelt.

His piratical-looking wife gave him a heavy-lidded gaze. "Well, surely some up-and-coming young Robotech admiral can figure out an appropriate plan of action to solve *that* problem, can't he?"

He smiled. "Haven't you heard? Night maneuvers are a Hunter specialty."

CHAPTER
SEVENTEEN

He had his own personal bestiary of unacceptable words, and chief among them was "defeat."

Constance Wildman, *When Evil Had its Day: A Biography of T.R. Edwards*

PHERIS PRESENTED A COMPLICATED SKEIN OF PROBlems unlike those of any other Invid-held planet on the Sentinels' hit list.

"We can't take *any* Protoculture weapons down there," Teal explained at a strategy meeting. "To do so would mean disaster."

"What're we supposed to fight 'em with, spit?" somebody groused from the sidelines.

Teal looked around toward the source of the voice, her eerie transparent eyes flashing. "Spheris is a planet of crystal structures," she snapped. "Protoculture-weapons emissions evoke certain harmonics from the very texture of my homeworld. Fire a beam and you're very likely to find that it will come back to hit *you*. Or it could sunder some of the delicate latticework that makes up the planet, and cause great death and destruction among my people."

"Hold, hold," Lron grumbled. "How then do the futtering Invid operate? Do they not use mecha?"

Teal nodded. "As I said in the intel debriefing, Protoculture-*based* mecha do no damage, because they're not as focused, as concentrated, as a weapons beam. But even the Invid dare not use *weapons* actuated by Protoculture, and so they employ a variety of conventional armaments. But those armaments are very effective."

"So are ours," Bela put in, casually flicking her thumb across the razor edge of her shortsword. She was also wearing a Badger assault pistol and a few grenades to complement her Praxian arms.

Others seconded what she had said: the Karbarrans with their pneumatic long-guns; the Garudans who had taken so quickly to REF conventional infantry weapons; Jack and Karen, who had seen for themselves that Invid could be hurt or stopped with projectile firearms if those firearms were used just right.

"You're not listening!" Teal barked. "The Invid will have the advantage in firepower. So, we must exploit *our* advantages to the fullest. And the Sentinels' main advantage is my and Baldan's access to the Crystal Highways."

With this Teal put her hand on the shoulder of her son, Baldan II. He sat by her side, gazing around at the Sentinels gathered at the meeting table and standing in ranks around it.

In mere weeks, he had grown until he was nearly his mother's height, a broad-shouldered, lean-waisted, postadolescent wearing a loincloth. People had simply taken to calling him by his father's name, leaving out the numerical. Talking to him, Lisa had found, was uncannily like talking to the original Baldan at times, but at others it was like conversing with a newborn.

"But you won't be going in blind," Teal said. "My son and I will descend first, to scout the way and ferret out our enemy's weaknesses."

There were some low-decibel remarks when the gathering heard that. Teal had never been very enthusiastic about the Sentinels' war—had stayed out of most of the fighting with a demeanor that had won her the nickname "Permafrost Princess."

But here was the Permafrost Princess, in the wake of Baldan's death and a motherhood she had detested at first, ready to take her son down on a first-in team op. Ready to lay her life and her son's, most emphatically, on that well-known line.

Rick rose now, in the midst of a lot of murmured debate among those present. "We *have* to apply everything we've learned to beat the Invid, because they've had us outgunned and outnumbered at every turn. Now, the subject populations of the planets we've liberated have always worked in our favor, and they've tipped the balance at least twice, maybe three times. So our most important trump cards here are Teal and Baldan.

"They will be delivered to the surface of Spheris by a stealth-insertion drop capsule and employ their innate skills to merge with the Crystal Highways. They will gather information and attempt to raise popular resistance, while we hold station and wait.

"They will communicate the results to us and coordinate our assault. If anyone has objections to this general outline, I want to hear them now."

Moments passed, while the Sentinels looked at one another and at Teal and Baldan II. But no one spoke.

Baldan, for his part, looked over to where Karen Penn was sitting with some of the younger REF turks along the sidelines. He had already heard of her deeds; his mother was rather taken with them. Karen was talking with Gnea and another young amazon. She suddenly looked up to meet Baldan's gaze, and he turned his face away, a radiance rising in his cheeks for no reason he could understand.

Rick Hunter was still speaking.

"You all know the tactical importance of this planetary objective. The Invid have found a way to mass-synthesize their nutrient fluid here—the best they have. Apparently, it's like high-octane to them. If we can cut off that supply, we'll be nailing the lid on their coffin."

He looked over to where Burak sat, at the edge of the shadows. The thing that was Tesla, the thing that made every Sentinel uneasy no matter how it protested its faith to their cause, had failed to appear for the planning session.

"And so at last we will have crippled their sources of new mecha"—Rick ticked off on his fingers—"their sources of new technology, their shipyards and their life-support supply line. We'll be set up for the campaign on Peryton."

Burak looked up suddenly at the mention of his home-world, like a thief surprised in the act. Rick met his gaze and wished he knew what was going on in the young buck's head.

One thing was apparent to everyone. Armageddon lay ahead, and not too far off.

There was almost a firefight between the REF factions.

Edwards was determined to have a face-to-face with Lang, but the security people at Lang's enormous complex refused entry to the convoy of limos, armored vehicles, and troop carriers. The Ghost Veritechs flying high cover were warned away on pain of getting their tails shot off, and no one was inclined to test the perimeter defenses of the Robotech sorcerer.

It was an open secret among Humans, and Tiresians as well, that battle lines were being drawn for a contest of wills and/or a power play in the REF. The surviving Ghost Riders and quite a few others beside were rallying to Edwards's banner, but as many and more were standing by

Lang and the council members who were in accord with him.

In addition to Lang's own security force there were Jokers and Diamondbacks, people from the technical and support units, Destroid types from the Old Ironsides and Walking Steel squadrons, and infantry doggies like the men and women from Hell's Hoplites.

Many were still straddling the fence, though, and Edwards's forces were organized, highly disciplined and motivated, and loyal to him alone. He and his opposition had one another in an uneasy stalemate, but everyone knew it couldn't last for long.

So, the request for a meeting with Lang, in Lang's own stronghold, had come as something of a surprise. The obvious lessons of the Trojan Horse gave the scientist pause, but the off chance that a power struggle could be averted made him agree to the confrontation in the end.

Edwards's VTs veered off in compliance with the warnings, and the general himself stepped forth from his armored limo once it was inside a garage-bunker. Edwards looked around warily before exiting the car; he had begun sensing some troubling and lethal presence near him in recent days—a menacing shadow he could never quite see out of the corner of his eye. Sometimes he thought it was a phantom image brought on by his brain-boost, and other times he was sure that there was somebody poised in the darkness, waiting to kill him.

But he had no qualms about going into Lang's den, really; fools like the good doctor always played by the rules, which was why they were always fated to lose.

Soon, the two were closeted together in Lang's inner sanctum, an alchemist's lair of bizarre experimental Robotech equipment, glowing retorts, and weird holographic displays of flora and fauna from that galactic region.

"We're wasting time and resources with all this bickering." Edwards got around to his pitch quickly. "I only want what's best for the REF! For Earth and the Human race!"

All the while, he was monitoring the sensors that had been built into his skullpiece, reading the alphanumerics and indicators that were projected onto the inside of his eye-lens. It was the crowning achievement of his technical staff, the ultimate debugger.

Edwards knew that Lang had several monitoring systems that the scientist thought would catch every word and movement in the room, but the remotes built into Edwards's belt and epaulets and the fabric of his dress uniform would counter all that. Lang was going to find himself with a lot of blank tape.

"How can I prove that to you and the others?" Edwards finished.

Lang hadn't batted an eye. "Remain neutral during the hearing of Wolff and the others, since you have no real evidence. Put all your forces under the direct command of the council. And most importantly, allow me and my teams to examine the Invid artifacts, or remains, or whatever else there is, under the Royal Hall."

"No!" Edwards forgot himself, his fist pounding a table so that minor items leapt off it and scattered on the floor.

"No?" Lang echoed mildly. "And why not, General? Nothing to hide, surely? So, when you permit me to investigate the catacombs there, which your people so closely guard, then we can talk about your dutiful beneficence toward the REF."

"You stay away from there, you damn *black magician*!" the general hollered.

"And another thing," Lang said mildly. "Major Carpenter and the Earth expedition are safely away. The warning's gone forth, and there is nothing you can do about it."

The general was stunned for a moment. He had had no idea that any of the new SDF-7 vessels had been fitted with a spacefold drive! And now one was on its way to Earth, commanded by an officer loyal to the council and to Lang, imperiling all Edwards's grand designs.

The general, provoked beyond words, lurched at the scientist, hands out to choke him.

Suddenly, Lang's hands were clamped around Edwards's wrists with a strength that threatened to crush them. The general was being forced back and down to his knees. There was a wild moment in which Edwards realized that Lang's strength wasn't Human—that Lang could quite easily kill him.

Edwards had come into Lang's bailiwick without bodyguards, though, because he was sure he had read the man. "Go . . . ahead," he gritted. "Finish it, if you think you can! Murder me! Isn't that what your precious Shapings are all about?"

The tremendous pressure from the scientist's grip fell away, and Edwards was left to rub numbed wrists. He laughed a little hysterically. "No, you can't, can you? That wouldn't be kosher with the Shapings of the Protoculture, would it?" He cackled to himself, struggling to his feet.

"Stop your subversion now," Lang said in a near monotone, "before there's any more bloodshed. Adhere to your oath, and abandon these megalomaniacal dreams."

Edwards drew himself up, lips coming away from his locked teeth. He would perhaps never again have a chance to tell Lang off in private; this would be the only moment when the two stood alone together out of the spotlight, as it were.

"*Here's* the oath I'll serve," he said in a voice so low it was barely audible. But as he spoke it became louder. "I swear to kill Wolff. I swear to exterminate Rick and Lisa Hunter and Breetai, after I've made them suffer enough. The rest of you will either bow at my feet or die. I swear to have Obstat and Huxley and all the rest of them on the council as my personal slaves—"

It was on the tip of his tongue to say that he meant to

subjugate Minmei, but that secret he managed to contain. "I swear to have the galaxy as my personal domain."

He backed away, flexing partially paralyzed fingers. "I swear revenge."

Lang didn't pursue him; indeed, Lang stood with hands locked behind his back now. "Then there's nothing to discuss. But—one last question, if you will, General."

Edwards flashed a grin like a shark's. "What?"

Lang's eyebrows met. "I understand why you despise Rick Hunter; his connection to your old nemesis, Roy Fokker, makes that obvious. But whence comes this loathing of Lisa Hayes Hunter? What has she ever done to you?"

Edwards forgot the pain, letting his hands fall to his sides. "You'll find out when the oh-so-saintly Hunters do: when it's too late."

He turned his back on Lang, striding out of the room so fast that the door barely had time to get out of his way.

Lang made sure the door was secure, then turned toward a dim corner of his sanctum. "Scott, did you get all that?"

Scott Bernard, Lang's apprentice and godson, emerged —a slender, dark-haired, unsmiling kid of thirteen or so, small for his age. "The machines are in some sort of flux, Doctor."

Heels clacking on the hardtop, Edwards walked back toward his limo as his personal bodyguards fell in beside him. The wrist module still read true; he laughed.

Nothing I say can be held against me!

That left a number of other concerns, but suddenly the most pressing among them was Minmei. Edwards made a rasping, pantherish sound as he slid into his limo.

God! It would be so easy to break her will by physical or chemical means—to turn her into something that would obey his every word and whim, satisfy his every hunger.

The hell of it was he wanted *Minmei*, not some brain-wiped zombie that looked and talked like her. *He wanted her to love him.*

And she would. If he had to turn the universe upside down and shake it like a toy to make her do so, she *would* love him.

The limo rolled out under the security spotlights, flanked by security vehicles, about to swoop under the security umbrella of Ghost VTs.

"Wait!"

Surface-effect braking thrusters blared; people pulled guns and Guardian-mode fighters swooped in, while the security net crackled with confused transmissions.

Edwards was out of the limo virtually over the lap of a hulking bodyguard. "Did you see him? There, up *there*!"

But the spot to which he was pointing, the top of a nearby building, was empty. Even as VT spotlights converged on it, he could see that.

Adams was out of the front seat. "What was it, sir?"

Edwards kept his eyes trained on the spot. *Don't let them see you sweat! You can't afford to show any weakness!*

"Nothing; a trick of the light. Let's get 'em rolling."

When the convoy was moving again, he replayed the split-second glimpse and couldn't convince himself that he had been wrong.

A human figure, poised on the roof almost nonchalantly. Watching.

Waiting . . .

CHAPTER
EIGHTEEN

The frictions among the Sentinels were many, and the Grail of defeating the Regent was sometimes the single thing that kept them from a disastrous falling-out.

It is noteworthy that none of them noticed how immune Tesla grew to their irritability, frustration, retribution, and so on. They were physical warriors, under attack—though they didn't know it—from a metaphysical foe who'd gotten inside their own lines.

Ann London, *Ring of Iron: The Sentinels in Conflict*

"WHAT'S THE MATTER, LIEUTENANT COM-
mander Baker? Don't I look 'strac'?"

Jack Baker eyed Gnea. "I, uh, I just wish my academy commandant could see you, is all."

Such an encounter would offer a chance to brush up on his cardiopulmonary resuscitation technique, Jack figured, because Commodore Steinfeld would certainly have a heart attack if she ever got a glance at Gnea.

Just as Lisa had taken to wearing Praxian accessories, most Sentinels pretty much dressed as they saw fit. Prolonged campaigning had seen to it that virtually nobody had a regulation wardrobe anymore, and people wore what came to hand or caught their fancy.

A case in point was Gnea. The ringmail G-string and studded dragonskin halter top were in keeping with Praxian fashion, but the REF dress uniform jacket was a bit of a shock. The high-waisted mess jacket was decked out with brush epaulets, decorations and ribbons, fourragères, and insignia.

She pirouetted to show off her new acquisition. "Commander Grant's exec and I are just about the same size, so we swapped," she said, brushing the embroidery on her cuffs. Jack wondered how the economy-size Lieutenant Commander Shimoda was enjoying her new gryphon-fur shawl. Certainly Gnea, a six-foot-four teenager with legs that wouldn't quit, did things for that jacket that, in Jack's private opinion, merited a medal.

"Anyway, what did you want to see me about, Jack?"

He realized guiltily that he had been admiring her long-waisted figure and gave a start, glancing around by reflex and expecting Karen Penn to be scowling at him. Dammit! The two were at one another's throat as often as they were caught up in their romantic friendship, and Karen had certainly never said or done anything proprietary. But somehow, he found, he couldn't look at another woman anymore without the fear of being clobbered.

"The admiral's noticed that Tesla's been keeping a low profile since the Haydon IV tea party," he said. "In fact, nobody's seen him. For that matter, Burak's been conspicuously out of sight, too. So I figured I'd sort of take a stroll and hunt them up."

Gnea had been a confidant of Burak's, at least back when the Sentinels first showed up on Tirol. So, enlisting her in the project was one of the first things that had come to Jack's mind.

"Yes, I noticed that," Gnea said with a pensive look on her face. "It's time someone found out just what those two are up to, isn't it?" She fell in next to him and they started off, she a half-head taller but both of them comfortable with each other's company.

"Burak and I don't talk much anymore, you know," the amazon went on. "I just—once he became acquainted with

Tesla, he started talking like some kind of savior. It was one thing to sympathize with him but a completely different one to put up with that—what would Humans call it? Napoleonic complex?"

"I dunno," Jack said. "I majored in Wood Shop."

Gnea let that pass without finding out what it meant; one had to understand that Jack liked to be obscure.

Burak wasn't in his quarters, and so they went to the compartment that had been assigned to Tesla. The Invid wasn't there—just as he hadn't been there for days. But Jack had learned the unpleasant facts of what it was like to turn in an unsatisfactory report to Rick Hunter, and so he snooped around the place, opening empty closets and looking through empty drawers.

But it was Gnea, studying the deck the way a Praxian huntress was expected to examine the ground, who came across something that merited their attention. "What's this?"

Jack squatted next to her. "Mung." He knew the look and smell of it well: a mixture of dirt and grease, moisture and machine oil. It was as common to certain starship ancillary power compartments as it had been a generation before to the power plants of nuclear submarines. The mung looked like it had come off Tesla's bare footsole.

Finding the right compartment didn't take long; looking for places near the ship's power section where the security monitors were out of service narrowed it down. On the third try, Jack and Gnea stepped through a hatch and found themselves facing Burak.

Jack was one of those who wore sidearms aboard ship nowadays, and Gnea had always practiced the habit. He had his Badger out and cocked, and she had two feet of glimmering blue blade in the air.

Burak looked subdued, almost frightened. But he

bowed, his long horns dipping. "We wondered when you would come."

Jack waffled, torn between the urge to get to the bottom of things and the impulse to call for backup. Then something moved in the shadows of a corner.

"Yes," a voice said. "We looked *forward* to it."

Two slits of red light, like miniature furnace mouths, opened. Laserlike beams leapt out at Jack and Gnea. Jack tried with all his might to pull the Badger's trigger, even though the muzzle was pointed away from Tesla; he was hoping the sheer shock of the assault pistol's report would free him up, let him slew the gun around at the Invid.

Gnea had raised the sword high, a very image of war, but she was as immobile as Jack while the rays from Tesla's eyes played across them exactingly, almost intimately.

Rocked as he was by the numbing impact of Tesla's will, Jack still saw that the scientist had undergone profound changes. He now resembled the artists' sketches that had been made to the Praxians' descriptions of the Regis.

The snout had pulled in; the mouth was now conventionally humanoid. Tesla was much bigger, though that was tough to judge precisely since he was sitting in a kind of lotus position. He was hairless, his musculature so well defined that he might have been a figure from an anatomy text, his nerves and blood vessels visible in a way that suggested he had no skin, no epidermis at all.

"Gaze upon me."

Jack and Gnea found that they had no choice. The emanations from the Invid's eyes saw to that. "You will be my eyes and ears in the ship, and among the councils of the Sentinels, and on Spheris," Tesla said. It sounded to the dazzled Jack like something that was his own idea.

"Keep the others at bay," the thing sitting on the deck said. "I need time to complete my Transformation. And then..."

The being in the corner of the compartment began to rise, like a Robotech *mechamorphosis* shape-shifting, until it stood with the top of its skull nearly touching the overhead.

A thread of saliva was dangling from Gnea's chin; Jack Baker's eyes seemed about to roll up in his head. But both of them made acknowledging sounds.

"Make yourselves available for the most important missions and find access to the most sensitive data," Tesla said. "Your lives are of value only in that they serve *me*."

Lisa considered her fighting stance and wondered if she shouldn't be a little lower, a little more straddle-legged.

After all, Bela was—what?—six six or so? And yet her stance was as low as Lisa's own, solid and yet fluid.

Not to mention those big hands, and the sheer muscle of the Sentinels' number-one amazon. Still, Lisa had learned to look for certain hints and signs of vulnerability, possible avenues of attack, that she would never have been able to spot a few months before.

Lisa faked a hand combination and came in low for a foot sweep. Bela leaped over it, kicking in turn, but Lisa wasn't where she was supposed to be; she had reversed course, her spinning foot catching Bela right over the ear.

There was a solid thwack, and even though Bela's sparring helmet and Lisa's footpads were thick, the Praxian was brought up short—more by surprise than by pain.

Nonetheless, she had Lisa's foot in those big-boned hands before Lisa, a fraction slow on the recovery, could withdraw it. In another second, Lisa was on the mat and slapping it in surrender, as Bela exerted pressure on the leghold she had gotten.

They rose and clasped one another's forearm, to signal the end of the match, then moved toward the sidelines as they removed their pads. Another amazon and Susan Graham, the young communications and public-info officer, were squaring off; a number of the REF women had followed Lisa's example and asked the Praxians to tutor them in combat arts.

"You faked me out," Lisa grated, cross with herself for falling for it. "I thought I finally had you."

"You *did*." Bela patted her shoulder. "But part of the fighting arts is to keep on coming at your opponent, no matter what."

She regarded Lisa for a moment. "But then, you already know that."

Karen Penn was sitting back on her heels at the edge of the mat, like other Humans and Praxians, waiting for her turn to spar. She was one of the few REF members there who could hold their own against an amazon opponent— could give as good as she got and, often, win.

There were no males of any species present. The Praxians didn't object to more general training sessions and tournaments, and in fact welcomed the chance to compete with and learn from their Sentinels comrades. There had been some monumental clashes, and the Karbarrans, in particular, demonstrated how much they loved a good-natured brawl.

But certain classes and workouts were reserved for females alone. Karen seemed to find a kind of serenity in them. Lisa had thought about confronting Karen with the *real* problem, but had more than enough command time to know that unless it was somehow impairing that person's professional performance, a subordinate's love life was best left for her or him to handle.

Certainly, the physical, mental, and emotional wringer of the Sentinels' campaigns seemed to have worked a change in Jack; anyone with eyes could see that he was more open and giving with Karen. But the two had worked up determined defenses against one another, and Karen was loath to drop hers.

If Penn and Baker never admitted to themselves or each

other that they were in love, it would be too bad, but a matter that others would be well advised to keep out of, Lisa decided.

The next bout was as good as Lisa and Bela's or better: two Praxian middleweights, veteran fighters and as fast as rattlers, were mixing it up. Blocks and parries came as fast as kicks and punches; the amazons at the sidelines began rooting and cheering. Neither woman on the mat could score a point on the other, though they were using everything they knew.

In the midst of it all, nobody noticed a newcomer enter the hold. Then the ref shouted the winning point as a blow landed, and somebody became aware of who was, against all tradition and decorum, standing there.

The amazons were less offended or outraged than amazed. Baldan II took advantage of the sudden silence that fell over the compartment to walk toward Lisa and Bela, who stood watching him.

His feet were bare, and yet they didn't make the glassy tinkling Lisa would have expected on the hard deckplates. Instead, there was a kind of steady rising and falling vibration, like someone running their wetted finger around the rim of a crystal goblet.

Lisa saw that the Spherisian wasn't looking at her, and stepped aside as Baldan came to stand before Bela. Bela held her padded sparring helmet in her long-fingered hands, her strange avian eyes as wary as a hawk's.

"You know the plan for scouting Spheris," Baldan said. "There are some few days yet, before I have to leave. I ask you to teach me some of the fighting skills you know, for I know none."

The amazons murmured, some of them holding their halberds uneasily or putting a hand to a shortsword hilt. No male was permitted to invade the sequestered training places.

Bela looked down at him. He was already, in size and

form, a being resembling a Terran nearing the end of his teens. Baldan wore only a brief waistclout.

He was not translucent, but rather seemed to give off light that he had gathered from sources around him. His facets, convexes, concaves, and planes without number had made him a being almost too beautiful to believe, shining with the youth that was in him.

Bela's voice, usually a hearty shout, was now only a husky near-whisper. "You must learn those things from others; no male is allowed here."

He was ready for that. "By your own laws, you cannot refuse entry to a godchild."

Bela looked up sharply, eyes wide, shock and anger and a sort of involuntary tenderness mixed together. "Godchild?"

"You saved my life, you and Miriya Parina. By your *own* laws, that makes me your godchild, and your responsibility."

A Chinese obligation, Lisa thought. She was thinking back on the moment when Bela emerged from Miriya's VT, cradling the quartzlike egg that was to become Baldan II.

Lisa figured that Bela's sudden lack of balance had nothing to do with the biology-as-destiny or melting-mama theories of instinctive female behavior. But it had everything to do with a feeling of connectedness, and a satisfaction in having done the right thing.

The amazon looked him over. "But—are you sure you won't shatter?"

He turned and did a diving roll along the deck, the singing of his shifting facets and angles sounding like celestial music. Coming to his feet in the same move, he faced her with a luminous smile.

"If I were breakable, I'd have been broken long since, Godmother."

Bela threw her head back and laughed, and other Praxians joined in, first a few, then all. Lisa stood to one side with Karen Penn, looking on as Bela handed her godson a complete suit of pads and a helmet. "Things have to change with the times,"—Bela shrugged—"even Praxian rules."

There are things coming out of this war, byproducts, that are almost *as important as victory,* it occurred to Lisa.

■□■□■□■□■□■□■□■□■□■

CHAPTER
NINETEEN

*You're free to be THE BEST "YOU" THAT YOU CAN POSSI-
BLY BE! You're OKAY! So take charge of your life and learn how
to be YOUR OWN BEST FRIEND!*

*Also, get PERSONAL POWER over your POTENTIAL and
LEARN HOW TO ASSERT IT!! Grok yourself fully during QUAL-
ITY TIME!! Dare to be great! Remember: TODAY IS THE FIRST
DAY OF THE REST OF YOUR LIFE!!!*

Kermit Busganglion, *The Hand That's Dealt You*

THE REF HAD ALWAYS BEEN INTIMIDATED BY THE
stupendous Royal Hall of the Robotech Masters on Tirol—
had never in their total muster been able to fill more than a
portion of it.

But now the Royal Hall was lit from one end to the
other, thanks to amblers and floating illumination drones.
For an evening at least a corner of it was free of the tyr-
ants' echoes. There, among ranked mecha, a court of inquiry had been convened. The Plenipotentiary Council sat
ready to discharge one of its gravest functions; defendants
and accusers waited silently or held quick conferences behind cupped hands.

It was going out to just about every outlet and terminal
under REF purview—with one special exception. In the
prairielike square outside, the throngs looked at the

screens, as people were doing elsewhere on Fantoma's moons, and on SDF-3.

Most of the accused—Wolff; Vince Grant and officers of the expedition that had been sent to bring back the *Valivarre*—sat at the defense table. Breetai was the lone Zentraedi there, seated off to one side in a monumental chair. Kazianna Hesh and the rest of the giants were still aboard the *Valivarre*, and while no one had made much mention of it yet, so was the monopole ore.

There had been some surprises for the returnees, the chief among those being that Wolff had been charged with the murder of the Regent/simulagent. But that charge had been set aside with their news—and indisputable proof in the form of sworn reports and battle recordings—that the Regent still lived.

The group had also brought back word of Janice Em's true identity. Vince feared that it would prejudice the case, since it might make people completely mistrustful of Lang, but that did not seem to be the case. Vince figured that Lang was so far outside of Human norms—a Merlin of Robotechnology—that people simply were not very surprised by *anything* he did.

And, since no one who had remained behind on Tirol (except for Lang) had any firsthand experience with Janice in her android persona, people seemed to take the news matter-of-factly. There was no sudden outbreak of paranoia.

For his part, Lang refused any comment once he had assured himself that Jan was in no danger. But Wolff thought he detected something more in the man's manner than a mere concern that an invention was functioning, or that a strategem might have backfired.

Counsel for the prosecution had been summing up his case when Edwards, no longer able to restrain himself, leapt up and intervened. No one was sure what transpired then; it was in low tones. The lawyer sat down with a look in his eyes like a hound called to heel, and Edwards stood forth to take up the argument.

"You have every documentation," he said to the silent council, "every citation, every particular. *There is no doubt here!* These people, and the others who've temporarily evaded capture, have defied and subverted duly constituted authority, and conspired to stage a mutiny. Or more precisely, a *coup*."

Edwards was about to throw his arms wide, but knew that grand gestures had long since lost their effect on the sort of people who made up the council. Instead he paused, pensive. "These were my brothers-in-arms. Don't you suppose this very scene is agony to me? But right is right, and treason is treason. And these people you see here . . . are guilty."

Wolff and the others were watching Edwards's grandstand play, but Vince Grant was keeping an eye on Lang. And when Edwards was finally done with his stemwinder speech (to some considerable applause both within the hall and from outside), Lang stood up.

Most of the onlookers and viewers were braced for an impassioned plea. Vince winked at Exedore, and Exedore winked back.

Scott Bernard stood to one side, looking proud. Once people found out his part in tripping up Edwards, he figured, a lot of folks were going to know his name.

In an altogether neutral voice, Lang rattled, "Hereby-submitted under my seal as council member, the following recorded data, pertinent to these proceedings."

There were REF screens rigged everywhere in that corner of the Royal Hall. They were all abruptly alight with the scene between Lang and Edwards, the scene Edwards had been so sure his scramblers would render private.

Edwards had been given to understand his interference devices—the ones in his epaulets and so on—would keep him safe from surveillance. They had done so in the past, hadn't they? But now he saw that that had only been because Lang wished it so, in order that Edwards be drawn into this trap.

Forewarned, certain council members had caused riot police and MPs to be stationed in strategic points, but throughout the playing of the recording, the Royal Hall and the streets outside were silent, just silent. There was a final scene of Edwards, slinking away and nursing the wrists Lang had bruised so terribly—had only stopped himself short of crushing by an act of will.

Edwards and his staff were on their feet, crying that this was some electronic/Protoculture forgery, but Lang's people were already submitting the authenticated taped originals that would prove differently.

Justine Huxley stood, too, severe and cold. "I think it's obvious that there are mitigating circumstances here. *Do I have a consensus?*"

Under her withering glare, with the undeniable evidence of the tapes, and the cries of the crowds rising outside, none of the would-be dissenting council members dared meet her eye. There was a tacit assent. All in an instant, Edwards saw that his plans were shattered and that, at least in terms of the council, he stood alone.

Huxley went on, "And so *all* the principals, General Edwards included, will surrender to the custody of the— *Stop that man!*"

This, because Edwards had vaulted the railing and sprinted for the door. Adams was a half step behind him, but the prosecutors froze, and the MPs closed in on them.

Over at the defense table, Wolff was nearest. He was up on his feet, dashing off after his archenemy. Vince and the others would have helped, but court officers had already moved in to restrain them.

Breetai came to his feet, but there wasn't any way for him to reach the general short of stepping in among the

Humans and trampling some. And armed guards had fanned out to see to it that he kept his place.

Wolff raced after Edwards like his own namesake, his blood boiling for a fight. Without warning, a blur came homing in at an angle in an attempt to tackle Edwards. It was Scott Bernard. But he lacked the weight to pull it off, and merely swung Edwards partway round just as Wolff was closing in.

Edwards tore Scott off him in a transport of rage and was about to break the boy's neck. Wolff had the option of going for Edwards and taking a chance that Scott would be killed, or grappling to save Scott. Everything in him told him to do the former; many lives had *already* been lost to the general's schemes, and it was worth the sacrifice to stop him.

But he found himself struggling to save the boy, hampered enough by the effort so that he couldn't get in the first blow. Wolff got Scott partway out of Edwards's grasp, but in the meantime the general landed a vicious flat-handed chop and nearly downed Wolff.

Edwards released Scott and was about to follow up and finish off the colonel, but his all-pervading sense of self-preservation halted him. Court officers were closing in. He pivoted and sprinted on.

The guards stationed at the doors were the biggest in the REF military-police contingent, and everyone expected them to grab Edwards and Adams, throw them down, and sit on them until such time as Justine Huxley said to stand up.

But Edwards caught the first MP's hand in some kind of take-away hold, levered her aside, then drew a handgun from beneath his jacket and shot the second, a massive sergeant who was trying to get his own pistol out.

Everyone was milling about, and that made it impossible for the court officers and other MPs to get through. In a moment, Edwards and Adams were through the inner door and Edwards was firing blasts through it. Adams was screaming something incoherent, but Edwards took no time to listen. Instead, he backhanded the man, then seized a fistful of his uniform and dragged him toward the front entranceway.

Ghost Rider sentries and escorts there already knew Edwards's whistled signals. As other REF troops tried to understand what was going on, the Ghosts got the drop on them. In another few seconds, Edwards was inside his personal limo with Adams, lifting away.

Adams curled up in a corner of the luxuriously upholstered back seat, whimpering. Edwards tried to think, though it felt as if his blood vessels would peel the scalp away from his naked skull. The driver was already headed toward HQ and the armored escort vehicles were falling in before and behind.

T.R. Edwards smiled in the dark, even as the rivulets of sweat poured down across his face and dribbled over his faceplate. The council thought it had him cornered.

You've got me where I want you.

Edwards gave a quick command. The rest of the motorcade went on, toward the landing areas and the shuttles, along the route the council would expect him to take.

But the limo veered aside and down a ramp, through a recessed hatch that led to the underground levels. There were loyal troops there to welcome him; Edwards emerged and led the way down and down toward the installation that connected him so appropriately with the Regent.

Behind the convoy, the street-access door rolled shut. No one was there to see a single figure, standing atop a building opposite, watch it close. Unmoving, the hunter poised and prepared himself. Tonight the hunt would end.

There were two Humans, a Karbarran, and a Garudan; they were purposely shoving toward the compartment hatch despite Gnea's protests.

"It's not just a request anymore," the Human, a junior officer Gnea recognized as Susan Graham, said. "Admiral Hunter says Tesla's to be braced *right now*, and answer a coupla questions."

Gnea looked around at the mixed posse. "And suppose I say no? Tesla is unwell, and I've been charged with seeing to it that he lives." She placed herself before them, big-boned and used to fighting, seemingly indifferent to whether she lived or died. She fingered her halberd and waited, throwing the ball back into their court.

Susan Graham brought up a pistol, and the others leveled weapons, too. "Then, you can either let Doc Obu here look at the patient or you can get your bellybutton microwaved, toots, and we'll *still* see what we came here to see."

Obu, the Karbarran scientist, growled and inclined his head gently. When he raised his eyes to Gnea's again, there was a frank sanity in his steady gaze. But there was mayhem on the backburners.

"I—I see the wisdom of what you say," Gnea got out. It was very nearly a whisper. "But don't you understand? You'll frighten him. Just when we were doing so well with him."

The Garudan, Quias, growled. "If we damage him, it's not much loss, is it?"

"No! You're wrong!" Gnea objected so quickly that they drew back a little. Something told her that she had made a mistake, and so she looked around to where Jack Baker stepped out of the shadows.

"We're not sure, but Tesla may be dying," he said quietly. "Those two Invid scientists, Pye and whosis, Garak, say they can pull him through—*maybe*. But not if you go in there and rough 'im up."

While the deputation was wavering, Jack took another step toward them, so that the light fell across his face now.

It was strangely composed and unsmiling, unlike the jaunty young man they knew.

This Jack Baker stood shoulder to shoulder with Gnea, smiling at them with his mouth but frowning with his forehead. "And that wouldn't do *anybody* any good, would it? Put that weapon away, Graham. Relay my respects to the admiral, and tell him I'll have Tesla on a remote hookup for questioning as soon as he can stand it. Well? You *heard* your orders."

Rick *had* put Jack in charge of the Tesla problem. Susan Graham slowly holstered her pistol. "I just hope you know what you're doing, sir."

"Move it!" Jack snapped.

He and Gnea watched the foursome leave, then made their way back to the compartment where Tesla now dwelt. When they were sure no one was near, they entered. Inside, they stood with faces blank, as the thing before them threw their shadows on the bulkhead with its intense light.

"Well done, my good and faithful servants," said Tesla.

The drop capsule was a miracle of the combined sciences of the various Sentinels races as orchestrated by the capable Obu. Despite the increased Invid sensor surveillance in the wake of their defeats on Karbarra and Garuda, the tiny lozenge-shape fell through the planet's atmosphere without raising a single alarm, transparent to enemy detectors. In many ways, the war had forced the oppressed to out excell their oppressors.

Rick badly regretted the limitations to the new techniques that restricted the size of an "invisible" drop capsule to something on the order of a padded commo booth. He would have liked to equip the *Ark Angel* with the same protection, but that was impossible as yet.

Impossible, too, to arm and equip Teal and her son with Human-style gear for their espionage mission; where they were going, no hardware could follow.

In due course the two Spherisians stood next to their abandoned capsule, looking out over the homeworld Baldan II was seeing for the first time.

It was a prismatic landscape, reflecting and refracting and breaking into spectra the light of Blaze, the planet's primary. Human and Invid and other offworlders required visors or other eye protection there, so they weren't blinded by the furious splendor of it all; but Baldan II gazed, unblinking and unshielded, on the planet he had never glimpsed before.

The capsule lay on a beach that scintillated like a field of stars, each infinitesimal grain throwing back its white or multicolored rays. The sea that crashed against the shore was as unreal as some computer construct, so radiant, its hues so quick-changing. Distant mountains shone like luminescent fountains.

Baldan felt his mother's hand on his arm. He turned to see Teal wearing an expression he had never seen on her before.

The arrival in the capsule had driven home to her, as nothing else had, how serious her circumstances and her son's were. What was bewildering her was that she was unexpectedly more concerned about his well-being than her own. That was a common phenomenon among some of the other races, of course—look how the Karbarrans had agonized over the fate of their young—but it was new to her, and troubling since it involved an offspring she had never wanted.

When had she come to love her son? Teal couldn't recall, and yet there was an abrupt welling-up in her, and a desperate fear for his safety. If the capsule had been capable of a return trip to *Ark Angel*, she would have taken it with Baldan, or at the very least sent *him* back.

But the road back was closed to them; they knew that when they volunteered. Teal studied the gemstone landscape for a moment, then pointed.

"There." She set off toward a seam of crystal that had been upthrust by a rift in the planet's surface. Baldan hurried to catch up. By the time he did, his mother was standing before the glorious light of the stratum and undressing.

"Wh-what . . ." he fumbled. Something within him was calling out, and something within Spheris was answering. But he didn't know how to be a part of the symphony all around him.

Teal stood unclothed—her chiton fluttering down around her ankles—but not naked. She stepped free of the garment and was like a magnificent beacon, moving toward the exposed seam before her with arms spread wide as if to embrace a lover.

She turned to her son. "Come; time for you to travel the Crystal Highways."

Baldan threw aside the half tunic he wore. As his mother did, he pressed himself flat against the glittering rock. The planet sang to them in high, clear tones.

For a moment they were half merged with it, like Mesoamerican bas-reliefs. In another moment they were gone, leaving their discarded clothing and the empty capsule behind. The only sound was the flashing sea striking rainbow surf from the diamond-dust sand.

"Well! My dear, dear General Edwards! What a delightful surprise!"

Edwards held his face in unrevealing lines, forcing himself not to curl his lip at the green goop streaming off the Regent—the nutrient bath, or royal jelly, or whatever the hell it was these maggots liked to splash around in.

He also contained his anger. The Invid ruler had taken his own sweet time about answering the general's transmission, as if knowing that he had the Human at a disadvantage.

"Things here have become rather . . . counterproductive,"

Edwards said, tight-lipped. "I think it best, strategically, that we unite our forces at once."

"Ah." The enormous liquid black eyes betrayed nothing as the Regent inspected the man. "In that case, do come here to the Home Hive, by all means! Er, how many ships will you be bringing, and how many troops?"

Edwards's jaw muscles jumped. "There's been trouble here. I'll require a bit of assistance."

Something moved up to sit next to the Regent—a Hellcat of extraordinary size, wearing a jeweled collar. The ones destroyed in the Haydon IV battle had been replaced, Edwards surmised. "How inconvenient," the Regent clucked.

The Invid threw his arms wide. "Because, as you can see, you're about to miss out on the opportunity to serve the One True Ruler of the Universe! My life will be a roll call of triumphs! All Creation will grovel at my feet, as my courtiers do even now!"

He lowered his voice craftily. "And *then* won't my wife, my precious Regis, come begging for forgiveness, eh?"

Edwards saw only an empty, echoing hall in the background behind the Regent. *Great suns! He's mad as a march hare!*

But he was the general's only hope for survival. "I want you to think for a moment what will happen if the council gets me now. The REF will be reconsolidated into a pure fighting force with nothing holding it back, and there'll be nothing to stop the combined forces of the near stars to come after *you*! Am I getting through to you?"

It seemed he had. The Regent swayed for a moment, a new clarity coming into his voice. "We can't have that, can we?"

"I want you to send your army to get me and the people loyal to me," Edwards pressed on.

The Invid asked guilelessly, "But why should I, when you have an army of your own right there?"

The Invid Brain! The Inorganics! "Damn you, explain!" Edwards grated. "There's no time for games!"

The Regent wasn't so demented that he had missed Edwards's point about the REF; he activated controls at his end of the connection that displayed instructions at Edwards's end.

"Do stay in touch," the Regent bade him, and his image vanished.

But Edwards was already busy, switching on the Living Computer, the artificial Brain the Invid had left behind under Tirol in the wake of their defeat. His personal guards looked on uneasily as the massive globe of specialized tissue came to life in its vat.

From the catacomb rooms where the inert Inorganics had, at his command, been stored like so much cordwood, Edwards heard stirrings.

His lips drew back from his teeth in a canine smile; his good eye became glassy. He looked as insane as the Regent.

CHAPTER
TWENTY

Consider humble clay.

Small amounts of it can speed chemical processes by a factor of 10,000. Its phenomenally intricate layered-sheet structure gives one pound (Earth norm) of it as much total surface area as fifty football fields. It can store information as patterns of ions. It's perfectly plausible that self-replicating crystals brought forth a "proto-organism" as the jumping-off point of life on Spheris.

But those who travel the Crystal Highways are unimpressed with such theorizing. They explain it all with a name.

A. Jow, *The Historical Haydon*

"MAX! *Pay attention!*"

"Uh?" He blinked.

Jean Grant, infinitely patient, still had a way of letting someone know that she wouldn't put up with their short-comings.

"Just take it easy, Max; babies've been getting them-selves born for ages now. Besides, this is only a drill, *ca-pisch*? All you have to do is help a little." She smiled down at Miriya. "Relax, soldier."

Miriya stopped her breathing exercises and chuckled tir-edly. She was pale and drawn from the ordeal that her second pregnancy had become. But she squeezed Max's hand, their *I love you* code.

Max squeezed back twice, but he was still worried. This pregnancy shouldn't even have *happened*. Apparently, conventional birth-control methods didn't apply to a Human-Zentraedi union.

Her first pregnancy had worked changes on Miriya's body that Jean still hadn't figured out completely. The physical readouts on her were getting more and more peculiar, and nobody, not even the saintly, floating Haydon IV healers, could say why.

Max resisted the impulse to sigh, there where Miriya could hear it. Instead he crouched by her, pointing at the window that ran from floor to ceiling in her bedroom.

"See there? The urban core's almost rebuilt, and about seventy percent of the underground systemry's back up to snuff. Vowad says the whole planet'll be like new in less than two months."

"It's good that—" A sudden spasm of pain overcame her, and she clamped down on Max's hand with a grip so hard that he involuntarily yelped in pain.

Jean was there in an instant, reading the bed monitors. The Haydonites had built Miriya's room so that it was a virtual duplicate of the quarters she and her husband had shared back in rebuilt Macross City—their happiest home —but the place was actually a well-camouflaged intensive-care unit.

"Code red," Jean called into the empty air; not two seconds passed before the wall slid aside and Haydonite healers floated in. Miriya was losing consciousness.

"Talk to her, Max," Jean whispered to him, then turned to her own job.

What to say? He wasn't used to making conversation; that was one of the reasons he had been a loner until he and Miriya found each other.

"And—and, the interstellar trade's already starting up again," he babbled, squeezing her hand but, to his terror, getting no response. "I've got a place all fixed up for you and me and the kid, outside of town—"

"Sorry, Max." Jean moved him away from the bedside

and he didn't resist. She and the Haydonite healers, and medical machines that looked like hovering seashells and airborne spores, all clustered around his wife.

Max Sterling stood at the foot of the bed. "We're losing her," one of the faceless healers said, and Max bit his lower lip until blood ran, so that he wouldn't scream.

"*Talk* to her, Max," Jean repeated, without looking up from her work. "Keep her with us."

"I . . . I . . ."

"You're fixing up a place for her," Jean prompted him, still without breaking her own concentration.

He drew a deep breath. "We can stay there until you're ready to go home, Mir." He felt like crying, but Jean gave him one quick look.

"C'mon, ace," she told him, and went back to what she was doing.

C'mon, ace . . .

"Dana's gonna be some big girl when we get back, huh?" he found himself saying.

The lifesign monitors made a slightly different sound; Miriya managed to form a word. "Dana . . ."

"Uh-huh! God, she wants so much to go to the academy, and Emerson says if she doesn't behave, he's gonna put her in a convent, remember?" He was wiping the tears from his face and his glasses. "And Bowie said that if Dana goes, *he* goes." He was laughing and crying at the same time.

"She'll be . . . a big girl," Miriya said.

The lifesigns were stabilizing. With effort, Max swallowed and said, "Think of all the things we'll have to tell her when we get home, Mir. She's gonna be waiting to hear them."

Miriya Parino Sterling smiled as she hovered on the edge of a coma then came back to him.

He stood looking down on her as she slept, after Jean

and the healers and the machines left. Miriya's pregnancy had seven months yet before it came to term.

But that was only by Human calculation. According to the lab workups, it could happen any time now.

In the barracks of the security forces posted to Dr. Lang's complex, the officer of the day lost patience with pounding on the door.

"Linc? Lincoln? Goddamn you, *fall in!*"

But Flight Officer Isle, REF Service # 666–60–937, wasn't there. The duty OD looked around and found the man's flight suit missing. Oddly, there were also hair clippings and shaving-lather residue in the cramped quarters' tiny sink.

Isle always was a strange one, but this was pushing it some. "Isle, you sumbitch," the OD muttered. "What now?"

They were like dolphins in the sea, or eagles cutting the winds.

Baldan soared, following his mother, through the netherworld of the Crystal Highways. The mineral lattices stretched away in every direction, making their own landscape for the beings who swam in the bosom of Spheris.

Baldan found that he *knew* his way around there. The emanations from the various compounds and strata were like signposts and streets—a three-dimensional highway system.

He zoomed over to catch up with Teal on a thoroughfare layed down from the molten condition. There was a lot of veering and dodging because of the magma chambers, but the scenery was spectacular.

Disembodied, they flew through the very structure of their world. Baldan found that he *knew* how to avoid metamorphic structures, *knew* how to slide along the crystallographic axes.

There was no gravity, except as a somewhat abstract force; electromagnetic and thermal and nuclear imperatives were the rules of the road.

And before long, he could hear the voices of his people.

Baldan understood that he was nothing but a disembodied intellect, seeping along the boulevards that molecular forces had drawn. But it seemed that he was corporeal, flying like some character out of the Humans absurd comic books, in an element that was his to command.

It was a world suspended in space: here, the juttings of a tectonic rift; there, the sweep of a rhodonite seam that virtually girded the planet. They navigated currents of chrysoberyl, emerald and corundum, rode the piezoelectric waves, fought through schist and bodysurfed in tourmaline.

Then he became aware of the songs, and they drew him. Teal noticed that he was veering away, and followed. They understood through unspoken communication that the longing he felt wasn't to be questioned. She gave in to an impulse that she had only marginally resisted until then, and found she wasn't one person anymore: she was two. Herself and her son.

In a place like a cathedral made of living mineral, or a megaplex encysted in a jewel of perfect clarity, he encountered the first of his race he had ever met aside from his mother and a few shipmates.

Their voices drew him, the sound resonating through the world. Baldan found to his surprise that emerging from the warp and woof of the planet was harder than melding with it, and understood a little better how his father died.

There was a tremendous strain as he fought to free himself from the Crystal Highway; it was as if Spheris didn't want to let him go. Baldan came forth halfway, like some tormented cameo; he was sucked back again and nearly consumed. He fought and kicked and flailed his way clear, reborn once more.

Teal was standing nearby, and he knew instinctively why she hadn't been able to help; there was only one road test for riders of the Crystal Highways, and it was very Darwinian.

Their very substance was changed. They were now of smokier stuff, harder and more given to sharp angles, than they had been above and in the ship. Baldan understood that each time he emerged from the Crystal Highways, he would be of different composition—would be of the stuff that made up the area from which he exited.

So; I'm truly part of my world now.

Teal and Baldan had come into a place that was dazzling with shards of pure light in a million shades and haunting in the tones that sprang from every cusp and facet. It was like heaven's own house of mirrors, a sound-and-light show that no non-Spherisian would ever be able to comprehend.

There were thousands upon thousands of his father's people there, contemplating eternity and the Universe in small nichelike chambers, or communing with one another, or working to enlarge the boundaries of their sanctuary. Some looked around in surprise at the arrival of newcomers.

One in particular dropped a caving tool that rang like a bell on the vitreous floor of the place. "Baldan!"

It was an elderly female of his race, Baldan II could see. Before she had taken two more steps, her posture and the aura she emitted changed. Joy and disbelief gave way to uncertainty. "But—you're not Baldan, are you?"

"I'm his son." On Spheris, it went without saying that a great deal of the parent was born again in the child. "Baldan is dead. I am Baldan II."

"My son is dead," the old one said as if the words were incomprehensible. "But then—who shaped you?"

Teal stepped forward. "I knew you would want to meet the boy, Tiffa."

"You!" Everyone knew the story: how a flighty female of no discernible talent or promise had coincidentally been taken prisoner with Baldan, a champion of his species.

Tiffa struggled for words, plainly displeased at having a new in-law thrust upon her, and one who enjoyed no great prestige or status at that.

"Do try to conceal your joy," Teal said dryly.

By now, there were a lot of other Spherisians looking on and listening in. They saw in Baldan II the image of their fallen resistance leader and hero.

Teal faced them. "We might as well get all this out in the open right away. This is Baldan's son, Baldan II. I Shaped him. I didn't ask for the obligation, but we don't always get to choose the Shapings of the Protoculture, do we? I want it known that I'm proud of this boy and I love him very much.

"Now, we've come back with allies, to free Spheris from the Invid. I know a lot of you would prefer to sit down here in safety and comfort and wait for them to go away rather than fight them, but I say to you that the Invid won't *go* away."

That had people murmuring to one another. They had hidden in the bosom of Spheris—a defense that had never failed them—but many were growing restive. No invader had ever been as tenacious as the Regent's hordes.

"The Sentinels have already removed the Invid from Karbarra, Garuda, and Haydon IV," Teal went on. "And we mean to do the same here. We're not asking your permission, because this war will be fought to the death whether Spherisians throw in their lot with us or not. But —the outcome lies in the balance, and your help could make all the difference."

Tiffa was looking at Teal with a troubled expression. Wasn't this the frivolous, whimsical girl who had been the despair of her parents and who, most had agreed, would come to a bad and probably meaningless end?

Who are these "Sentinels," Tiffa wondered, *that their companionship should bring Teal home so vested with wisdom and purpose?* Perhaps the Invid had met their match at last.

But there were voices from the crowd now. "Leave us in peace and go!" "We want no war!" "We're not fighters!"

"Yes, you are."

Teal had been about to try to shout the doubters down, but Baldan spoke first. Now he took three steps forward, so that they could all get a good look at him.

"Yes, you are," he repeated. "The memories that Baldan gave me tell me that. These nice safe strongholds in the planetary womb are no protection anymore; the Invid will crack this world apart with their protoculture devices if it comes to that.

"Spherisians have fought before, long in our past. Now it's time to fight again—that, or kneel and wait for the hammer to fall on our naked necks."

He walked a few steps to one side, to where a spar of shimmering agate stood out from the wall of the sanctuary. "I mean to raise rebellion. I mean to rally every Spherisian who remembers how to fight or is willing to learn. I mean to throw the Invid off this world or die trying."

Teal went over to stand by her son proudly. A wisecrack of Jack Baker's came back to her, and she decided this was a good time to use it. Putting her arm around her son's strong young shoulders, she fixed Tiffa with her gaze.

"Maybe we're not much to look at, but *we're all you've got.*"

"From here we go to the Great Geode, to ask for aid there," Baldan announced. "Follow us, any who are willing, or carry the word to other sanctuaries." He hesitated, unsure if the last thing he wanted to say was fair, but the impulse was too strong to deny.

His voice dropped an octave and became the voice of Baldan I; a different look came into his eyes. Through him, his father said, "It is good to see you this one last time. I love you all."

Baldan II vibrated a little, coming back to himself, then turned to merge with the spar of agate. A moment later, Teal was gone too.

The Spherisians looked at one another, the sanctuary resonating with the hurrahs of some, the doubts of others. There were troubled glances everywhere.

That was when Tiffa stepped to the outcropping where her grandson and daughter-in-law had disappeared. She spread her arms like a high-diver, leaned slowly, and melded with the stuff of Spheris.

In another few seconds, people were thronging to the walls of the place, or lying flat to dissolve into the very floor. Those who doubted or had other reservations found themselves in a dwindling minority. Many remained behind, but now the sanctuary was a hollow-sounding, mostly deserted place of more silence than sound, more emptiness than life.

Out along the Crystal Highways the folk of Spheris flew, energized by a force before which piezoelectricity and Protoculture and logic itself must bow. Toward a thousand destinations on the planet's crust and under it they went, to free their homeworld.

CHAPTER
TWENTY-ONE

This may sound strange, coming from me, but I want to take a moment here to speak in defense of the Ghost Riders—a unit with a long and proud history going back to United States naval aviation—until those events on the SDF-3 mission.

I believe that some of those men and women were swayed by Edwards's Faustian lure—there are bad apples in every barrel. But I've reviewed the citations and decorations of the Ghosts, going back decades, and I'm convinced that some force beyond mere human fallibility had enslaved them to their general by that night.

It would be a stain on the memory of brave and selfless service members not to point this out: Edwards's greatest crime, among his many, was in making us Earthers fight our own.

Justice Justine Huxley, *I've Been to a Marvelous Party*

THE MAN WHOSE NAME TAG READ ISLE, L. KNEW FROM the start that Edwards's breakout would be unstoppable at its source.

Hundreds of Inorganic bipeds had flung open the doors of the Royal Hall's underground warren and poured forth, inflicting terrible casualties, in response to the general's silent command. It was only good luck that an officious security OIC had insisted that the Plenipotentiary Council evacuate the building after Edwards's escape—she had practically been forced to *wrestle* some of the council members into armored vehicles.

She was exonerated a few minutes later, when the Crann, Scrim, and Odeon boiled up from their catacombs, spreading death. Justine Huxley, gazing at it in horror through the rear viewslit of an APC, wrote later, "Words will not serve to describe the carnage there. I do not think the REF had a darker moment."

A few loyalist VTs brought down death from the skies within minutes, but Edwards's army was already on the move. Now Flight Officer Isle watched them come toward the REF HQ complex, as he knew they would.

Poor rebuilt Tiresia was being razed again, in a grotesque Mardi Gras of Robotech warfare. Excaliber Mark IXs and Crann whirled, fighting hand-to-hand in the streets; Spartans and Scrim stood flat-footed and shot it out at point-blank range in alleys; Battloids and Odeon rolled, locked in mortal combat, crumbling buildings and tearing each other to shreds.

What Ghost VTs there were were primarily occupied keeping Lang's security fliers busy. The conflict was pretty much a ground battle.

The man released the nametag he had ripped from his flight suit. It fluttered down on the wind as he watched the battle move his way. Edwards was using his Invid troops cleverly, feinting and redeploying, subtly opening an avenue of attack on the HQ. REF Command wouldn't consider HQ much of an objective for Edwards, Flight Officer Isle knew; Command would consider it a dead end, and would be watching for an assault on the spaceport. They didn't know that the most precious thing in the universe was in the headquarters building.

No, Command was busy dealing with diversionary strikes by Edwards's loyal Ghost Riders and shoring up its faltering ready-reaction groups in the western and southern parts of Tiresia. Edwards was one up on them.

The council acted quickly on Lang's plea to secure SDF-3 against mutiny. But what they weren't prepared for was a mass desertion by Ghost elements then on the superdimensional fortress. And while there were sufficient loyal troops to hold the bridge, power section, and other vital points against assault, there weren't nearly enough to stop Edwards's people from decamping.

Some of the Ghosts headed for the surface of Tirol, to provide air support for their general's escape. But the bulk of them drove directly toward the new SDF-7 ship, sister to the *Tokugawa* and the *Jutland*, that was just nearing completion. Since Edwards had to take flight, he meant to do so in a ship with its superluminal drive in place.

Inorganics were already breaking through onto the huge square outside the rocketlike HQ building. The man who had called himself Isle for so long drew a deep breath and leapt from the parapet on which he stood.

Ten feet below, he touched down soundlessly on the tiles of a balcony, eased himself onto a ledge that ran round the building, and sidled along it, back to the wall. He negotiated the corner and saw the mecha he had seen fifteen or thirty seconds before: a Scrim lumbering in behind the first wave of Inorganics to assault the doors of the HQ.

He swung himself out with a grip on the evercrete of a flying buttress, his fingers, as strong as steel, finding purchase where few other Humans' could have. When the Scrim passed under, he made a daring deadfall, clinging to a ridge of armored backplate. The Scrim stopped and turned, but saw nothing behind it. It charged after its companions, bringing up the rear, as they breached the headquarters' main doors.

In another instant, the man was inside the building that had for so long resisted his every effort to gain entry.

He saw his chance and sprang, with nearly superhuman strength and precision, to a darkened surveillance camera mast, just as the Inorganic he had been riding came under intense fire from a gun emplacement. The fighting in the lobby and the halls was hideous and without quarter, the Humans as willing to die as the Invid. Cool and capable as he was, he was staggered for a moment by the blind, unyielding carnage of it. Edwards's advantage in numbers and firepower were quickly reduced by sheer Human stubbornness. The Invid mecha paid heavily for every inch they claimed.

But there were other things to think about. He slid away like a flickering shadow, knowing the floor plan from diligent study. He had waited so long and patiently, so humbly. And now the moment was his.

Reports had it that Wolff's damnable Wolff Pack were advancing to back up the loyalist Destroids in repelling the Inorganics. Luckily, only a part of the Hovertank unit had been permitted to make planetfall with their commander, and most of the rest of the troops who had gone to Haydon IV were still in orbit aboard ship, too far away to be of any tactical importance.

Edwards didn't care, just as he didn't care how many lives he had to spend to take the HQ citadel. Troops and mecha were things that he could replace; Minmei wasn't.

Adams was yammering something in his ear; Edwards looked aside from his screens and readouts. "What?"

"HQ building partially secured but still putting up resistance, sir," Adams repeated. "I think we should stand fast and wait till—"

"We're going in," Edwards cut him off. "Where's that SDF escort?"

Adams told him calmly, "Rendezvous is still on schedule. They're beginning orbital insertion now. We only have twenty-three minutes, General."

More than enough time. "Drive on! Hit hard!" Edwards hollered over the tac net. "I want some *results*, people!" Relaying orders back to the Living Computer by means of a receptor band that looked something like an Invid slave headband, he worked the Inorganics into a killing frenzy.

He left the limo behind to take personal charge of the raid. His forces mowed down all opposition, slew and demolished, melted superalloy and blew apart walls. At the entrance of the brig section, he was obliged to leave his Inorganics and Ghost mecha behind because the corridors were too small. Ghost Riders deployed with rifles leveled, securing the area.

Minmei had imagined the cell door opening, had imagined it so many times that she thought her mind was playing tricks on her now that it was happening. *Oh, God! I'd rather be dead than crazy!*

But when Edwards stepped into the open doorway, she knew she wasn't imagining it and started to scream. Sinking her fingers into the black hair that hung around her face, squeezing her eyes shut, she shrieked.

Edwards pounced on her as Adams and two lesser officers brought up the rear, guarding the door. The general cuffed her face, back and forth. "Shut up, *shut up!*"

Then he had her shoulders, shaking her, as she shuddered with long, wracking sobs. "Minmei, you're coming with me! Do you hear? You're *mine!*" He slapped her again. "Not Hunter's! Not Wolff's! *Mine!*"

Somehow she stopped crying. Minmei raised her eyes to Edwards with a look he had never seen from her before. She wiped away the tears and saliva and mucous with the back of her hand.

She looked her foe in the eye. "If you don't leave me alone you'd better kill me, T. R. Or else *I* am going to kill *you.*"

He felt such sudden misgiving that he raised his hand to hit her again, expecting her to flinch. But she kept her eyes fixed on him. "I'm going to make you beg me to forget what you just said," he whispered.

Minmei drew a deep breath. *"No, you're not."*

A hand closed around Edwards's upraised wrist from behind; a voice told him, *"No, you're not."*

Edwards was pulled aside, his wrist nearly broken. He

was spun at the cell wall like a child's top, his burnished facemask ringing against it, his nose banged so that he smelled metal and blood. He clawed for purchase but found himself sliding down the cold alloy, leaving a red stain. A foot pressed his head to the deck, nearly crushed it, then relented. Then the foot was abruptly gone.

The general shook his head to clear it, glancing about drunkenly. Adams lay sprawled in the doorway, perhaps unconscious, perhaps dead. Edwards could see the up-turned toes of one downed guard's boots in the corridor beyond. Minmei was on her feet with a look on her face that Edwards had always longed to force her to direct at *him*. But it was for the man in the REF flight suit who had appeared out of nowhere.

Edwards felt numbed in certain ways, superalert in others. The light danced in Minmei's eyes as she slowly raised her hands to her rescuer.

"Lynn-Kyle! Oh, Lynn-Kyle . . ."

Her distant cousin and, in the opinion of some, a reflection of the dark side of Minmei herself; her onetime lover and the most renowned martial arts fighter of the Robotech age. The haunted and saturnine, the brilliantly gifted but ill-starred, the undefeated and cursed Lynn-Kyle.

Kyle's face was thinner than when he had been a movie star. The fine, silky black shag was showing some gray. He kissed his cousin's forehead, then took her hand. "I'm taking you home." There was something as much penitent as loving in his voice.

Home! She couldn't really think what the word meant anymore. But she felt weightless, her hand and her body and her soul buoyant beyond belief, as she entrusted her grip to his, her feet seemingly free of the cell floor.

Edwards lurched and grabbed her ankle with a failing grip. "No! I won't let you go!"

Kyle was kneeling on Edwards's biceps, Edwards's head clamped in his hands, so quickly that there was no sense of transition. The general heard the bones of his upper spine creak and knew that his life lay on the line.

The dagger in Edwards's boot, the energy derringer in his jacket pocket—those might as well be on the SDF-3, or back on Earth, for all the good they could do him. Kyle was as quick as a lightning bolt, and there was simply no defense against him. He was more like an elemental force than a man.

"I've never taken a human life." The words seemed to come so slowly, though Edwards knew Lynn-Kyle was speaking very fast. "But I'll kill you if you don't lie still!" The heel of Kyle's hand lay, pressing upward in warning, under the general's nose, poised to execute him in an instant.

Edwards, defeated, kept still. In Kyle's place, he would have killed; but he would never *be* in Kyle's place, he knew now. He had lost.

But he couldn't resist croaking, "Go ahead; take the little slut, then. She's a waste of time in bed anyway. . ."

Kyle seized a handful of Edwards's hair, preparing to kill him. His fist hovered, middle knuckle cocked forth, and Edwards's eyes nearly crossed, focused on that single Damoclean striking surface hanging over him.

"Kyle, *no*," Minmei said, as her cousin drew quick breaths and gathered his resolve. "Kyle, we *need* him!"

"*I* don't need him." The wrist turned upside down, the cocked knuckle drawn back tight and high under Kyle's right armpit, aimed at Edwards's Adam's apple. The general squirmed, trying to move his arms, but he was helpless.

"Kyle, the war's over. Just hang onto him, and we can end it all *today*." She swiped the long, damp night-black hair out of her eyes. "Kyle, you're not a murderer. The war's over."

"The war's over." Saying it didn't give Kyle the satisfaction he thought he would have back at the beginning—

back when the SDF-3 mission was recruiting; back before he and Minmei and the rest had passed into the flames once more.

But it was enough. He would settle for it. "War's over, General. You're going to stand up and order your troops to surrender. We'll strike a peace with the Regent. And then we're all going home, right?"

Edwards's mouth moved, but he was unable to speak. Yet he was careful to nod unmistakably, his hair pulling against Kyle's grip, as he looked up at that one single knuckle that jutted out like a battering ram. "Urr. R-right."

Kyle smiled, nodding. "'The wolf shall dwell with the lamb.'" He grabbed the front of Edwards's dress uniform jacket, ready to lift him up.

"'And the leopard shall lie down with the kid.'" Kyle stuck his fist close to Edwards's face again. The fist was like some gnarled piece of iron with a scruffy skin-covering on it. "And we're all going to live happily ever after, isn't that right?"

Edwards almost said something, but thought better of it. He swallowed, then nodded. Kyle leaned forward to pull him to his feet.

There was a sudden scuffling behind him and Kyle whirled, rising. Edwards's eyes flickered that way at the same time, to see Adams grappling with Minmei, the bright edge of a combat knife reflecting the light.

"Kill her! *Kill her!*" Edwards screamed, not because he thought Adams would necessarily follow orders, but rather because it would keep Lynn-Kyle diverted. It was no surprise that Kyle unthinkingly sprang to Minmei's aid. Edwards was digging for his gun, even as he thought, *Kyle must know I'm armed! Why...*

Adams's eyes opened wide, the edge of his blade drawing a trickle of blood from Minmei's neck. Kyle came at him, unstoppable and almost too fast to see, with a strength like something out of Robotechnology.

Adams felt himself horribly hurt and sent pinwheeling, but there was nothing he could do about it; he was propelled into a corner, black-red blood bubbling on his lips, knowing he had only a few moments of life left. Minmei was safe, except for the shallow cut on her throat.

Kyle spun on Edwards, but the general already had his derringer in his hand. It didn't make any difference; Kyle leapt at him anyway.

The gun was small, only good for two rounds, but graphically effective at short range. Edwards shot Kyle twice while he was in the air; the body that landed on the general was almost dead.

Edwards pushed Kyle off, while Minmei came to her cousin's side, knelt, and brushed his raven's-wing forelock out of his eyes. She took his head into her lap tenderly, as Edwards labored to regain his breath and get to his feet.

Kyle's eyelids fluttered. "Minmei . . ."

"Shh-hh."

There was no saving him; she kept her trembling hand at his chin, so he couldn't see the melted fabric and bloody mess that was his chest. Kyle coughed, "The war was almost over. We'd *won*."

"We'd won." She nodded. "You won it *for* us, Kyle." She was about to faint, holding a human body that was half blown open, but she found reserves of courage from someplace she had never delved into before, and smiled down at him instead.

There was a final, galvanic bit of life to him. "Tell me you love me, Minmei. Let it be the last thing I hear. Please."

Once, she would have hung back from conceding that, but she had suffered so much since joining the Sentinels . . . it seemed that last words were all she knew anymore.

"I love you, Lynn-Kyle. Now and forever."

Minmei locked her mouth to his, and felt Kyle go cold and lifeless. She held him close, rocking as she embraced his head, crooning a little children's song he had taught her a thousand eons ago.

There was the sudden grip of bloody hands, and Edwards dragged her away from Lynn-Kyle's corpse. He was speaking into a rover commo unit through his smashed face. "Rally here! Rally here! Make pickup at this location at once!"

There was a burst of static as someone acknowledged from the assault units. Minmei knew she was still a captive and that Edwards might still win the day, but all of that was unimportant to her now.

I'm not a prisoner anymore. I have my own part to play now.

She glanced around the room, and everything she saw seemed to be an edged weapon or a bludgeon. Edwards, still trying to arrange for a rendezvous, was suddenly troubled when he saw Minmei's slow smile.

CHAPTER
TWENTY-TWO

Strange, that the "Loki" of the Sentinels campaign should have a namesake so renowned in Earth's scientific history. But the Human Tesla invented polyphase systems, dynamos, oscillators, and so much more, whereas there is no record of his Invid counterpart making any contribution whatsoever—beyond the abominations that are already so notorious.

Simon Kujawa, *Against All Worlds: A Biography of Tesla the Infamous*

"WHAT'S YOUR HURRY, JACK?"

Karen tried to make it sound joking, but some of her concern slipped through nevertheless. Jack paused, there in the *Ark Angel* passageway, to face her.

"Tesla's due to speak to the leaders," he said in an emotionless voice. "I'm making final arrangements, and I'm very pressed for time, so if you don't mind—"

"What are you now, that big slug's *errand boy*?" she sneered. "Does he keep you busy kissing his feet? Is that why you and Gnea are holed up down in that compartment with him all the time?"

Wrong tone, girl, she told herself. But she couldn't help it. She was angry at him for avoiding her, she was suspicious of all the time he was spending together with Miss Teenage Amazon, and she was worried about what Tesla might be cooking up. And she was PO'd at herself for caring so much about Jack Baker.

He had that same distant, dispassionate look he had been wearing lately, studying her like she was something on a microscope slide. "You're an idiot," he said, and about-faced and marched off on his way.

She fought the urge to go after him and put his lights out. *Violence never solves anything unless you happen to live in certain parts of New Jersey*, as someone—W. C. Fields?—put it.

There was some slight reassurance in the fact that Tesla was about to make his long-postponed appearance before the Sentinels elite. Rick Hunter had decided he wasn't going to put up with any more stalling, and had in fact been in the process of organizing an armed contingent to drag the Invid before a board of inquiry—even if it meant clapping Gnea and Burak and Jack Baker in irons and giving the alien scientist a taste of the business end of a cattle prod.

But Tesla's relayed announcement—that he had something of great importance to lay before the leadership—forestalled all that. There were a hundred different scuttlebutt theories about what was about to happen, and some of them were awfully disquieting.

But apparently Jack Baker wasn't about to clarify anything. Karen Penn found that she had curled her hands into fists. *Idiot, huh?* She went after him with every intention of dumping him on his keister.

It surprised her almost as much as it did Jack Baker when, grabbing his elbow and dragging him around on his heel, she kissed him instead of belting him. She put one hand behind his head and the other on his cheek and went to it.

It wasn't the first time they had kissed, but Karen made it something that said a lot more than the friendly/competitive necking they had occasionally done in the past. She knew then that Jack definitely *wasn't* his normal self; it was like kissing some unyielding stranger.

But then the kiss changed, and for a moment Jack felt stirrings of his true self and his own free will. He put his arms around Karen and kissed her back, as astonished crewmembers of various species detoured around the two or stopped to stare. A few whistled and cheered and applauded.

Tesla's mindlock reasserted itself, though, and Karen felt Jack go distant and emotionless. He held her at arm's length, his hands on her shoulders. The kiss had left her breathless, but he was behind some strange emotional barrier once more. The interplay of his features told her that there was a struggle going on somewhere inside.

"Let's see you shrug *that* one off, Jack," she whispered to him, her hands pressed to his cheeks. He lurched free, staggering a bit, and continued on his way. There were a few sniggers from the sidelines. Karen spun to face the onlookers.

"What're the bunch of ya doing standing around *leering*? Haven't you perverts got sex lives of your *own*?"

Her temper was well known. In five seconds she had the whole passageway to herself.

My god! Maybe we should shoot him right now, before it's too late! That was Rick Hunter's first thought when Tesla appeared before the Sentinels' leadership.

The scientist was now fully as tall as the Regent, but more strongly resembled the Regis. He reminded Lisa of a store mannequin or an ancient statue, his bodily structure and face now clearly defined along Human lines but still devoid of any real identity.

Tesla had had robes made for him—by Baker and Gnea, Rick supposed; the two were doing all his stepping and fetching in alarmingly devoted fashion these days—robes like those of the Invid monarch himself. He even wore the jeweled collar Lisa had once fastened around his throat; but now, Rick assumed, the Tango-niner explosive charges had been removed. Tesla looked . . .godlike.

What Rick couldn't figure out was how the big grub was *doing* all this evolving. There had to be a technique or medicine or *something*, but no one had a clue as to what it might be. Of course, Burak and Jack and Gnea might know, but they were now over in Tesla's camp, and weren't talking.

The Invid spread his huge five-fingered hands and spoke from his new mouth in a saintly voice. "I'm here for just one reason, my friends: to bring an end to these unfortunate hostilities between your races and mine. I propose to begin my great mission by alleviating the suffering and oppression down there on Spheris."

"And how will you do that?" Rem asked in clipped, precise tones. More and more, he found himself a sort of moderator among the Sentinels, since he had a certain diligent impartiality and a need to repair the damage done by his species.

Tesla raised a single, Human-looking forefinger dramatically. "The Invid were a peaceful race, since time out of mind; we didn't know the meaning of war until our Flower of Life was stolen from us.

"We can go back to our peaceful ways again! For us, it would be like the Humans returning to the Garden of Eden. But for that to happen, the old leaders must pass away."

He pressed on before anybody could raise an objection. "Self-actuated changes lie at the heart of the Invid psyche; this is well known. That is the form of existence the Flower decreed for us. Now, I am already more highly evolved than the Regent himself. I therefore intend to go to the garrison on Spheris and command the officers and Inorganics there to lay down their arms."

"Just like that," Lisa heard Janice Em mutter. The Artificial Person wore the aspect of a human female just about constantly nowadays, yet something of the cold android logic bestowed on her by Lang had informed her persona.

Tesla had caught it. "Yes, Miss Em, just like that. Think of the lives saved and the suffering and damage that world will be spared!"

"What if it doesn't work?" Kami of Garuda said, inhaling through his special breathing mask. "What if you fail?"

Tesla's wax-museum face turned toward him. "Then, proceed with the battle plan that Teal and Baldan II are prosecuting. And remember me with what compassion you can spare, for I shall be dead."

That had people talking to each other, and Crysta, banging the gavel she manned as current chairbeing of the leadership, was some time in silencing it.

"I don't trust 'im,' Rick said out of the side of his mouth to his wife. He was looking at Burak and Gnea and Jack Baker, who stood behind Tesla and gave every indication of rooting for him.

"Whatever Baker and the rest've caught, I hope it's not contagious," Lisa agreed.

"And what are the alternatives?" Tesla forged on. "Fighting the battle and suffering the casualties you'd planned on anyway? *Give me a chance to make up for what my people have done!* That's all I ask of you! This can still be a galaxy of peace and mutual understanding!"

Not a dry eye in the house, Rick thought sourly, with a feeling he knew which way the voting was going to go.

As for Tesla, he felt a spreading warmth within him as he sensed victory. How did the line from that Human story go? *Don't throw me into dat briar patch!*

Or in this case, into the midst of an Inorganic garrison he could commandeer. Into a Protoculture garden where new varieties of the Fruit of the Flower of Life waited to speed Tesla's unprecedented evolution. Into a power base from which he would launch his campaign to dominate the entire universe.

Once, an age ago, realizing that his star was on the ascendent, the Regis had asked him, "Tesla, why are you so *wicked*?"

And he had answered with a bored mental yawn, "Mistress, only mediocre intellects can endure the tedium of being *good*."

Contacted deep within Spheris, Baldan II and his people agreed to try Tesla's plan. The carnage that had accompanied previous battles with the Invid was well known now, and any idea that might prevent such ruin on Spheris was worth a try.

Teal was wary of it, though; once reassured that others would take up the fight for them, the Spherisians might be difficult or impossible to work into a fighting mood once more.

The Odeon's hornlike energy projectors gushed fiery bolts at him, but Wolff's Hovertank slewed aside, firing a close-in salvo from its own massive main gun.

The Inorganic went up like a roman candle as the rest of the Wolff Pack followed their commander, battling their way through the determined Invid resistance toward the REF HQ building.

The Hovertanks were making only the slowest progress; the Inorganics were being incredibly obstinate. Something to do with Edwards's control over them and the man's military zeal, Wolff supposed. The Inorganics had seemed paralyzed for a few moments a while back, and Wolff thought for a few seconds that the general was dead, but the alien mecha had shaken themselves awake and plunged into battle once again.

When the Invid onslaught began, Wolff's first impulse had been to get his Hovers down into the catacombs under the Royal Hall, where the Brain that activated them floated in its vat. But even before the Wolff Pack could get organized for the assault, the Inorganics had established almost unassailable defensive positions in the catacombs. Detectors said that something big, involving a lot for Protoculture, was going on down there, but nobody could figure out what.

Since Edwards couldn't leave the Living Computer behind without losing the bulk of his fighting strength, Wolff deduced that preparations were being made to move it. But whatever was being done, it was no impediment to the combat capabilities of the Inorganics.

Edwards and a major part of his force had made their break for the HQ building. Jonathan Wolff and most of his available mecha pursued. In the meantime word came of the hijacking of the SDF-7 cruiser; Wolff knew time was short.

Much of the Hovertanks' success was due, pure and simple, to the colonel's single-minded determination to get through to the headquarters. There could only be one reason that Edwards would delay his escape and divert his troops in the way he was doing: Minmei. Though Edwards had declared to the council that he had no idea of her whereabouts, Jonathan Wolff never believed it for an instant.

Assuming Tank, Battloid, and Gladiator configuration in compliance with his instructions and his deployment of them, his armored forces slugged their way closer and closer to the HQ. The Inorganics were making them pay for every yard of ground they gained along the elevated highways and wide, straight boulevards. Luckily, fully three quarters of the awakened enemy mecha were tied up in the fight by the Royal Hall or had been engaged by other REF and Human Sentinels fighters.

Reinforcements from SDF-3 and elsewhere on Tirol would be some time in arriving, however, and the Inorganics would have the numerical advantage for another critical half hour or so yet. Wolff was undaunted, though:

the key to victory lay not in the sheer attrition of set-piece battle, but rather in striking the head from the monster—literally. By killing Edwards.

But Wolff's timetable was changed as Exedore's voice came up over the tactical communications net. "Colonel! We have Invid Terror Weapons rising from the Royal Hall! Some are heading for immediate rendezvous with the SDF-7, but others are coming your way!"

So, that was Edwards's other ace in the hole. The Regent had left more than just troops and the Living Computer behind in his haste to abandon Tirol. The Invid Brain was no doubt on its way to safety already.

Even as Wolff was getting the bad news, the Inorganics began disengaging, pulling back to defensive positions, awaiting evacuation. Soon, the way to the HQ was clear, but the building itself was alive with alien biped mecha putting out murderous, concentrated fire.

Within a minute, two of the bizarre-looking Invid dropships were descending toward the roof, accompanied by skirmish fliers. With their increased fire superiority, the enemy craft drove back the few VTs the Humans still had in the air. Inorganics were soon embarking for their escape.

Wolff saw that there was no way his force could stop them. He switched to Edwards's command frequency and broadcast in cleartext. "This doesn't end it, General! I'm coming after you! D'you hear me?"

Unexpectedly, the static of on-line encrypted traffic broke, and Edwards's face appeared on a display screen on the tank's instrument panel. He looked like he had been in a fistfight, but had apparently come out the winner, because he still radiated that cynical, superior air of his. Wolff could see from the background that Edwards was already aboard a Terror ship.

"That's fine with me, Colonel. You were lucky I was too rushed to finish you back there in the Royal Hall. I still have a score to settle with you.

"But until we meet again, here's someone else you might want to say good-bye to." The camera pulled back, and Wolff swore helplessly.

Minmei stood there, eyes glazed—looking catatonic. Wolff breathed her name.

"Why, Minmei!" Edwards smiled at her. "Aren't you going to tell the big, bad Wolff how much you love him? He's come home at long last to rescue you, after all."

She looked up at the screen in the dropship that displayed Wolff's face. "Love? The man I love is dead."

"Minmei, don't say that! Just hang on; I'll save you, I swear it—"

"I don't want anything you have to offer, Jonathan. The man I'll love forever is dead."

She wanted to be with Edwards so she could kill him as soon as she got the chance, not thrown back into the company of the colonel who had abandoned her—as she regarded his going off with the Sentinels now—after she had begged him not to leave. There was nothing Jonathan Wolff could do for her ever again.

But there was one thing *she* could do, to take some of the weight off her conscience and vent the bitterness she felt toward the whole world in the wake of Lynn-Kyle's death. She could make the break clear and final.

"Why don't you go back to your Sentinels buddies, Colonel?" she said, narrowing her eyes at him. "Or better yet, why don't you go home to your wife and kids? Remember *them*, you two-timing *pig*?" She reached out and broke the connection herself.

Edwards exulted at this sudden turn of luck. He had hoped that Minmei's grief and mental turmoil would make her rebuff Wolff—he had had nothing to lose by letting her and the colonel speak to each other once more. But this was simply marvelous! He vowed that he would make Minmei love him, as he had once before. She would come around in time.

The dropships were rising over Tiresia, laying down suppressing fire to keep the REF's heads down. The hijacked starship was swinging low for pickup, its bays opening.

Of course, it was a tragedy that Lang hadn't installed the new spacefold drive in the stolen starship yet; otherwise, Edwards could have had his ticket back to Earth, and a loyal army at his back.

No point mourning that now. The Ghost officers aboard the ship were asking nervously what course they should set, to be ready for immediate departure.

"Optera," the general answered curtly, and broke the connection. The Regent had already been of service, but that was nothing compared to how useful he was about to become to Edwards's dream of conquest.

CHAPTER
TWENTY-THREE

> *In summation, it is important to bear in mind how the "social insect" organization of the Invid renders them immune to certain politico-military strategems. Among the things we CANNOT do to the Invid are:*
> *1) Wreck their (nonexistent) monetary system*
> *2) Establish an underground or resistance*
> *3) Cause racial or religious friction*
> *4) Employ propaganda techniques*
> *5) Insert double agents*
> *6) Subvert them with things like material wealth, freedom, erotic literature, or baseball.*
> *7) Appeal to their better nature*
>
> from *Limited Options: Warfare and the Invid Infrastructure*, submitted to the REF Strategic Studies Group by Dr. Boscoe Highwater

LRON, RICK HUNTER, AND OTHERS POINTED OUT THAT in the wake of the ruse Tesla had used against the Invid garrison on Karbarra in the Sentinels' attack on that world, the enemy on Spheris wasn't very likely to roll out the red carpet for him.

"That incident will be of no consequence here, because I am Evolved," Tesla said grandly. "Nothing you Mortals can understand, but take my word for it: my people will recognize my divine right to command."

One thing in his favor was the fact that Gnea and Jack Baker believed so strongly that Tesla could deliver what he was promising. But Rick had his own suspicions about the two; they were too eager in their attitudes, too ready to back the Invid.

Another troubling factor was Burak. The Perytonian had conceived a sort of jealousy toward Jack and Gnea—a proprietary air concerning Tesla. He was also acting more and more messianic, as if Tesla *was* contagious.

But there was no derailing Tesla's plan now. The leadership had agreed on it and the Spherisians were demanding that it at least be *tried*, in the hope that it would prevent needless carnage and damage on their world.

Much disagreement had arisen as to how Tesla should actually make his appearance on Spheris. Combat drops and commando insertions would produce the wrong effect, he insisted. In the end, Veidt took him down in one of the cone-shape Haydonite fliers, with Burak, Jack, and Gnea acting as retinue and security.

At Lisa's insistence, Tesla's jeweled bib had been wired up with explosives again, to prevent any double-crosses. Jack Baker carried one firing switch, and there was another on the bridge of the *Ark Angel*, which still lay hidden from enemy detection.

, On the approach, Tesla considered putting Veidt under his mental control, too. But the Haydonite's mind powers were strong, and Tesla would need all available power to take over the garrison below. He therefore settled for masking his dominance over Baker and the others.

As the flier descended, the thin atmosphere began to buffet it slightly. Spheris lay like an imperial orb, heavy with gems and wrapped in the cotton of clouds, below. The dazzle of it was intense; Human, Praxian, and Perytonian were wearing wraparound sun visors, as most of the Sentinels would have to do on Spheris during daylight hours.

The passengers shifted their feet on the thick, resilient padding that carpeted the passenger compartment. "What if they fire?" Veidt wondered calmly.

"They will not fire," Tesla parried. "I have willed it so." Jack and Gnea smiled at one another conspiratorially. Burak glowered at them.

The surface drew near. A shining city appeared below, like a masterpiece of venetian glass. Tesla, looming over the others, commanded that communications links be established, and Veidt's apparatus did it instantly.

"Loyal hordes of the Invid race! Hear my voice, a voice you know!" Many figures in the city seemed to freeze, looking up. Jack could spy Inorganics, Enforcers, and Hellcats.

As Tesla ordered, Veidt brought the flier down by a landing platform near the garrison's main hive, a megastructure out of place amid the delicate beauty of the city. Tesla emerged radiating a rainbow aura, and the Invid there stood transfixed.

"I come to save you from the aimless strife and the privation of your long exile. Too long have the Invid fought wars for no reason; too long have you wandered in search of a new Garden of the Flower of Life. I come to lead you—"

He spread his arms wide, as tall as a tree, gorgeous in his robes and glimmering collar. "—to Paradise!"

The city seemed to ring with a wordless, reverent sound the Invid made in unison. Mecha bowed their heads or dropped to one knee, holding fists and weapons aloft to salute him. Hellcats roared their worship, touching foreheads to the high-gloss pavement.

It was as Tesla had foreseen. The brain that controlled the planet's garrison was of lesser power and he had managed to subvert its authority through his evolved mental force. He broadcast a thought-impulse, voicing it aloud as well.

"Come to me, my children! Gather and do homage, that I may see you and you may heed my commands, to prepare for your joyous new life on a new Optera!"

The things began making their way toward him from the hive and from all over the city. "As soon as we have secured the city," Tesla said, "we will proceed to the Protoculture orchid in the hive and secure the local Fruit of the Flower."

The Invid were already gathering below the landing platform, a swelling lake of them promising to become an ocean. They looked unusual in that they were armed not with the usual Protoculture weapons, but rather with projectile and chemical devices. The Invid, too, valued Spheris—primarily for its production of unequaled nutrient fluid—and had no wish to inflict unnecessary damage to it.

Veidt objected. "There was nothing in the plan about you ingesting Fruit of the Flower. Keep to the agreed-upon timetable, or I notify the Sentinels!"

Tesla didn't respond, busy basking in the glory as the Invid mob began hailing him with un-Human sounds. Veidt turned to Gnea. "Stop him! He's betraying us, I can sense it now!"

But she spared him only a sinister smile. Veidt turned to the control panels of his flier, sending out mental signals. A communication device lit up, preparing to send Veidt's warning to the *Ark Angel*.

Gnea turned her Badger assault pistol on it and blasted the apparatus; explosive bullets were about as good as Protoculture bolts for a job like that. Then she shot up the rest of the controls, disabling the craft. Jack and Burak did not seem to notice, showing the same adoration for Tesla that the Inorganics did.

Tesla was radiant in his triumph, but the moment was short-lived. A Terror ship threw its shadow across the scene. Tesla howled a curse; the Brain wasn't so feeble that it couldn't exert influence of its own.

The dropship landed nearby and its landing ramps descended. Officers emerged by the dozen, leading troops whose loyalty Tesla couldn't bend to his will. He was already extended to his limits with the many he had taken over, and in addition found that the more highly evolved Officers put up too much resistance to the subjugated.

Since Gnea had destroyed the flier, his path of retreat was cut off, but that mattered little. Tesla hadn't come to Spheris to retreat *or* be beaten. He still had most of the city's garrison—a major part of the entire planet's complement of Invid—under his sway. He sent out the order to his loyal host, "Slay the unfaithful! Cut them down! In the name of Tesla!"

They turned to do just that, the two waves of mecha closing with each other. Tesla spared a moment to snap, "Baker! Burak! Go, and fetch me the Fruit at once! Gnea, keep watch on Veidt!"

The two males dashed away, on a roundabout path, guided by his unspoken directions. Veidt looked at Gnea and knew it was no use trying to reason with her. As for Tesla, the scientist's now-uncloaked powers were astounding, strong enough to resist anything Veidt could muster against it.

Helpless, Veidt watched with Tesla and Gnea as Invid closed in mortal combat with Invid.

"There's fighting below on a large scale, Captain," a bridge crewmember told Lisa. "It's some kind of Invid civil war, apparently."

Lisa had more than half hoped it would be some sign of treachery by Tesla, especially after contact with Veidt's flier was lost. That would give her all the justification she needed to throw the switch and trigger the charge in Tesla's collar and blow his damned head away.

"I guess Tesla can't fool all of the Invid all of the time," Rick mused. "I'll say this for him, though: he's created a diversion."

"But we don't know how long it'll last," Bela said, fists planted on girded hips. "The time to move is now!"

The leadership came to a quick decision; Rick could see that his once-cautious wife was in accord with the amazon way of thinking now. Orders went out for the combat drop operations to begin.

Perhaps the conventional weapons with which the Inorganics on Spheris had been armed couldn't produce the planet-rending effects Protoculture firearms did, but the ruin they spread in the gorgeous capital city of Beroth was appalling enough. Explosive shells, armor-piercing rockets, and the mecha's own brute strength shattered buildings and sculptures, stately columns and illumination pylons. The Inorganics pounded and shot and dismembered one another throughout the city.

Jack and Burak found that the combatants were totally uninterested in them, but that didn't mean they were safe. A Scrim's stray shot or a wrestling Odeon's foot would kill them just as dead as a well-aimed missile. Following Tesla's silent guidance, they picked their way through the madness toward the hive. They had no idea how to distinguish between the local Brain's loyalists and Tesla's faction, but obviously the Inorganics did.

At one point they were nearly cut to ribbons by a shattered wall that fell like a waterfall of needles and razors, knives and guillotine blades. Seconds later, they just reached cover before a thermal warhead went off in the midst of a cluster of Crann. Two Hellcats, trying to tear each other apart, rolled from a higher esplanade and nearly crushed them.

But they ran on without pause and in perfect cooperation, because that was Tesla's will. At the entrance to the hive, Burak led the way, being more familiar with the layout of such places.

There, too, the Invid seemed to be distracted to the point of utter carelessness—at least where non-Invid interlopers were concerned. The pair made their way through the shadows, as reinforcements went pounding up and down the corridors. Navigated by Tesla's hold on them, they came at last to the place where the Flower of Life had brought forth its burden.

Here, too, the Fruit had only appeared recently, so much so that it wasn't quite ripe yet. Therefore, it hadn't been harvested yet for shipment to Optera. Tesla took that as another sign that *he*, not the Regent, was destined to rule his species and the universe.

"The Invid are fighting it out sure enough, sir," Karen reported back to Rick over the command net, "but there's no way to tell who's who!"

She completed her close pass in the Fighter-mode Logan VT, weaving among stray shots and deliberate ones, missiles and autocannon both, that drew lines through the sky around her.

"Suggest you delay drop, I say again, *delay drop*, until we can figure out what's going on."

"Understood." In the *Ark Angel*'s tactical information center, Rick switched to his link with Lisa up on the bridge. "Did you get that?"

"Acknowledged." She swept the ship around into a holding pattern, as it was jarred by the atmosphere. In the mustering points, hundreds of troops cussed at the delay and wondered what was wrong; the waiting, the veterans knew, could sometimes be the worst part of all.

Karen brought her VT about and went to Guardian configuration for another pass. She finally spotted her objective. "I've got Tesla sighted! Gnea and Veidt, too, but I don't see Burak or Jack!" She felt her heart sink within her.

Just then Gnea's voice came over the net. "Attention, Karen! Jack and Burak are inside the Invid hive, stealing a, um, special weapon that Tesla says can win the battle. Make the pickup on them at the main intersection south of the hive; Jack will have his comset keyed for a homing signal.

"Also be advised: Tesla will instruct his troops to emit blinking signals with their optical sensors. I say again, troops with blinking signals are friendlies."

"Roger that," Karen said. She relayed the information to Lisa even as her VT leapt away through the sky, thrusters bellowing, to make the pickup on Jack and Burak.

Below her, Tesla took his concentration from the battle for an instant to tell Gnea, "Well done."

The faster the Fruit was brought to him, the better. And, having a Veritech at his disposal would enhance his situation, too.

This time, the Fruit was as yellow as a sunflower and grew in a shape that was nearly a perfect pyramid.

Jack and Burak had bundled up as many as they could in their jackets, and crept out of the hive once more, like raiding mice among the hurrying giant Inorganics.

At one point, they felt disoriented as Tesla wondered if it wouldn't be worthwhile to send them on a suicide attack to the Brain. But the moment passed as the scientist realized that the Brain would be far too well guarded for two lightly armed humanoids to tackle. Besides, he must have the Fruit, before something happened to it.

When they reached the intersection, Jack, by Tesla's decree, keyed the homing signal. He and Burak got ready to put the rest of the plan into effect.

Zooming down in a wash of thruster fire, Karen could see no sign of either Jack or Burak. And yet, she was getting a strong signal from the comset.

The only building still standing in the area was a sturdy-looking structure suggesting a bunker of polished opal. Karen checked her instruments; the signal was coming from there. Its entrances were far too small for a Battloid.

Jack's voice came up on the net. "Karen, get in here and help me with Burak; he took a bad hit."

The fighting had moved from the area, but she still considered Jack's proposal dubious. "Can't you get him to the entry? I can pick him up with the Battloid's hand."

Jack sounded weak and weary. "Goddamn you, it's all I can do to keep him from coming apart in *pieces*! And I caught a hit or two myself."

Karen imaged the mechamorphosis, and the VT, back in Guardian shape, knelt with its radome almost touching the ground. She was out of the cockpit and running in another second or two, sidearm drawn. She passed into the dark interior, calling his name.

Something hit her from behind, and the next thing she knew, Jack and Burak were standing over her with drawn guns.

CHAPTER
TWENTY-FOUR

I've been accused of over-romanticizing certain aspects of the events that day. Maybe so, and if that's the kind of thing that irks you, then don't read on.

What you should do to keep yourself busy, though, is make sure you try the glass slipper on every appropriate foot that comes your way. You might change your mind—or your luck.

Jack Baker, *Upwardly Mobile*

FLOWING DISEMBODIED ALONG THE CRYSTAL HIGHways, Baldan II implored his people.

"We know which mecha we must strike at now! Tesla's troops and even the Sentinels may not be enough! We *must* help them!"

But everywhere it was the same. "We are safe here in the bosom of Spheris. Let the outworlders fight their own battles!"

The heart he had put into them was gone again, now that someone seemed ready to hand the Spherisians peace and freedom on a platter. Baldan brooded, and wondered if such a gift could ever be trusted, and how much harm it would do Spheris in the long run.

Teal spoke across the mineral medium to him. "What shall we do? Baldan, if you want to fight, I am with you."

"There is one thing we might do," he said. Reorienting his mind-spirit along new vectors, he headed toward Beroth. Teal rose after.

Karen knew her flight helmet had saved her from being killed; from the positions of the two as they stood looking down at her, she presumed Burak had struck the blow.

She tried to move and realized she was trussed up with her own flight harness and their uniform harnesses.

Burak was tucking her dropped pistol in his gunbelt. "I'll get the Fruit. Make sure she's secure. And don't forget to bring her helmet."

Jack removed the helmet, but then stood looking down at her uncertainly, weighing his Badger. "Jack, Tesla's making you do this, isn't he? Jack, don't listen to him! Stop and think what you're doing, before—"

"Silence!" Burak was back. "Be grateful that Omnipotent Tesla directs us to spare you, or—"

Then his expression became a little vague, as did Jack's, as they both listened to something she couldn't hear. Burak glanced down at her with a devilish grin, his horns silhouetted against the entrance.

"It seems you're not indispensable after all, Penn." He turned to Jack. "Finish her, while I load the Fruit." Burak had no compunctions about killing Karen—not under Tesla's coercion. But he was much more concerned that the Fruit stay in his possession, giving him some minimal leverage with the Invid.

"Jack, don't do this," she whispered.

He holstered his gun like a man in a trance. His forehead was covered with rivulets of sweat. Hooking his hands in her bonds, he began pulling her up. A part of him felt that he couldn't simply leave her body there; that he must move it further into the darkness to hide his terrible crime. Another part simply wanted to lift her up and bear her away—away from the danger.

Her infighting moves were severely limited: ankles and knees were strapped together, her hands bound behind her at elbows and wrists. But as he lifted her up, she made her play; it had nothing to do with knocking him unconscious.

Lurching against him, she pinned him between the wall and herself, putting her mouth to his. The zombielike dullness slipped from him, and after a surprised instant, he kissed her back, arms going around her, supporting her. He buried his fingers in her hair and hugged her tight. Time stopped for both of them.

"What are you doing?" Burak's footsteps clicked on the floor.

Jack could only release her and turn to go for his gun in a desperate contest. Karen tucked her chin in and managed to avoid having her head cracked open as she toppled over backward in a painful fall.

Jack didn't have time to unholster his pistol, because Burak was practically on top of him, though one of the man's groping hands blundered open the retaining strap that held his comset in its pouch. But he managed to grab Burak's wrist and give it a practiced twist, sending the Perytonian's handgun bouncing across the floor. Then Jack hit him with a right cross, sending him staggering into the wall.

Tesla sensed what was going on and strove to reassert his dominance over Jack, sending a mental bolt at him just as he went to grapple with Burak. Jack somehow endured the attack, but he was off balance.

Knocking aside Jack's clumsy defense, Burak used an instinctive attack, one the Sentinels hadn't seen from a Perytonian yet, and that Jack wouldn't be looking for. Rather than use hands or feet, Burak faked, then lowered his head and gored Jack Baker.

The long, dart-keen, tapered horns ripped through the tough fabric of the man's uniform and through flesh and muscle, opening twin channels across his midsection. One horn hung up on a rib, and Burak was pulled off balance. Jack managed to land a hammer blow to the base of Burak's neck with his fist, but the Perytonian lifted him from his feet and dropped him like a bull tossing a mata-dor.

As Jack fell, Burak looked around dizzily for his gun. But a burst from a Badger made him duck, and he rushed madly for the bunker's entrance. Karen fired again, but with no way to aim, she was lucky she just stitched a line of shots across the ceiling.

Lucky I didn't shoot my own young tush off! she told herself.

As it was, she had through some miracle managed to squirm over to Burak's gun, rolling over it backward to get it.

As Burak fled, he kicked something that skittered ahead of him. He instinctively scooped it up as he ran, barely breaking stride: Jack's comset, which had bounced loose in the struggle.

Karen fired one more burst blindly, then let Burak go and set the Badger aside. She went back to work on the makeshift bonds. By the time she had her wrists loosened up a bit, the rumble of her ascending VT shook the air.

Burak didn't have the flight helmet, but with luck and a little skill he could get back to Tesla using sheer manual controls.

Other hands, slick with blood, fumbled to help Karen free herself. In seconds she was kneeling by Jack, and he curled back on the floor. The goring had been savage, and he was losing blood fast. But she could see that he had shaken off Tesla's influence.

She looked around for her flight helmet to call for a medevac but saw it lying in pieces, an inadvertent victim of one of her own unaimed bursts.

Jack managed a pale ghost of one of those maddening grins. "Isn't *Prince Charming* supposed to awaken *Sleep-*

ing Beauty with the kiss? Penn, can't you get anything right?"

Armed with all the non-Protoculture weaponry they had been able to muster, the Sentinels dropped into Beroth to throw themselves in on the side of the blinking Invid.

If the Brain had been more devious, it might have had its troops imitate Tesla's strobe signals and confuse things again. But, an aging and somewhat obsolescent organism, it practiced only the standard, brute tactics of Invid warfare.

The Sentinels had come in armed with everything from Karbarran pneumatics to Garudan slingshots, but most were carrying REF-style non-Protoculture weapons. Even the Praxians had put aside their polearms and swords and dart-throwers willingly for submachine guns loaded with explosive bullets, heavy machine guns that fired discarding-sabot rounds, and portable recoilless rifles.

There were also mortars, flame guns, Garudan things that squirted molecular acid, blowtorches, and a lot more. The VTs and the few remaining Hovertanks couldn't use Protoculture weapons either, of course, but there had only been time to retrofit a few of them with old-style autocannon and rocket pods. Still, even lacking firearms, a multi-ton mecha throwing armored punches or swinging a superalloy club as long as a utility pole could do a lot of damage.

It was easy to sort out friend from foe; Tesla's new subjects' cyclopean eyes flashed brightly. The Sentinels launched themselves into the fray with that same hunger for revenge and victory that they had brought to other battles.

But Tesla was beginning to feel misgivings. Burak was already on his way back with the Fruit—slowly, because he wasn't used to handling a VT, and certainly not without the special thinking-cap flight helmet—but the Sentinels might discover Tesla's treachery at any time, if Baker or Penn could get word back somehow.

Was it luck or was it the Shaping of the Protoculture that Penn's helmet had been shot up and Baker's comset taken by Burak? Tesla steeled himself against doubts. Though every Inorganic he could command was sorely needed in the battle, he detached several and sent them toward the bunker, to do away with two troublesome Humans before they could interfere any further.

In the meantime, sensing the deployment of the Sentinels and the manner in which the battle was taking shape, he began a series of strategic withdrawals, in order to shift the burden of the fighting over to his former captors. He would need his own troops for other things.

On Optera the Regent, still dripping from nutrient immersion, viewed a recording of the brief fragment of message that his Spheris garrison had managed to send.

"Under attack by—"

Then the screen went blank, because the main communications installation had been the first thing against which Tesla directed his troops' fire.

But the Regent could hardly know that. He could only quake with rage and fright, that an enemy could so suddenly overwhelm his most important remaining stronghold outside of Optera.

Burak barely survived his landing, crumpling the Guardian's powerful leg under it with a creaking of metal, and stoving in the radome.

"Can *you* fly it?" Tesla demanded of Gnea.

She shook her head somewhat groggily; leakage from Tesla's mind let bits and pieces of the fierce battle through into her own. "Not without a helmet."

Tesla roared and reached out to swat her like a bug; she never even flinched. But he stopped himself, realizing that she might be of some further use. Burak emerged from the keeled-over Guardian hobbling, somehow contriving to carry the bundled Fruit. The ring of flashing-eyed troops that Tesla had drawn around the area to protect himself opened for Burak.

By the time the Perytonian was dragging himself up the ramp to join him on the landing platform, Tesla was already issuing new marching orders to his usurped army.

Just then a contact signal came from the communicator on Gnea's belt. It was Lisa Hunter's voice over the command freq. "Tesla, get your eastern and northern elements going in a pincer movement, do you read me? What they're doing now is worse than useless!"

Tesla took the comset in his now-dexterous hand. "Oh yes! I read you, female; have no fear."

He broke the contact, but continued what he was doing. His objective now was the troopships on the other side of the city; the Brain was too well guarded, and he had sworn never to go back into Human captivity.

The VTs the Sentinels had been able to field had already hit some of the tanker ships in port, sending tidal waves of nutrient fluid washing outward. But the troopships stationed there in long-term ground positions were, in accordance with military procedure, camouflaged against space attack—just as the Terror Weapons on Tirol had been. They were still there awaiting Tesla's pleasure.

"And then on to Optera!" he cried, shaking his fist at the sky.

"No!" It was Burak, limping toward Tesla with a wild look on his face and Jack's blood still glistening darkly on his horns. He dropped the bundles of Fruit and stepped back from them.

"Not Optera; *Peryton!* You promised!"

Tesla, furious, sent out a mental bolt that almost flattened Burak. How the Perytonian had slipped his mental leash, Tesla had no idea, except that Tesla's concentration was divided among so many things.

But Burak withstood the bolt somehow and held up Jack Baker's comset. His thumb was on its special switch, the one that would trigger the charge in Tesla's resplendent collar. "Pery . . . ton," Burak got out between locked teeth.

Tesla felt immense amusement and savage wrath at the same time. "Is that so? *Behold!*"

Suddenly the unpickable locks that clasped the collar around his neck clicked open. At the same time, Burak found that he couldn't move, not so much as the thumb that rested on the deadly button.

Tesla took the collar and hurled it far from him; there would be more of such baubles than he could count once he had taken his rightful place. He reached out to push Burak's thumb; there was a loud report from the exploding bib, down somewhere in the lower levels of the landing platform area.

Tesla still had three valuable hostages, an army of Inorganics, and his newfound powers. He had no doubt now that he would prevail.

"Very well, all of you; we're going to—"

But as he turned, he let out an enraged bellow. Veidt was gone. Gnea was befuddled, swearing that he had been there, with her Badger trained on him, only seconds before. From where he had floated, cornered, Veidt could only have plunged over the edge of the platform and down into the darkened levels far below.

Only, who knew what such a fall meant to a Haydonite? No time to wonder now. Tesla issued a mental order, and Gnea and Burak gathered up the Fruit, then closed ranks behind him. Together, they descended to fall in behind a flying wedge of Inorganics, to battle their way toward the spaceport.

Odeons lifted them up and carried them swiftly.

* * *

The Invid had thought the arms room a place safe from
Spherisian intrusion—firstly, because it held Protoculture
weapons the locals dreaded; secondly, because it was an
enclosure cut off from the Crystal Highways.

The invaders never thought to consider their own thick
bundles of fiber-optic filaments—thick cables of silicon-
based strands. That same system was accessible elsewhere.

In one corner of the room, two cables swelled and
swelled, expanding, drawing in more material from floors
above and below, until at last the insulation around them
was blown away in shreds. The filaments curled and fused,
taking on humanoid form.

This time, Baldan found himself all but transparent, the
light shifting within him as if he were a fortune-teller's ball
come alive. Teal was now composed of the same clear
stuff, though her body was still unmistakably female.

He shook his head to clear it of the ringing. The last
stretch, through the Invid cable system, had been resonant
with their incomprehensible battle signals rather than with
the songs of the Highways.

"Why are we here, Baldan? And where are we?"

He set off among the rearing racks of outsize Invid
weapons. "We're here because it isn't right that Spherisians
let others do their fighting and dying for them. It isn't just.
It cheapens freedom."

He's not using Baldan II's voice, Teal told herself.
Those are his father's words, and no mistaking it.

He came at last to what he was searching for: a row of
heavy Enforcer rifles. They weren't even locked up. He
lifted one, making sure that its charge was full. As heavy
as it was, he handled it easily; his structure was stronger
than that of ordinary flesh and blood. Teal saw that he was
drawing on Baldan I's memories as much as he was upon
the training Bela and the others had given him.

He heard a quiet clicking and turned to see Teal checking over a second rifle. "No!" he said softly. "Where I go from here you cannot follow."

She held the rifle resolutely. "You complain because Spherisians won't fight, and now you lose your composure because one *wants* to! Make up your mind, young man."

The features of his face slid around into a wry look, then straightened again. "Keep your head down, Mother."

They stole out along Invid-style corridors, through the great hive. They were near the innermost sanctum, having bypassed ring upon ring of sentries and guardposts and surveillance by means of the Crystal Highways. In moments they hung back in the shadows of a structure like a huge fibroblast, looking out at the Invid Brain that held sway over most of the occupying army.

It was pulsing and emitting strange sounds, so agitated and apprehensive that even the two intruders could sense it clearly. The battle wasn't going well.

There was a handpicked elite of Officers and Enforcers around the Brain, conferring in low tones and attending it. Baldan looked to his mother, raising his chin and brows inquiringly.

What misplaced practical joke of the Protoculture brought me here? she carped to herself. All she had ever wanted to do was enjoy life and the attentions of admirers, to let her beauty speak for itself and languish in the adulation that everyone seemed eager to accord her.

But she nodded to her son that she was ready. The two leapt out to either side of the cover, rifle muzzles at waist level, firing Protoculture blasts.

CHAPTER
TWENTY-FIVE

*Tesla was very troubled in the last hours before the attack.
When I braced him about it, I expected one of his evasive numbers
or egomaniacal silences.*

*But he seemed to need to talk to someone. He was psychotic by
then, I think; the lab people conjecture that he'd actually been
increasing his chromosome numbers.*

*At any rate, he said, "I have had a recurring dream lately. A
great phoenix of mind-force rises from a small blue-white world
and soars away to another plane of existence. It fills me with
apprehension."*

Lisa Hayes Hunter, *Recollections*

KAREN HAD SEEN TO JACK'S WOUNDS AS BEST SHE
could, but he went into shock, still losing blood. It came
down to a simple choice of leaving him there and going for
help, or staying with him and watching him die.

Then the decision was taken away from her. A Hellcat
bounded into sight at the bunker's entrance, showing its
glowing fangs. Its eyes were flashing rhythmically; it was
one of Tesla's.

Three had originally been dispatched by Tesla to keep
Karen and Jack from getting word of his treachery back to
the Sentinels. But an ambush by the Brain's forces had cut
down the other two 'Cats.

Tesla had picked the feline-shape for the job because it
was smaller and more limber than the biped Inorganics.
Now, it slunk into the entranceway of the bunker on all

fours, belly scraping sparks from the gleaming floor, yeowling at its prey.

Karen was already trying to drag Jack back to safety, but the side doors were all secured. So at last she wound up crouched, with Jack, against the dead end of the entrance-way's rear wall. The Robobeast edged nearer, its strobing eyes lighting the darkness, claws gouging the quartz-hard floor.

Karen raised Jack's pistol and her own side-by-side and opened fire. The 'Cat screamed and lowered its head, shielding its eyes, but kept coming; it had little to fear from a conventional handgun. One paw reached out to slice her wide open.

But it missed because it was being yanked backward. It turned to grapple with something Karen couldn't see, unable to get any fighting room in the confinement of the entranceway.

Then it was gone, dragged into the open, and there was a monstrous clash going on outside. Karen rushed to the entrance, looking for Skull colors; nothing short of a mecha could have jerked the Hellcat out of the bunker tail-first.

She was right. It was an Odeon, rolling with and slugging the smaller 'Cat. Another Odeon joined it, its nose-tentacle flickering out to ensnare the Hellcat. In another moment, they were socking and kicking the thing, dismembering it. Their optical sensors were *not* flashing.

Karen thought about making a dash for it, but she couldn't leave Jack behind. The Odeons were rising from their savage battle and turning their attention to her.

She backed into the shadows once more; they closed in. But as the nasal whips curled and snapped at her, a stream of depleted-transuranic slugs the size of candlepins hit them.

Karen spun and threw herself headlong, shielding her face. The Odeons, holed through and through, leaked green nutrient fluid for a moment as their systemry fizzled, then they collapsed, smoke and flame belching from their split seams. They ruptured open with explosions that mingled with the sounds of a descending Alpha's thrusters.

Karen had sat up again, face smudged and pallid. The VT was in Guardian mode, its canopy raised now as the pilot stood. Blaze's light reflected off a well-remembered flight helmet, one cast in the image of a Praxian war helm.

"Well, well! Maybe when we get a moment, you can tell me why two *enemy* slugs killed a *friendly* 'Cat that was in turn just about to eat a *Sentinel*!"

It was Bela.

"Tesla! *Ark Angel* to Tesla!"

"Still no acknowledgment, Captain," the Human commo officer told Lisa.

"Keep trying anyway," she said. To the mike, she repeated, "Your troops' lines are collapsing in all sectors! You *must* get them to stand fast!"

She switched off her mike and told the officer, "Keep on trying to raise him." Then she switched to ship's net. "Rick, he's not answering. I think it's a double-cross." She looked intently at the duplicate trigger, on her command console, for the explosives in Tesla's collar.

"All right; make another approach," he answered from the drop bay. "I'm taking in the last of the reserves, to get our troops back out."

It was on her lips to object, but she held it in. The lessons of the Praxians had subsumed those of the Academy. Of *course* you don't leave your buddies in deep trouble, no matter what the cost. She knew it as well as he. It was just that she wished she could make the assault with him and the other units.

She brought the ship onto a new heading, bearing down on Beroth at low altitude and steady helm, coming to dead-slow. Luckily, the Invid had used up most of their missiles, and their conventional cannonfire and smaller rockets weren't powerful enough to do more than dent the starship's armor and blow away noncritical superstructural features.

Ark Angel nudged over or smashed a lot of local architecture on its touchdown, lying almost smack in the middle of Beroth. At Rick's command the combat teams charged out to provide fire support for the Sentinels elements still trying to disengage, now that Tesla's forces had abandoned them.

Lisa saw from the tactical displays that it looked very grim. It was clear that Tesla was leaving them in the lurch, having some plan of his own, but there was little the Sentinels could do about it; the Brain's Inorganics were after *them* now.

At that moment even the shaky timetable of the withdrawal was set aside. There were sounds of Protoculture weapons fire in the city. Spheris itself cried out in torment.

Baldan and Teal hosed the Brain and its attendants with steady streams of riflefire, cutting Officers and Enforcers down and leaving streaks of blackening tissue across the sides of the heaving Invid monstrosity.

The attack had come so suddenly that all opposition was mowed down before there was any chance for the Invid to return fire. With wild elation Baldan thought, *We've taken them by surprise! We can kill the Brain and end the battle here!*

But even as he thought that, the floor was heaving beneath him. Protoculture weapons had been fired, and Spheris was reacting in pain.

His affinity for his world let him understand what was happening. Sympathetic vibrations of a sort only Protoculture could evoke were sending fractures along and between the Crystal Highways, like fractal daggers driven into Spheris itself. Somehow, the mere explosions of mecha didn't produce this phenomenon—perhaps because such bursts were undirected. But the riflefire, minor as it was in comparison to the warfare going on in Beroth, was a different matter entirely.

Baldan and Teal were knocked off their feet and the Brain was sloshed around in its nutrient pool. Baldan tried to get to his feet and shoot the Brain again, but Teal shouted. "No, or you may doom us all! Come, come! Before the Inorganics get us!"

The floors were already drumrolling to the heavy tread of running Inorganics coming in answer to the Brain's agonized summons. Baldan rose at last, taking his mother's arms and dragging her off the other way. She dropped her rifle and clung to him. They tottered away as the hive shook on its foundations.

The bend in a corridor brought them up against a sealed security door; the sound of the Inorganics came closer. Baldan backed off and fired at the door over and over, even though he knew it would do no good.

As the biped mecha came lumbering around the corner, Teal saw the method to Baldan's madness. The floor quaked and shifted, and a prow of icy crystal thrust itself up into sight. Spheris was reacting against its source of pain.

The upthrust had cut the Inorganics off from their quarry for the moment. Baldan threw down the rifle, took his mother's hand, and veered at the crystal as the hive tilted again. They melded with it and were safely away.

Churning in its nutrient pool, nearly insane with the pain of its wounds, the Brain lost all control. If the slave races were going to use Protoculture weapons, *protoculture weapons it would be*!

Tesla, too, nearly lost his balance as the planet convulsed. The Brain demonstrated its ire a moment later. Weapons pods set on tall masts around the hive opened up.

The blasts were highly accurate, hitting Tesla's blinking-eye Inorganics and blowing them part.

"To the ships! The ships!" he howled, an echo of his mental command. The disguised troop transports were only yards away, but most of his loyal troops were still covering his retreat.

He dithered, racked by indecision. To flee without the army he had gathered would leave him a wretched outcast once again, but to stay was to be killed, either by the Brain, the Sentinels, or the very planet! Better to live to fight another day.

"We raise ship immediately!" he screamed, so loud that Burak and Gnea winced.

The Crystal Highways themselves spasmed. The planet bid fair to tear itself apart. The Spherisians who had trusted the safety of the underground looked at one another.

"Get everybody back! Disengage!" Rick was nearly hoarse from shouting his commands over the tac net. "Prepare for pickup!"

It felt as if Spheris was going to come apart at the seams, and the only thing to do was try to get his Sentinels to safety. He had no idea what the upheavals meant for the Spherisians themselves, but there didn't seem to be much he could do for them, except—

He switched to command freq. "Lisa! Do *not* use Protoculture weapons! It'll only make things worse down here!"

That didn't seem to bother the Invid Brain, though. Rays and annihilation disks streamed from the hive's defensive batteries, wiping out every mecha that flashed the signal of Tesla, and whatever Sentinel targets they could find as well.

The tide of the Inorganics' battle had definitely turned, with Tesla's mecha fighting dispiritedly or simply turning to run, while the Brain's war machines came on relentlessly. Still, for some reason none of the Inorganics were using Protoculture weapons. Some programmed proscription?

The Brain's gunners were really pouring it on now, and the planet rocked. Rick despaired of ever getting his troops—or himself—out alive.

Around the perimeter of the hive one head rose from the living rock as if being born from it. Then another emerged, and another. Soon scores were there as the planet swayed and bucked under them. They exchanged looks and unspoken words, then sank back out of sight.

Tesla wailed as a sudden tremor knocked him from his feet and overbalanced a Crann that toppled across him.

He fought to keep hold over his troops, to maintain dominance over the transport crews he had taken under his control, and to ward off the Brain's mental attack. But in this latest setback, something had to give.

Gnea felt her mind pried loose from Tesla's bond. She shook her head, hearing a ringing and seeing lights before her eyes. A voice in her mind said, "Gnea! Quickly! Over here!"

She spun around and saw Veidt poised not twenty feet away, on a flying carpet. His robes were blackened and punctured where shrapnel or bullets had plucked at them. "Make haste! There are only seconds!" She realized that he had freed her from Tesla's grip.

Other Inorganics were trying to separate Tesla from the one that had sprawled across him. Gnea grabbed Burak's shoulder. "Come! We're leaving!"

Burak tried to shake her loose. "Let me be!"

She knew nothing about the unholy alliance into which Burak had entered with Tesla—how much deeper the Invid's hold was over the Perytonian than over Jack and herself. She just assumed Veidt hadn't been able to wrench Tesla's mental grip off both victims at once.

So, with Praxian directness, she yanked Burak back around and swung a roundhouse right that tagged him precisely on the chin. His knees buckled but she had him up and over her shoulder in one move. Legs driving like pistons, she crossed the space between herself and the hovering carpet in three bounds, nearly overturning it when she landed on it.

Veidt kept it steady, however, and it zoomed off toward the approaching *Ark Angel*, keeping low because of all the conventional firing still going on, and the blasts from the hive. Gnea noticed with interest that the carpet was actually the resilient floor matting from Veidt's cone-flier—a novel way of making an emergency escape conveyance serve double duty.

Evidently, Haydonites *could* survive falls from considerable heights, she decided.

Firing from the hive was getting heavier, and all Spheris was straining and shaking. "It seems the Regent's forces will have their revenge no matter what."

Veidt shook his head serenely. His mental powers had given him a glimpse of the latest developments. "I think not. See there?"

Gnea looked where he was pointing and the breath caught in her throat.

CHAPTER TWENTY-SIX

*At least Kyle had victory in his grasp and died with a certain
serenity. I guess I just don't deserve either one of those things.*

Minmei

T WO GLITTERING FIGURES STOOD, HAND IN HAND,
gazing at the vast hive of the Invid.

All around the place, a ring of thousands upon thousands of Spherisians was rising, head and shoulders, from
the body of their planet. As that was happening the
weapons pylons and gun emplacements toppled or settled
into the rock, swallowed by it. The last few, out of kilter,
blasted uselessly into the sky then were gone.

Other batteries were still firing from the hive proper at
mecha and parts of the city—the *Ark Angel* being too far
off yet. But the Spherisians were too close to the hive to be
in its fields of fire.

And, safe in that fashion, the thousands rose to join the
first two, until they were standing around the hive in a

circle several miles in circumference. From where she flew, Gnea could see still more heads appear and then bob back down again, in the direction of the hive, like porpoises heading under a ship. It seemed that the landscape rippled.

The first two Spherisians to appear—Gnea somehow had no doubt who they were—held out their free hands. All the others linked up, all around the great ring. There was a strange moment of silence then, the Invid guns ceasing fire.

Spheris shook again, then vast faceted dowels of crystal the size of skyscrapers thrust their points up out of the planet's crust, angling in from every side, going up and up until they formed an irregular apex over the center of the hive's dome.

The hive trembled—and began to sink.

Gnea thought there were great counterforces fighting back; the hive seemed to be trying to fight free like a fish caught by a sea anemone. Rock and dust and segments of the hive foundation were flung up all around its sides. But inch by inch it was pulled down.

A liquid, lucid substance gushed up slowly, hardening as it went, trapping the dome and everything in and around it like flies in amber.

Veidt had the carpet at a hover now. The firing had stopped everywhere. He and Gnea watched as the Invid stronghold was pulled low and disappeared from sight, the ground closing over it like something alive—like the landscape of Haydon IV, and yet different from it.

A single united psychic scream came from the Brain and the Invid immobilized in the amber-stuff, as they were drawn, forever unmoving but still alive, deep into Spheris. Every Sentinel and Spherisian winced at it. Then it faded and was gone.

The Spherisians began melding with their world again,

all but the first two, who stood looking at the spot from which the Invid had ruled.

Tesla had no time to be outraged at the defection—that was how he thought of it—of Gnea and Burak.

The Brain was gone! The Invid garrison was his to command!

But at the same time, he was aware of the terrible fate the hive had met, and knew, too, that the *Ark Angel* was in the area. Though he had an army under his control, he dared not use it there on Spheris.

He heard a clanging sound and turned to find that some of the more simpleminded Inorganics had gone back to fighting one another. With a mental shriek, he began rallying his forces. They began pouring toward the camouflaged transports.

"Getting strange power readings from the spaceport," someone relayed the report to Lisa. "Could be Tesla. Inorganics are disengaging and withdrawing that way."

She jabbed her fist into her palm. He had to be stopped! First Karen Penn had made her report over Bela's comset, then Gnea returned on Veidt's carpet, to fill in gaps in the story; all of it proved that Tesla must be reimprisoned or perhaps even eliminated. And yet there were still wounded being loaded directly into the *Ark Angel*. She couldn't just seal up and go chasing off after Tesla.

"Have one Beta do a recon of the spaceport. Get all other available VTs over here to fly security," she snapped. "And have all non-Protoculture weapons stand ready. Keep the Hovertanks on landing-zone-perimeter patrol."

Rick was helping lug a stretcher over to a cargo lift—all the powered gurneys were long since full—when the sound went through the city. He thought it was an aftershock. But word of movement came from the VTs flying cover; in moments everyone was watching as buildings out at the starport began to fly apart.

Since Spheris didn't react in pain, Rick assumed the Invid had rigged some sort of repulsion charges rather than using Protoculture explosives. In any event, pieces of what had been assumed to be a hangar complex were thrown outward. Something began rising from the spot where the structures stood.

Somebody shouted, "I-Invid troop transports!"

Three of the clamshell vessels were lifting off—troopships bigger than any the Sentinels had encountered before. Rick expected them to open up on *Ark Angel* for a parting volley, but apparently the appalling fate of the hive had intimidated Tesla.

The starships rose higher and higher, throwing shadows across the city. Rick wasn't surprised that Lisa held fire; Spheris had been wounded enough, aside from the fact that the planet might react just as violently to the Sentinels' flagship as it had to the hive.

Tesla watched Spheris sinking away beneath him with a mixture of relief and wrath. His victory had been so close!

But—perhaps it was better this way. Surely, the Shapings of the Protoculture were leading him toward his rightful, Evolved fate. "Optera," he whispered to himself.

He had the greater part of the Inorganic garrison with him. From what he could glean from communications logs on the ships, the Regent was now presiding over a Home Hive guarded by a badly depleted army. If he struck before the Regent heard of the outcome on Spheris and could reshuffle forces, *Tesla would have the numerical and tactical advantage*.

"Optera," he said, a little louder, to his bridge crew. They hastened to plot the course.

Once he had slain the Regent and assumed control of

half the Invid species, Tesla would lead his race to triumph. There were ways of coping with the Sentinels and the Robotech Masters and the rest that the devolved maggot hiding on Optera couldn't begin to conceive. And once Tesla had the universe beneath his heel, there would be the Regis to win. But how could she resist him, Evolved as he was? No doubt, he would conquer her without firing a shot.

"Optera!" he exulted, and took his first bite from one of the sunflower-yellow, pyramid-shaped Spherisian Fruits of the Flower of Life. The juices ran down his chin and moistened his magnificent robes.

His aura shone brighter.

Because the new starships still under construction had no drive units or functioning weapons, Breetai's *Valivarre* was the only hope of catching Edwards.

The fact that the hijacked SDF-7 mounted more firepower and had more fighting mecha aboard didn't deter the Zentraedi giants for a moment; Edwards had made himself their blood enemy. Skulls and others were quickly boarding in their VTs and Hovertanks, even as the *Valivarre* was casting off, but Wolff hadn't been able to get back through the press of battle.

"Sorry, Colonel," Breetai said sincerely when Wolff pleaded with him to wait. "Every second counts if I'm to catch that devil."

But Wolff had his own schedule, and he kept it by getting three Diamondback VT pilots in Battloid mode to add their boost to his own Hovertank Battloid's back thrusters. It was a near thing, but he managed to grab the aft section of *Valivarre* without being roasted by its thrusters, and drag himself to an airlock.

"Welcome aboard," Breetai said dryly over the intercom.

Edwards refused to stand and fight, and wouldn't even

answer their transmissions. "It's a drag race now," as one Human officer put it. Both ships increased velocity toward lightspeed, but bit by bit the SDF-7 pulled away. And, once superluminal, she could multiply her lead many times.

"We're losing him," Breetai said in his bulkhead-shaking basso. *Valivarre* had never even gotten within weapons or VT-strike range.

Wolff, standing near on one of the high catwalks Humans used for face-to-face conversations with the giants, begged, "At least let me try a commo channel with him one more time! He'll talk to *me*, I *know*!"

Breetai hid his pity behind a stern military mien, but ordered that it be done. The colonel said, "Edwards, this is Wolff. Answer me! Edwards, I challenge you to answer me!"

He was about to give up in despair, the SDF widening its lead on the Zentraedi ship. But to everyone's surprise Edwards's contemptuous smile appeared on the main screen.

"Jonathan, old man! Sorry I can't dawdle, but *tempus fugit*, and so must I. You understand."

"I challenge you," Wolff said again. "One on one. VTs, Hovertanks, bare hands—name it."

The Zentraedi on duty on the bridge grunted a certain grudging respect for Wolff then, even though he had shown certain weaknesses; *this* was a challenge worthy of a Zentraedi!

But Edwards shook his head in mock exasperation. "Still the romantic, eh, Jonathan? Well, I'm afraid I haven't got time to play black knight to your Galahad. I've other things to do, as you can see."

The camera angle shifted to a long shot, and Wolff moaned.

He and the others in *Valivarre* were staring at the most outlandish wedding scene conceivable. Inorganics formed a guard of honor. Ghost Riders stood in ranks in a "chapel" that was a vacant hold. The altar appeared to be the un- adorned spacefold mountings, presided over by Benson, one of Edwards's aides.

The pickup followed Edwards as he went to the altar. Waiting for him there was Minmei, still wearing the clothes she had worn in her cell but with the addition of a veil improvised from gossamer antivermin netting.

The pickup zoomed in on Minmei. She seemed a little pale, but her eyes were bright and adoring as she took the general's hand. She turned to the camera for a moment.

"Good-bye, Jonathan. I've found happiness at last. I do really think it's time you go home to the family you de- serted and try to make amends to them, don't you?"

Then she and Edwards knelt before Benson, as he raised his arms to the crowd and intoned, "My fellow Edwardsian warriors, we are gathered here—"

The commo link was broken at the SDF's end.

Wolff was sobbing and shaking his head. "It's a trick! It's a phony tape, or he's got her drugged!"

"Intel officer?" Breetai snapped crisply, turning to his staff.

"Voice-stress and imagery-interpretation computers con- firm authenticity," a giant tech officer answered. "No indi- cations of coercion or chemical manipulation."

"That can't be!" Wolff howled, then put his face in his hands. Some of the other Humans got him off the bridge.

Breetai's eyes stayed with his instruments in the vain hope that a power failure or a change of mind would put Edwards back within his grasp. He castigated himself for not giving in to one of his hundred impulses to kill the man, despite his Zentraedi oath of fealty to the REF.

And he felt a pang of sorrow for Wolff. Breetai, as much as anybody, knew what hurt the love of Minmei could inflict.

* * *

The Crann, Scrim, and Odeon watching the wedding service hadn't the vaguest idea what it meant, so they weren't surprised when the bride went berserk, just as the soft music began to play.

The Humans *did* understand, but tried to ignore her rising shriek as she leapt up from her kneeling position and turned on Edwards, trying to claw out his good eye. Edwards hissed out a few perfunctory vulgar words as he fended her off. The two Hellcats flanking the altar backed away, spitting.

He had come so close. Experimenting with the power of the Invid Brain he now controlled, he had learned how to bend Minmei to him. The effort had taken the major part of his will—to the point where the Inorganics were little more than awkward puppets—because somewhere deep inside, Minmei was fighting him every inch of the way.

It had almost been perfect; his Living Computer control of her made it almost seem as if she really loved him.

It was that damned music! Song had always been her unique power, and when the bland strains played over the PA system, the innermost part of her began to sing along. With that, she had thrown off his hold over her in moments. He fought to reassert it, but something told him that she would never be vulnerable to that particular kind of domination ever again. Not while the voice within her lived.

Edwards lost patience and swung his fist. Minmei dropped, senseless. He tried to insinuate his mind into hers, greedy to have her as his living puppet again. But the song was still there; he was shut out of her mind and her love forever.

Minmei came to blearily, in discomfort and pain. She felt like vomiting as she blinked her eyes open. It took seconds to realize where she was and what had happened to her.

She was shackled to a crudely hewn wooden X that had been erected on the bridge of Edwards's stolen starship. Before her were the screens and consoles, and loyal Ghost Riders who ignored her moans.

Edwards, noticing that she had come around, left his command chair to put his hand under her chin. "I want you to enjoy the ride, darling," he said, showing his teeth. "After all, you're my most important passenger."

The soul-song that protected her from him had made him remember how her voice played a pivotal role in Earth's victory in the Robotech War. Undeniably, Fate had been working in his favor when he fought to take her with him on Tirol. In addition to the SDF, his own loyal troops, the Brain, and the Inorganics, he had the secret weapon that had won the war!

Now the problem was how to use it. "My beloved," he added, kissing her cheek, tasting the salt tears there.

Deep within, her newfound patience settled in again, so that she could wait however long it took, bear whatever she had to, until she could kill him.

"We asked you here, Commander Grant," Lang said, "because we require your opinion. Despite the setback of Edwards's mutiny, we shall be ready soon to send an expedition back to Earth. The new ships will be quite spaceworthy within weeks."

"But—the fold drives—" Vince objected.

Exedore tut-tutted. "They are already completed, as in fact was the one for the ship Edwards pirated. The drives are all in safekeeping here in Dr. Lang's complex."

Strolling along in the middle of Lang's Robotech wonderland, Vince rumbled with laughter. Good old Lang, one jump ahead all the way!

But a sudden thought stopped Vince. "I hope you gentlemen aren't about to ask *me* to volunteer." Much as he ached to go home to his son and the world he loved best, to leave without Jean was unthinkable.

"No, no" Exedore was saying, placing a small hand in the center of that massive, V-shaped back. "But we want your opinion on the person we *have* chosen."

He explained quickly the circumstances of Edwards's escape as Breetai had relayed them. "And the *Valivarre* will be making planetfall soon. We want to put Jonathan Wolff in overall command of the expedition back to Earth."

The REF was an expedition; it sounded strange to be talking about an expedition *home*. But the more Vince thought about it, the more logical a choice Jonathan was, what with Rick and Lisa, Max and Miriya unavailable and Vince himself unwilling.

If reports were true, then Wolff had no motive to stay and every reason to go home again, reunite with his family, and put Minmei and the REF behind him. More to the point, he was a brilliant and capable commander—diligent and honest.

And, with the threat of the Invid and the Robotech Masters on the loose, somebody had to carry the warning to Earth. There had been no reply from Carpenter's expedition; it was time for a recon in force.

"I'd say that for once, Hobson's Choice has given us a winner," Vince told them.

CHAPTER
TWENTY-SEVEN

> *The more information we accrue on the subject of the being known as Haydon, the more convinced I am that my work is only beginning.*
>
> Dr. Emil Lang, personal notes on the SDF-3 mission

"**L**ISTEN TO ME, HONEY: I WANT YOU TO PUSH again now. Okay?"

Miriya caught her breath, stopped sobbing, and nodded.

"That's my girl," Jean Grant said, the encouragements automatic as she concentrated on her job. "Max, are you holding her hand?"

"Yes." Max and Miriya exchanged finger squeezes, but hers was so weak.

"Okay, Mommie and Daddy; let's do it," Jean said. "Bear down, hon."

Miriya did, biting her lower lip until it bled, then groaning in pain. No battle wound had ever given her suffering like this; no enemy torture could be more horrible.

Jean didn't have time for an indecent turn of phrase. Medical advances had made the safe, relatively painless delivery of babies a run-of-the-mill thing, but those advances didn't apply to a Zentraedi woman impregnated by a Human male when by all rights it should have been impossible. Or a gestation period that only lasted a few months but had, by all indications, come to full term. Or a pregnancy that had come close to taking the mother's life several times for no discernible reason.

"What is it? What's wrong?" Max asked Jean, as there was a flurry of activity. He couldn't see what was happening from where he sat by Miriya's end of the delivery medtable, holding her hand.

"We're bringing a baby into the world. Isn't that worth giving your wife a kiss?" Jean said distractedly through her mask. But inside, she despaired. Miriya was hemorrhaging badly, and nothing Jean could do seemed to help.

Miriya screamed, and Max, clasping her hands and babbling words of reassurance, saw her eyes rolling up into her head. He ripped his own mask off.

"Mir! Mir! Don't do this! Please *please*, stay with me!"

She began convulsing, and Jean, checking the vital signs, thought, *We're losing her*.

Max was bending against his wife, holding her head to his, weeping and begging her not to die. "Jean, do something!"

"Shhhh! I'm trying, Max." But it was hopeless.

Don't worry, Mother; I am with you.

Max wiped his eyes. "Wh-what'd you say, Jean?"

"I didn't say anything, Max. I thought you did." The nurses and techs and two other attending physicans had nothing to add.

Put your minds at rest. All will be well; you'll see.

Jean didn't have time to wonder if she was going nuts—hearing voices directly in her mind. Miriya's convulsions stopped and her vital signs rose and stabilized. The hemorrhaging slowed to a trickle, then ceased.

And other developments continued. There were a few

busy seconds, but Miriya went through them with her eyes closed and a blissful smile on her face.

"You've—got yourselves a beautiful little daughter, folks," Jean said. The child was crying heartily. Miriya's eyes opened and she and Max laughed and wept, hugging each other.

But Jean, seeing to the umbilical word, felt a cold wind blow through her. She was no obstetrician, but she had delivered plenty of babies.

And this was the first newborn she had ever seen come into the world already breathing, with eyes open and teeth already sprouting.

The baby moved feebly, but its eyes fixed on hers.

Thank you, Jean, that same voice said.

"We have to move with all deliberate speed, Admiral," Burak told Rick in a controlled/impatient tone. "Tesla's efforts to liberate Peryton are welcome, of course, and I'm grateful that he's led the vanguard, but *I* am the one who has been chosen by Destiny to free my people and become their Lord.

"While I sympathize with the Spherisians and the rebuilding they must do, the fact is that they have been freed, while my folk lie under a terrible curse. You can see my point, I'm sure."

Burak was cleaned up and dressed in new garments, Jack Baker's blood washed from his horns. Rick had been avoiding him for days, but at last the Perytonian had buttonholed him, on his way to another strategy meeting.

"Um, I see what you mean, Burak. I'll make sure everyone in the leadership understands."

"Please see that you do. I will await word in my quarters."

Burak turned and strode off in kingly fashion, followed by a few of his people. Rick couldn't figure out if they were just humoring Burak out of loyalty and pity, or if they really believed all his claptrap about being the messiah of his planet.

Certainly, nobody could disabuse him of the conviction that Tesla had gone off to begin the liberation of Peryton, even when they showed Burak the tracking plots on Tesla's escaped ships headed in the direction of Optera.

Rick had been ready to chalk it all up to Tesla's hypnosis, or whatever the Invid used, but Gnea and Jack showed no signs of any residual effects while Burak was still walking around talking like a locked-ward case. He shrugged to himself, and made a note to have security keep surveillance on the Perytonians.

Ironically, Burak's home planet *was*, at long last, next in line on the Sentinels' long campaign. But before that battle could be mounted, the Sentinels had to tend to their wounded and bury their dead. There were also repairs to make to *Ark Angel*, mecha, weapons, and equipment.

And, despite his increasing behavioral quirks, Burak *was* being more cooperative in that he and his followers showed more willingness to answer the intel officers' specific questions about their homeworld. Though the general consensus was that they were holding back a lot, the Perytonians had given the rest of the Sentinels more to ponder with regard to that tragic, cursed planet.

There was also the plight of the Spherisians to consider: their cities in ruins, their economic and industrial infrastructure—the aboveground portion, at any rate—wrecked. Though they could survive in the planet's interior and rebuild on their own, in time, the Sentinels felt it their duty to help the Spherisians as much as possible before lifting off.

A partial message had been received from Max Sterling, and though Rick and Lisa were gone at the time, they were overjoyed to hear that Miriya had given birth to a baby girl the couple had named Aurora. The tape of the transmission was fuzzy and broken up by static, but Rick thought Max looked troubled, even though mother and daughter were both reported to be doing fine.

Of more importance to the mission was the fact that the Haydonites had established intermittent contact with Karbarra. The big ursinoids there had many of their technical problems licked, and production of REF-type mecha and smaller craft was due to start within weeks—as was construction of a prototype SDF-7 class cruiser. That didn't change the Perytonian invasion timetable, but it heartened the Sentinels—the Human members in particular. The fleet that would take them home was now a-building!

The Regent paced through his vaulted organic halls, followed by his faithful bodyguard. He had lost all contact with Spheris, and could guess the rest.

He had issued orders to strip all outposts and planetary garrisons, to bring home every Invid trooper to protect the Home Hive. But he knew that if an enemy was on its way from Spheris, there was no time for reinforcements.

He stood at last before the Special Children, the bio-manipulated embryos left behind by the Regis with the exhortation that he let them grow into what she had intended them to be, and respect the things she had designed into them.

"Bah! What use are they to the Invid if the Home Hive falls?" He had refrained from violating her wishes in the constant hope that someday she would return to him; he preserved her Special Children as a sign of his longing for her. But what good to honor her request if it meant his defeat and death?

He swept his hand out at the ranks and ranks of silent, glistening eggs. "Quicken and hatch them! Feed in the richest nutrients and do all other things to maximize their potential!"

He spun on his bowing entourage. "See to it that all

defenses are prepared and on alert. And make ready my combat armor."

If it was his fate to preside over the end of the Invid empire, he would see that it didn't overtake him gently or at small cost.

Once Jack was out of danger from his wounds, his love-hate relationship with Karen began swinging quickly back to its old sweet-and-sour tune.

There were a couple of days there—he was awake on and off, but in guarded condition and as weak as a kitten—when she was actually sweet to him. Especially when he managed a little sheepishly, "Thanks for riding to the rescue, Lancelot."

However...

"As soon as I'm well enough to *do* anything about it, y'turn back into Attila the Penn," he sneered.

She eluded his embrace nimbly and threw a clean, bundled uniform in his face. "The doc says you're on convalescent status now, you drooling sex fiend, so you're gonna *convalesce*! Veidt's flier meets us on the roof in ten minutes, so move it, Mister!"

Jack started undoing his hospital gown, but she was out the door before he could moon her.

Actually, his first excursion out of sick bay promised to be the trip of a lifetime. Numerous Sentinels had already made the journey; all had received heartfelt invitations from the grateful Spherisians.

It so happened that today was the first day the Hunters could get away to make the pilgrimage, and Gnea, hearing that Jack was to go, decided to come along, too, for a second visit. Burak announced with august dignity that it was only fitting that he witness the most guarded shrine in Spheris. Veidt, his flier repaired, felt it was a good time for a test flight.

Teal and Baldan II, learning who would be on Veidt's flier, insisted on showing the Sentinels around personally.

Veidt was perfectly comfortable hovering several inches off the deck, but seats like long-legged director's chairs had been provided for others. In addition, a picnic lunch lay in a pile of thermal canisters at the rear of the bubble-domed passenger space.

"Still not ready for volleyball, Baker?" Rick asked innocently as Karen helped Jack to his seat. Jack snorted a laugh and then groaned in pain, but he didn't complain; it was just the sort of thing he had done to other people, and he had no intention of being accused of dishing it out but not being able to take it.

Though Karen might abuse Jack, however, she wasn't about to see anybody else do so. "*Admiral!* Unless there're enough people here with matching blood types to give Lieutenant Commander Baker transfusions in the event he should rupture a gut, Sir, I respectfully suggest we go easy on him."

Rick coughed behind his hand to hide his grin. "Of course; quite right." Lisa elbowed Rick, then looked out over the devastated but rebuilding Beroth, throbbing silently with laughter.

The ice-cream-cone flier took them out across the crystal countryside, to a volcanic chimney the Spherisians had opened so that their liberators could see their greatest treasure. They descended past sights as wonderful as anything they had seen on their journeys so far.

At last they came to rest with the narrow promenade flange that encircled the little passenger dome even with a cut-glass walkway. They were miles deep, yet the temperature was comfortable, the air pressure little different from that above. Rick wanted to ask how that could be, but he was sure the Spherisians would only confuse him again, as they had the Sentinels engineers and scientists.

The party stepped out and followed Teal and her son

along, through an immense archway of lava pulled and braided like multiple strands of taffy. On the other side, they all fell mute except for a few loud, indrawn breaths.

No outworlder had ever seen that representation of Haydon until the Sentinels were invited into the lower domains of Spheris. It was set in the middle of a cavern from which light shone in darts bright enough to bother the eyes of the non-Spherisians. It stood in the polished, faceted glory of the planet's most beautiful gem setting, a form a thousand feet high.

A figure of clay.

The stuff was a nondescript color, impossible to discern there where fantastic light-shows changed from instant to instant. The matter of material strengths and the impossibility of such an immense amount of the stuff holding its shape was barely worth mentioning, because the reality was there before them.

The clay was unfired, looking like it had been molded only moments ago; yet it had stood there since the epoch of Haydon himself. It was as if a divine artist had been called away, for a moment, from an unfinished work. Again there was that lack of features but the definite strength and nobility of the outline. It agreed in form with the others the Sentinels had seen.

"Haydon was the living model for its shape," Teal said in a proud, distant voice. "Come; look closer."

She led the way toward an ascending path a yard or so wide which connected to a network that spiraled around and up and down the stupendous cavern. Awed, the rest began falling in automatically.

Except for Jack, who took one look at that corkscrew webbing of trails and knew he could never make it. In fact, he was already feeling a twinge in his mending middle from the activity; the nurses had made him promise to sit in the flier and not move at all, and he had already disobeyed them.

Karen was about to help Jack to Veidt's flier, but Gnea intervened. "I've been here once already, Sister. I'll give him a hand."

The others were already wending up the steep pathway except for Burak, who was still immobile before the clay Haydon. Karen nodded and let go of Jack's arm, then hurried after. Jack hobbled along, more or less leaning on Gnea, letting go a blissful breath as she helped him into his chair again.

"I'm not an invalid anymore, Gnea. You can go on with the others; I'll be all right."

She eased into a chair next to him and patted his forearm. "No problem, bucko. Are you hungry?"

"No, I—"

"Well, *I* am!"

"Well, you're a growing amazon," Jack pointed out.

CHAPTER TWENTY-EIGHT

Perhaps the most intriguing aspect of the Regent-Tesla conflict is one that cannot be verified but was a persistent rumor among the Invid.

It was alleged in various quarters that the count of Special Children eggs left behind by the Regis upon her departure was one short. Further rumor had it that she'd chosen to raise one of the select brood as a secret experiment, telling no one about it, not even the Special Child—and that she raised it as a Scientist.

Perhaps Tesla's crimes were, like something out of Greek drama, even more enormous than he imagined.

Lemuel Thicka, *Temple of Flames: A History of the Invid Regent*

THE PILGRIMS TO HAYDON'S SHRINE BECAME SEPA-rated, going off along various paths that wound the cavern walls, to view the stupendous icon from assorted angles and distances. Karen was walking alone when Baldan emerged from the glittering wall to stand before her.

He was as tentative as any adolescent male approaching an attractive older female. "There is—something I thought you might like to see," he began hesitantly. "I'd like to show it to you—to thank you for helping teach me the fighting skills."

She came with him into a passageway that reminded her of a cut and polished ice cave. It led to a sort of domed gallery or rotunda, where objects were set near the chamber's walls. The things he had brought her to see were like nothing so much as diamond footballs, or stylized Easter eggs, as big as a small groundcar. They were per-rate pedestals that were aligned along a complex celestial design in the window-clear floor.

Baldan led Karen over to one. "Stand on that spot, so, and look into the Microcosm."

She took her place, and the egg before her lowered itself a bit so that its tip was level with her eyes. It was wondrously crosshatched with lights and colors even though it was clear, but she saw nothing coherent. She was about to ask Baldan if she was doing something wrong when the world seemed to fall away on all sides.

She found herself looking at a place that had been ravaged worse than Tirol or even Spheris. Yet, somehow she knew that it had once been a thriving scene. She shuddered at the windswept tors, bleak wastelands, and dank, treacherous bogs. Off in the middle distance, though, something began to come into focus.

It was an Invid hive, far larger than any she had ever seen. Its central dome alone was bigger than Glike, Beroth, and Monument City put together. It, and the satellite structures connected to it and one another by a network that shone as red as canals of lava, covered much of one continent.

"Optera," she heard Baldan say. "And the Home Hive of the Invid."

She backed away and the vision faded. "Baldan, what are these?"

"They are our *fenestella*—mental looking-glasses for viewing other worlds. Seeing the Invid hive has upset you, hasn't it? I'm sorry; stupid of me to begin with that one—"

"No, no!" She laid a hand on his arm. "It was amazing! Was I actually seeing what's going on at this moment on Optera?" The G-2 intelligence staff would go wild over this!

But Baldan was shaking his head. "These are representations—depictions. And there are more pleasant ones:

Garuda and Karbarra and others the Sentinels have never visited. Let me show them to you."

"I'd like that."

As they went, he talked about the different worlds and their histories. She could tell that Baldan I was coming more and more to the fore in him.

"To the Regent and Tesla and their folk, Optera is a beautiful world," he told her, "even though it's not the paradise it was. Part of the purpose of this place is to remind us that Spheris is only part of a much greater scheme of things."

He spoke like a person with an *old soul*, as she had once heard someone put it. "I think you're a very wise man, Baldan," she told him.

He looked subdued. "Baldan I was in many ways the sum of our race. He was slated for great things, great accomplishments, before the Invid came. His death was a very untimely blow to all Spherisians. So I have a very great deal to live up to, you see."

Gloom had settled on him. Karen slipped her arm through his and pressed her lips to the glassy, strangely warm cheek. "You're going to do just fine, I know it. Now c'mon; show me some more!"

Aboard *Ark Angel*, Rem bent to his studies. Cabell would expect him to sift through as much of the data gained on this voyage as possible, and to have furthered his own studies as well.

There was a tone from his quarters' hatch signal. When he gave it leave to open, Janice Em stepped into the room.

She was wearing the guise of the Human, as she usually did with him—and around most crewmembers, to put them at ease. Even so, there were many who kept their distance from her now that they knew she was an Artificial Person.

Rem himself had no such prejudices; one reason was

that he had been on the receiving end too many times. But there was another, far better one.

"It's late," she said. "Haven't you studied enough for one evening?"

She turned out the light over his work station and took his hand, kissing his neck and lips as he kissed hers. Together they went to his bed.

Max Sterling fought the urge to hang onto Aurora, to see to it that she didn't hurt herself. But his daughter was screaming bloody murder, eager to practice her walking there on the carpeted floor of his quarters.

He tried to keep from dwelling on how crazy it all was. Here she was, only weeks old, taking her first steps. Max let go, and Aurora tottered toward Miriya, who knelt a few yards away.

The changes in Miriya were more subtle than the ones taking place in Aurora with every passing minute, but they were unmistakable. The peerless champion of the Quadronos no longer seemed the least bit interested in getting back on flight status or resuming her military career in any fashion whatsoever. Whenever Max brought up the subject, she simply gave him a serene smile and changed it.

It was as if the almost-fatal pregnancy and the birth of Aurora had given Miriya a secret wealth of knowledge.

Baby Aurora was doing splendidly, just as she did everything, when she abruptly went as stiff as a board, like someone suffering a seizure, and keeled over. Max and Miriya almost knocked heads, rushing to her. To their immense relief, she was breathing again, and the seizure seemed to have passed. But she gave no sign of hearing them.

Instead, she lay with eyes wide and focused on the ceiling. They heard her tiny voice but it took a few repetitions to understand what she was saying. And when they did,

Miriya let out a cry of pain, as Max felt the hair on the back of his neck standing straight up.

"Dana, the spores! Beware the spores! *Dana, beware the spores!*"

"Not very subtle, is he?" the Regent scoffed, looking into the screen. "Where's all this Evolved refinement we keep hearing about?"

It was true: Tesla's battle plan lacked finesse. Apparently, he thought the appearance of his force would in and of itself oblige the Regent to sue for peace.

"Fool!" the Regent reflected, his nasal antennae flashing. "He doesn't realize the true strength of deevolution!"

Outlying strongholds and defensive bases had been neutralized, and the central dome of the Home Hive itself was Tesla's straightforward objective.

The transports began sowing their crop of Terror Weapon dropships and skirmish fliers. While these went on ahead, the transports descended to let forth rank after rank of Inorganic bipeds and packs of Hellcats. The troopships fired in support of the assault but kept well back, since the hive's mammoth guns were shooting in answer.

The smaller invading craft and ground units advanced fearlessly, though. Suicidal attacks by a number of Tesla's Terror Weapons resulted in awful losses but succeeded in knocking out most of the big cannon—something that would have been inconceivable in the days when the Home Hive was operating at full efficiency and power.

It was fratricide, carnage between identical twins, as Inorganic fought Inorganic. As it turned out, on Spheris Tesla's soldiers had picked up tricks of battle concerning such duels that the Regent's fighters had never had occasion to learn. That was one more thing in the challenger's favor.

In an infernal landscape of Protoculture blasts, dismembering hand-to-hand combat, and fanatic killing and dying, the outnumbered loyalist army was pushed back and back toward the hive.

When he thought that the time was right, the Regent turned to one of his toadies. "Release the Special Children at once."

He turned back to watch as they rose from forward positions in camouflaged bunkers. Tesla's soldiers were caught off guard as new enemies burst into their very midst.

Though it infuriated him to think about it, the Regent's own scientists were very much the Regis's rejects. She had wanted only those who were energized by her Great Work, the seeking of the Ultimate Invid Form. Others, she banished from her presence.

Therefore the Regent's scientists—mostly culls—hadn't been able to fathom all the potentials and secrets of her Special Children. Several savants had died before the Regent's fury. The Invid monarch finally decided that he didn't need geniuses or great biogenetic artists, ESP savants or spiritual guides. "Give me living, breathing killing machines," he commanded.

And so it was. The things that began hurling back the invaders' advance were bigger than any other mecha the Invid were ever to field. They resembled the Enforcers that the Regis was later to develop on Earth, but were bigger and of greater brute strength, bearing heavier armor and firepower.

But like the Inorganics, the Special Children had multiple upper limbs. These were provided with pincers, tentacles, great scythelike ripper-blades, weapons muzzles, and more. The things could defend and fight on all sides.

They waded into Tesla's attack waves, slashing Inorganics in two and hurling the pieces in different directions, blasting them apart, tearing them limb from limb, or simply stomping them into the ground-up soil of Optera. The advance was stopped, the lines breached; the Special Children spread out, visiting destruction upon everything in their path.

But Tesla, in the safety of his transport ship, breathed a sigh of relief. Only in his Evolved state had he finally understood some of the things for which the Special Children were designed. One of those functions was *to absorb and store Protoculture energy*.

Brought to term properly, the Children wouldn't have been particularly imposing specimens or doughty fighters, but they could have stopped Tesla cold by draining all energy from his soldiers. The Regent, however, had approached the situation with exactly the devolved simple-mindedness Tesla had foreseen.

"Second wave," he ordered.

In his hive, the Regent shook the walls with his ire when twice again as many Inorganics were sent in by Tesla. Again, the renegade was willing to suffer horrific losses in his drive to victory. For every Inorganic that the Special Children slew, three more swarmed up at them.

The irreplaceable Special Children began to suffer losses, driven back toward the hive though they fought like demons every foot of the way. One of the Invid's greatest genetic treasures was being spent, at a hellish rate and to no great effect, in a few minutes of a battle between equally unworthy leaders.

"Commit all reserves!" the Regent ordered. "And establish a direct link so that I may speak to Tesla face-to-face!"

The defending lines wavered but held. The last power of the hive was supercharging the Regent's fighters, and Tesla suffered more attrition. But it didn't matter.

In his command ship, he vowed, *I* will *rule the Invid*!

The following chapter is a sneak preview of RUBICON —the final book in the Sentinels saga!

CHAPTER

ONE

> *Don't talk to me of Science! The only reference work I consult is the Encyclopedia of Ignorance. All Science has done is force us to narrow our definitions, categorize our thinking. It offers us false security at the expense of spontaneity. I have no use for it. I create my world and change its rules and guidelines as I see fit. I am the only god this dimension has ever known; the only one it will ever know!*
>
> T. R. Edwards, as quoted in Constance Wildman's *When Evil Had It's Day: A Biography of T. R. Edwards*

"AT LEAST I WON'T BE PIRATING IT THIS TIME," Jonathan Wolff told Lang as the retrofitted SDF-7–class cruiser nosed into view. The venom in his voice was palpable, but the scientist either misunderstood or refused to acknowledge it.

"Engineering and astrogation have already been briefed on our modifications to the Reflex drives and spacefold generators. Improvements, I should say," Lang added, turning around to face Wolff.

Wolff tried to take a reading of the man's transformed eyes, but staring into them only made him think of black holes, unfathomable singularities. He let his gaze linger on the starship instead, his ticket home, whatever that meant.

"We've moved away from reliance on the Ur-Flower peat toward a more conventional dialogue between the monopole ore and the Protoculture itself. Your ship has a bit of the SDF-3 in her, Colonel."

Wolff smirked. "Then maybe it'll find a way back to Earth on its own, Lang. A milk run."

The scientist cocked his head to one side, offering an appraising look. "It wouldn't be the oddest thing, commander."

Major Carpenter, whose ship had left Fantomaspace more than six months ago, had not been heard from. Lang's Robotechs were attributing this to malfunctions in the ship's deep-space transceivers—a wedding of Tiresian and Karbarran systemry—but privately Lang had confessed to misgivings about the very nature of the ship's drives. Not so with this ship, Wolff had been assured. This was the one the R&D people were puffed up about. This was the one that would give Wolff the edge; spirit him through space-time in the blinking of an eye, overtaking en route the Earth-bound spade fortresses of the Robotech Masters.

Wolff continued to regard the ship from the SDF-3's observation blister without much thought to Lang's reassurances, or what may or may not lay at mission's end. To him the ship, this sleek and substantially scaled-down version of the Super Dimensional Fortress, was simply *a way out*. There had been flashes of renewed faith these past few weeks, moments when he saw himself as reborn—on Haydon IV, for instance, or at seeing the look on T. R. Edwards's face when his treachery was revealed to the council—but all that had been emptied from him on the bridge of the *Valivarre*. Minmei's words still rang in his ears like a curse; her marriage to Edwards, that sick and sinister ceremony, replaying itself in dreams and every other waking thought. *I've found happiness at last*, she had shrieked from that black altar. *Go back to the family you deserted . . . make amends with them!*

As if it were possible.

He had convinced himself that it wasn't Minmei who was sending him away—not any flesh and blood Minmei at least. He had succeeded in depersonalizing her, divesting her of the power to inflict such grief. She was a symbol of the world gone wrong and Jonathan Wolff's false steps through it; a symbol of hope's turn toward evil. A symbol of transformed love, of broken promise. A world once turned on her voice, and now that voice raged against what it had redeemed.

"The ship's databanks contain a complete record of the mission," Lang was saying, "along with updated material covering the recent events on Tirol."

Wolff abandoned his dark musings and registered surprise.

"Longchamps and Stinson, the others who backed Edwards, are holding their ground. But we've won the battle, as it goes."

"Edwards is halfway to Optera, and they're still not convinced," Wolff seethed. "They're hedging their bets. They figure he'll be coming back here with whatever's left of the Invid fleet."

"Possibly that," Lang was willing to concede. "But I think it has more to do with Earth than Tirol. We can't be certain but there's some chance that the Southern Cross apparat has gained the upper hand. That would place Edwards' in a strong position there, despite what has transpired here."

Lang was downplaying things considerably, Wolff realized. *Some chance* meant sure thing, no matter how Lang chose to deliver it. An awareness of the Shapings—Protoculture had left him that talent when it drained the hazel from his eyes.

"Field Marshall Leonard. Zand, Moran . . ."

Lang nodded. "Exactly. Longchamps wants them to know where the lines were drawn."

Wolff muttered a curse. "So we could end up dealing with Edwards all over again. On Earth this time."

"Which is why I want you to hand-deliver a special report to Major Rolf Emerson."

Wolff's pencil-thin eyebrows arched. "Emerson?"

"He's the only member of the General Staff we can trust. We don't know what Edwards's next move will be. Perhaps he'll attempt to convince the Regent to move against Earth. It's clear now that the two of them have been in collusion for some time—at least as far back as the assassination of the Invid's simulagent. If Carpenter's ship made it back safely the tale of our schism has already been told. But who knows how strong Leonard has become in the interim, how he might respond to reports of indecision among the Council members . . ."

"Earth would welcome Edwards with open arms."

"Edwards *and* the Regent. He could conquer the planet without loosing a beam."

Wolff glanced at the ship, then uttered a short laugh as he swung around to Lang. "The goddamn frying pan to the fire."

"Not if we can hold Edwards here," Lang told him. "The Zentraedi have volunteered to spearhead an invasion."

Wolff was aghast. "Against Optera?"

"Breetai's forces are our only hope. Hunter and the Sentinels have only just left Spheris, and their destination is Peryton, not Optera."

"That's lunacy! Show Hunter the transvids of Minmei's *wedding* if you want to light a fire under him. He'll say to hell with Peryton."

Lang made a calming gesture with his hands. "I think you're mistaken, Colonel. But we're trying just that in any event. The *Tokugawa* under General Grant's command will launch for Haydon IV shortly after your departure. There he'll rendezvous with a Karbarran force and proceed to Peryton."

Wolf felt a wave of anticipation wash through him. What chance could his one lone ship have against a combined enemy force in Earthspace? But to have a chance to stop Edwards from leaving the Quadrant, to go to guns with him on Optera, put a personal end to his evil reign—

"So you understand just how critical your mission is," Lang said, as though reading his mind. "It is imperative that the Defense Force on Earth be fully appraised of the situation—even if the result is further factionalism. I trust you follow me, Colonel."

Wolff bit back a half-formed argument on the merits of his remaining on Tirol and nodded, tight-lipped and near-spellbound in Lang's gaze.

The starship was fully visible now, gleaming in the light of Fantoma's primary, an arrow in the unseen wind.

"There's one more thing, Wolff," Lang said after a moment. "Your ship has the capacity for a roundtrip."

"In case I change my mind."

Lang folded his arms. "If you should fail to make contact with us, we want you to return. We must be informed of the situation."

"That's a hell of thing to ask, Lang. Especially when nobody was figuring on the Expeditionary mission ending up a one-way ticket."

Lang seemed to consider it, then said: "It's not a request, Colonel. It's an order."

Lang attended the Wolff Pack's final briefing and shuttled down to Tirol while the starship was being readied for launch. After a protracted exit from the Fantoma system, the ship would initiate the first of more than a dozen spacefold jumps that would eventually land it in Earthspace, clear across the galaxy. Wolff was to communicate with the SDF-3 after each defold operation, and the fortress could thereby monitor the ship's progress. The Robotech teams had taken no such precautions with Major Carpenter's ship, which was to have completed the same trip in two jumps, dematerializing once some seventy-five light years out from Tirol before it re-manifested in Earthspace. But the sensor probes of the abandoned but still-functioning Robotech fortress there had relayed no indications of the ship's emergence or passage. For all intents and purposes Carpenter was lost in space.

Tiresia, in the wake of Edwards's embattled departure, brought to mind the city as Lang had first seen it shortly after the Invid conquest. Much of what Robotechnology had rebuilt had been damaged by the awakened Inorganics, and vast areas near the pyramidal Royal Hall where the fighting had been thickest were leveled. And yet Lang couldn't help but think that Tiresia had never seemed so at peace with itself. Certainly the native populace felt it, and —as his limo whisked him through the city's evercrete streets—Lang believed he could detect the same sense of release on the face of the clean-up crews. Those Hellcats and Scrim Edwards had left behind had been destroyed; skirmish ships and terror weapons brought to the ground. But more important, the Invid brain was gone—that slumbering malignancy Longchamps and the rest had let Edwards keep to himself.

Lang's last face-to-face with Edwards was still strong in his thoughts, stronger still in his hands, which curled now at the very recollection. He had to ask himself why he hadn't killed Edwards then; it was just the two of them in the lab together and who would have been the wiser? At the time he told himself that humiliation would be a greater indignity than death; but in truth it was the Shaping that persuaded him to ease his hold on the man's throat. An overriding signal sent to his hands that was meant to save Edwards for some other fate. No good or evil was attached to any of it; simply a kind of desolate awareness of *the appropriate*. God knew Lang himself hadn't given it any shape. Nor did it spring from any vestige of humanity. He and Edwards both were long past that now. As they all were—a mission of men and women beyond *Human* in any primary meaning of the term. They were warped, reshaped, and transfigured by wars that spilled across the galaxy, contact with a dozen lifeforms from as many star systems, and the urgings of Protoculture itself, the Flower's bad seed.

"How did he react?" Exedore asked when Lang entered the lab.

The Zentraedi stood poised beside one of the room's numerous consoles, a Tiresian data card in one hand. Lang recounted his conversation with Jonathan Wolff. "I had the feeling he would just as soon mount his own mutiny as return to Tirolspace."

"But he understands how critical it is that we learn of the Earth government's evaluation?"

Lang nodded vacantly. "At this point I'm more concerned with the spacefold generators. We could be sending Wolff off to his death. If only there were time to experiment with these monopole drives—"

"There is no time, doctor," Exedore interrupted him. "The Robotech Masters have been traveling at superluminal speeds for thirteen Earth-standard years now. Cabell himself thought the journey from Tirol to Earth might require as little as fifteen. That leaves us two years at best. Two years to ready a fleet for our return. Two years to arm those ships with sufficient firepower to defeat the Masters' fortresses." Exedore shook his head. "No, doctor, there is no time. Wolff must leave as planned."

Lang waved a hand. "I know all this. I'm asking for assurances where none exist."

"Here, or anywhere."

Lang paced for a moment, hands locked behind his back. "There is a chance we've overlooked something.

Some way to conjure the Protoculture we need." He crossed the lab to a window in a partitioned-off section of the room and pressed his fingertips to the permaplas, gazing in on the shaggy creatures held captive there.

"Cabell has told us all he knows," Exedore said, joining Lang at the window.

The creatures bore a resemblance to terrestrial moptop dogs, save for their knob-ended horns and unearthly eyes. They were the Flowers' pollinators—Lang understood as much—indigenous to Optera, which had been stripped of their presence when the Flowers were stolen. They subsisted on a farinaceous mix Cabell claimed to be composed of crushed stems and leaves from the Flowers themselves.

"Suppose we were to bring them into contact with the Flowers Zor planted, on Karbarra say, or Garuda, it makes no difference."

Exedore thought a moment and said, "We would perhaps succeed in raising a viable crop. But we would have only flowers, doctor, not the matrix in which to contain them. And I'm afraid Zor took that knowledge with him to his grave."

The Pollinators, who were most often heaped together in a corner of the small chamber, were on their feet now, watching the two scientists with a mixture of curiosity and expectation.

"Perhaps not," Lang mused.

"Lang?" Exedore said, the way he once called Breetai *commander*.

Lang turned and put his hands on the Zentraedi's shoulders, still misshapen under the confining cut of the REF jacket. "If we can believe our reports from Janice . . ."

Exedore raised an eyebrow. "The Zor-clone."

"Rem," Lang said. "We must learn what he knows."

"Go ahead, question the Zor-clone if it's an explanation you seek!" Burak pointed an accusing taloned finger at

Rem. "It was his seeding of our world that drew the Invid into our midst! Make him speak!"

The Perytonian contingent rallied behind their self-appointed savior, raising fists and tapered forehorns, a gathering of demons in medalioned black robes.

The Sentinels' ship, the *Ark Angel*, was approaching superluminal speeds in the outer limits of the Spherisian system. Blaze was behind them, off in Earth's direction, a cool white and distant disc. Beroth was restructuring itself without the Sentinels' assistance, a refulgent city in the works under the guidance of Tiffa and the planet's crystalline elite.

Rem felt Burak's hatred clear across the ship's hold, and looked at Jack Baker, who was still recuperating from an encounter with the Perytonian's horns. Burak was thought to have been under Tesla's spell at the time, as both Jack and Gnea were; but Jack's clenched fist told Rem that all had not yet been forgiven.

Nonetheless, Rem wished that he had something to offer Burak. Being a clone of Zor, it was possible that Rem could call up some data regarding Peryton from his neurons, just as the Regent's scientists had used the Garudan atmosphere to prompt memories of prelapsarian Optera, Optera before the fall. Those memories, though, were but half-remembered dreams now, isolated parts of some other's thoughts and deeds, and Rem considered himself a mere conduit for their emergence. It weighed on him like an unshakeable burden—the very fact that he had been cloned, instilled like a Zentraedi warrior with a false past, lied to by the man who had been father as well as mentor, *creator*, more like it. He and Cabell hadn't had occasion to discuss the matter of his laboratory birth; the old man had been successful in avoiding him after the battle on Haydon IV, and Rem thought that Cabell's decision to remain there was more personal than anyone on the *Ark Angel* was aware. Only Janice seemed to understand this; and it was she who came to his defense now—this not-quite human, who had revealed her true face to the Sentinels in the depths of Haydon IV's inner workings.

"He knows nothing!" she told Burak, pointing a finger of her own. "You confuse Zor with his offspring."

"Then let him speak for himself, *Wyrdling*," Burak shot back, using the Praxian term. Janice was in her lavender-haired human guise, but it was the artificial person most of the Sentinels chose to see.

"We have told you all we can."

"Enough!" Rick said, loud enough to cut through an eruption of separate discussions and arguments, Perytonians and Praxians hurling insults at one another, ursine Karbarrans muttering to themselves. "This isn't helping anything, Burak. We understand that Peryton has been in a state of perpetual warfare. But you've got to give us more background on this supposed *curse* if you expect us to intercede."

"'*Supposed*' curse?" Burak mimicked, repeating it for his camp, who shrieked a kind of angry laugh in response. "There is nothing *supposed* about it, human. You will see for yourselves if we ever reach Peryton."

"We *will* reach Peryton," Rick snapped. "And that's the last I want of hear of that. You have our word that we'll do everything we can to liberate Peryton—you've had our word from the onset."

"Your word," Burak sneered, horns lowered, red eyes glaring at Rick. "Words mean nothing. *We* have tried words. And we have tried weapons. To no avail." He swept his arm around the room. "You all know this. Words are *useless*. Weapons are *useless*. You think I am unaware of what transpires here? You think I am unaware of your secret plans to move against Optera and leave Peryton to fend for itself? Now that Spheris has been liberated, you see no need to delay, to involve yourself in my world's insignificant dilemma. It is just as Tesla warned."

Teal pushed her way to the edge of the circle as the arguments recommenced. "If that were the case, we wouldn't be here," she told Burak, indicating her fellow Spherisian, Baldan. "We would have stayed on our own world."

Burak only snorted a laugh. "A babe and a newborn warrior. How comforting."

Rick strode to the center waving his arms and motioning everyone silent. "Peryton is our priority. Anyone who disagrees better step forward now and present a case, otherwise it's settled, once and for all."

When no one moved to contradict him, he swung around to the Perytonians, showing them a determined look. "I'm as short of patience as this ship is of Protoculture, Burak. Tesla's not around to feed you any more lies, so you're going to have to begin dealing with us. You don't seem to want to believe that he's on his way to Optera, but there's nothing we can do about that. What I want to know is what you need from us. Tesla has you convinced that it's your destiny to save your world, and maybe that's exactly the case. But you'll need backup and all we're saying is that you'll have our complete cooperation."

"Then squeeze the Zor-clone for all he's worth," Burak said menacingly. "Or, by Haydon, we will do it for you!"

In his quarters an hour later, Rick positioned himself in front of a security camera to get a good look at himself in the monitor. He had been as thin as a ribbon since Haydon IV and suspected that the Haydonite scientists must have tampered with his physiology when they were cleaning Garuda from his system, because he hadn't been able to gain any of his weight back. Stepped up his metabolism or something. He turned profile for the camera and ran a forefinger along his larynx, which seemed to be, well, *protruding* lately. Could they have taken out his thyroid? No, that wouldn't have done it. He thought about Veidt as he stared at his on-screen image, flexing the muscles in his arms and legs, thankful that Haydon IV had left him with those at least.

There were other things to wonder about as well: whether Vince Grant, Wolff, and Breetai had been successful in clearing the Sentinels of charges; how Max and Miriya were faring with their new girlchild; whether the ship under Major Carpenter's command had been heard from; and just what the hell the *Ark Angel* was going to do when it arrived at Peryton.

Despite the bold front he had displayed in the hold, he couldn't deny that Burak's remarks were not far off the mark. It was true that the Sentinels had given their word to the Perytonians, and it was certain they would stick to it; but at the same time there was a kind of mutinous restlessness plaguing both crew and command—a feverish compulsion to push on to Optera and put an end to the war. They had had the Regent on the run ever since Haydon IV, and the sidetrip to Peryton—while an honorable undertaking—was only going to permit him to regroup his forces and fortify his homeworld stronghold. Rick could only hope that Tesla's troopships were in pursuit of the Invid leader. From all reports, he had actually *strangled* the Regent's simulagent onboard the SDF-3, and there had been that persuasive speech before the turnaround on Spheris. But who knew what Tesla had planned for the day after tomorrow? He was no longer the same being they had encountered on Tirol almost three years ago.

Rick had no way of knowing Dr. Emil Lang was nursing similar thoughts about change and transformation clear across the seas and nebulae of the local group. He knew only that victory was no longer a guarantee of order; in fact, there seemed to be a measurable quantity of *disorder* attending the Sentinels liberation campaign. An entropic dispersal; a scattering and depletion that grew more pronounced with each world set free. Half his command returned to Tirol; the Praxians uprooted; Cabell, Max, and Miriya on Haydon IV; Janice Em and Tesla reconfigured; Burak crazed . . . And indeed his own image seemed to bear this out: his nearly shoulder-length hair, the mismatched pieces of uniform and weaponry.

Rick turned to glance at Lisa, busy at a terminal which by rights had no place in their bedroom. She was outfitted in knee-high boots, leggings, and a hide skirt the Praxian Zibyl had given her on Haydon IV. Her admiral's jacket was worn over a Garudan fringe vest, and a kind of techno-headband kept her long hair back. There were Karbarran air-rifles in one corner of the room, Badger assault pistols near the bed, clips and bandoliers, halberds and grappling hooks. And it wasn't just this room but the whole *Ark Angel* that looked like this; not just Rick and Lisa Hunter but the entire crew. If they were not really the pirates the Plenipotentiary Council had branded them, *they were certainly dressing the part*!

"What is it?" Lisa asked over her shoulder, catching Rick staring at her.

Rick smiled and shook his head. "Nothing. I guess I was just daydreaming."

Lisa narrowed her eyes. "About?"

"Maybe about the first time we met," he said, coming over to her, taking her upraised hand and kissing it. "You in civilian clothes. Kim, Vanessa, and Sammie."

Lisa laughed and leaned back to glimpse her reflection in the monitor screen. "And you and Roy all duded up, two hot-shot flyboys on the make. 'Mr. *Lingerie*!'"

"Macross," Rick said, sighing.

She squeezed his hand. "We've come a long way baby."

"Yeah, look," he said, gesturing to himself and laughing.

She reached up to straighten the collar of his jacket. "I think you look terrific. I was proud of you today, Rick, the way you handled Burak."

"Even though you knew I was faking it."

"You weren't faking it," she countered. "We're committed to Peryton—obligation or not. Nothing will change that. Burak has to be made to understand."

"Not even a chance for a quick end to the war."

Lisa tightened her lips. "Not even that."

Rick looked away from her.

"Let me hear you say it, Rick," she said, suddenly concerned.

"Not even that," he bit out.

Elsewhere in the ship Burak was meeting in private with Garak and Pye, the two Invid scientists who had been with the Sentinels since the liberation of Garuda. The Perytonian had the two pinned up against the bulkhead of their quarters/jailcell, his hands at their throats. Behind him at the door stood two of his devilish cadre, who had neatly disposed of the rooms' Karbarran guards.

"Do I need to ask again?" Burak said in the lingua franca, his horns poised for a pass.

"We know nothing!" Pyre gasped, pleading for his life.

"You had the clone on Garuda. Your scanners peered into his mind. What did they reveal? How is Peryton to be spared? Speak, or die by my hands!" Burak held their ophidian eyes in his gaze, willing the truth to surface. The two had been present when Tesla had first worked his magic; they had seen for themselves the transmogrification, the link the Invid had established with Burak that day in this very hold. "Speak!" he commanded them, trying to summon a similar psychic bolt from his depths.

Just then the door to the hold slid open and Janic Em sidestepped in, her Badger in an upraised two-fisted grip.

"Hold!" Burak ordered his companions.

The two moved back.

"Release them," Janice said, gesturing to the Invid.

Burak grinned and opened his powerful hands; the sci-

277

entists slipped from his grip and fell gasping for breath to the floor.

"They can't tell you anything, Burak."

"You never know until you ask, changling. And the Zor-clone was not available."

Janice moved toward a corner of the hold and brought the pistol to her shoulder, pointing it toward the ceiling. "I can tell you what you need to know about Peryton."

Burak traded looks with his cohorts and relaxed his stance some. "Speak to me from your true face, then. Unmask yourself."

Janice complied. Without visible effort, her skin lost color, becoming transparent and leaving the blood vessels and human-made musculature of her face revealed. Her eyes emitted an eerie light, and what there was left of her expression became flat, unblinking, and inhuman.

"You would make Tesla a lovely bride."

Janice ignored the comment and said, "The Awareness opened my eyes to some things that bear on Peryton's curse, some things which you are meant to understand. Zor believed he would be helping your world by seeding it with the Flowers of Life. If you seek someone to blame, you must go further back—to Haydon."

Burak made a disgruntled sound. "Haydon? Then I may as well blame the Great Shaper, the Great Geode . . ."

"It would all mean the same," Janice told him. "When the Invid came they sealed off Peryton's one chance for salvation; but there is still time to rescue your world from the brink."

"But how?" Burak asked, eager now, captivated.

"The hive is the key."

Burak took an anxious step forward. "The hive . . . But tell me, changling, do I delude myself, am I to be the one?"

The light from Janice's eyes waned, then grew brilliant again. "You are the one."

Burak threw back his head and roared. "And Tesla," he sneered after a moment. "Does he have a role to play in all this, or were his words empty?"

"Tesla has a role," Janice said, "an all-important one."

ABOUT THE AUTHOR

Jack McKinney has been a psychiatric aide, fusion-rock guitarist and session man, worldwide wilderness guide, and "consultant" to the U.S. military in Southeast Asia (although they had to draft him for that).

His numerous other works of mainstream and science fiction—novels, radio and television scripts—have been written under various pseudonyms.

He resides in Ubud, on the Indonesian island of Bali.